Another Night in Paris

ELLIS ROSE

First Edition Published in 2016
by iponymous publishing Limited
iponymous Swansea United Kingdom SA6 6BP

A CIP record for this book
Is available from the British Library

(Physical Book) ISBN 978-1-908773-890
(EBook) ISBN 978-1-908773-425

www.iponymous.com

ALSO BY ELLIS ROSE

One Night in Paris

Another Night in Paris

Last Night in Paris

CONTENTS

ELLIS ROSE

Originally from Swansea in South Wales, Ellis Rose, studied modern languages at Cardiff University before moving to Paris to follow a career in Public Relations. After 30 years of working in a variety of marketing and PR related roles in Europe and the UK, in 2009 she moved back to her home town where she set up her own independent marketing consultancy, to allow herself time to write her first novel. Ellis now lives with her partner and two daughters on the beautiful Gower Coast.

CHAPTER 1

The February weeks just flew by. They were really busy at work with normal routines plus gearing up for the office move and the conference in Brussels. Josie also had to take nearly two whole days to get her Carte de Séjour sorted out. She hadn't needed one when she joined Chemfast as she had been employed from the UK and her salary was paid directly into her UK bank account. At Renseignements she would be paid directly into her French account by a French firm, so a Carte de Séjour was essential.

After queuing for nearly two hours the first time she went to the British Consular, she discovered she had all the wrong documentation and needed a letter from Jacques Fredet confirming her employment and start date with Renseignements.

"But when I called to make the appointment, I was told I would only need my passport and my last three pay slips," Josie told the disinterested woman behind the glass partition. The woman just shrugged in that annoying Gallic way which frustrates every other nation under the sun, as if to say, 'it's not my problem'.

So a week later Josie went back. This time she arrived early, before the Agency opened, hoping to be first in line. No such luck. The queue at 8.30 am was snaking down the road and she realized she was in for a long wait. Josie was eventually seen three hours later and did her best to hide her frustrations from the same woman who had been so unhelpful on her last visit. With only a few days to go before starting her new job she needed the Carte de Séjour and was determined not to leave without it.

1

The French woman seemed to have two paces: slow and even slower. Josie waited patiently whilst the she held a ten minute conversation with a colleague about the state of her health. Josie bit her tongue and said nothing; she couldn't risk not getting her card. After what seemed like an incredibly long wait she eventually left the embassy with the all-important document in her hand. She decided to treat herself to lunch before going back to the office. Although the government bureau was in the same arrondissement as her offices, it was along the Rue d'Anjou and she had never ventured along this street before. She found a small café tucked away down a side street and ordered a coffee and croque madame - cheese on toast with an egg on top.

While she was enjoying her lunch, her mobile bleeped to say she had a new message. It was from Christian asking if it was okay to call her that evening. She texted back to say it was. Josie hadn't seen him since their last date at the Pizzeria due to the pressures of work (her) and a skiing holiday which ran over two weekends (him). The message from Christian cheered her up and she was in really high spirits when she arrived back at the office.

Libby wasn't in such a good mood. The Americans were refusing to pay for her accommodation when she returned to London to help set up the new offices. This would mean she would have to live with her parents in Berkshire. The company had agreed that she could keep her flat on in Paris and would cover the cost of her rent while she was away. But they knew her family lived close to London and so were digging their heels in. JC had tried all manner of persuasion on her behalf, but had got nowhere. Personally Josie thought Libby was asking too much but then her friend had always been more mercenary than she was. "I'd probably be better off if I was more like her," she thought as she listened to Libby and JC discuss the pending move to London, "But I'm not sure I'd be much happier."

Josie had been too busy over the past few weeks to give much thought to Max or Paul. Neither had been in contact and she was grateful, for different reasons. She also hadn't heard from Jane and now assumed that she wouldn't be hearing from Anna either. She was determined to avoid the cricket club and the gang who hung out there for as long as she could. The previous weekend Daniel had invited her and the girls over to the club for Sunday lunch but they had all declined, having made other plans. "Wild horses wouldn't drag me back there for a while," Josie told her friends, "but don't let me stop you going."

Chrissie had already made plans with Claude, and Josie wasn't sure if Libby was included in the invitation. So they turned Daniel down, but feeling sorry for him Josie invited him to join them for supper on the Sunday evening. During the meal Daniel avoided any mention of Max or Paul, but afterwards, while he helped Josie with the dishes, he told her that Max was absolutely livid. Daniel informed her that Max was telling everyone that Josie was a mad creature who had been pestering him for months.

"I don't really care," replied Josie, although she couldn't believe just how much it hurt her. "People I know and care about know the real truth. If there are those who believe him, then so be it. I can't do anything about it. Have you seen Paul at all? How is he?"

"I haven't seen Paul lately but I have seen Anna. She and Paul are going out together now," he replied.

"Really?" Josie was genuinely surprised. She didn't think Paul was that taken with Anna. Although a small part of her was genuinely relieved, she couldn't help but feel a little hurt. She knew she had no reason to be, "It's just one vicious circle isn't it, Dan? I wonder how Max feels about it!"

"Not too bloody happy from what I gather," he said, "but he has no right to feel that way. Max treated her very badly. Well, he treated everyone badly, you especially."

"I still don't understand why he told me he loved me when he was seeing that Spanish girl. I just don't get it, I never will!"

"That's Max for you, Josie. He always wants what he can't have. And he doesn't want to share what he does have."

Josie remembered the passionate sex with Max. She would be lying to herself if she didn't admit that she missed it. But she had made the right decision. Max would always be the same, he had betrayed Anna. He had betrayed her and seemed incapable of any form of commitment.

"Anyway, how's your love life these days?" Dan asked her.

"Well I've been out with Claude's friend Christian once. He's really good fun but it's nothing serious, which suits me for the moment. I don't need any distractions just now. I'm starting my new job tomorrow."

She was very excited about the next day and had her outfit

already washed and ironed. It had obviously been very sad leaving Chemfast, although it didn't really feel as if she was leaving. JC had taken her aside and told her that she would be supporting them for the Brussels conference, along with the rest of the accounts team from Renseignements. Jacques and Thomas both thought this would be a good transition into the new job. Josie was really pleased that they thought she would be able to handle the additional responsibility.

The Madames had each given her a present and they had all gone to lunch on her last day. Unfortunately JC had been away on business, but had promised to take her out for lunch another time. Muriel had joined them and had been really funny throughout the meal. They all had a lot to drink and not much was achieved that Friday afternoon, even by the Madames who were usually very restrained.

Josie had chatted with Christian for ages on the Friday evening, and on Saturday they had all gone bowling. It was Josie's birthday the following weekend and they had arranged with the air traffic controllers to go to one of the main Parisian nightclubs – La Scala. Unfortunately Claude was unable to come as he was working, but Christian and Yves were looking forward to it and promised to bring along Joel, a fellow air traffic controller who, they promised, was a lot of fun. Libby, whose birthday was on the same day, was going home as she was due to spend the following week in London sorting out the new offices.

"We'll celebrate together when you get back," Josie told her friend, "that way we'll have two birthday celebrations each. What do you think?"

"Can't wait," Libby said, although her response seemed a bit half-hearted. Josie knew that Libby was already fretting about going home, mainly because she wanted to see Matt. But Libby didn't know how they were going to be able to rekindle their affair, especially whilst she was living at her parents' house.

Once supper had been cleared away, Josie headed off for bed and an early night. She could hardly sleep a wink, thoughts of Max and Paul kept her awake. Josie realised she was better off without both of them, but couldn't help feeling sad at the ways things had turned out. Eventually she drifted off and awoke with a start when her mobile started bleeping at 7am. She had set the alarm for 7.30 and she realized it was a text message that had awoken her. The message was from Paul wishing her good luck on her first day, and Josie felt heavy-hearted as she got out of bed. Paul was a very caring, thoughtful man and she wondered if she had made a big mistake in not giving their relationship a chance. Once she had showered and prepared breakfast, her mood perked up. Chrissie was also up early and gave her a little present as apparently it was her saint's day – a good omen, she thought, thanking her friend for her thoughtfulness.

As Josie emerged from the Métro station at Sèvres-Babylone, the sun was shining in the late winter sky. During the short walk to her new offices, she began to feel a little nervous but excited too. Thomas had told her to arrive at 9 am rather than the usual time of 8.30 am. It was her first day and she was looking forward to meeting the entire team.

She had noticed that the dress code at Renseignements was less formal than she was used to but she still wanted to look smart on her first day. She had chosen a knee length plain navy skirt with a pale pink angora cardigan (which was unbuttoned as low as she dared, in order not to show too much cleavage but just enough). Josie was fully aware of her assets and how to use them to the best effect. The walk took just a few minutes and once again she was impressed with the different shops and restaurants that she passed on the way to her new job.

Josie was greeted warmly by Claire who immediately called Thomas from his office. Her new boss greeted her like a long lost friend. Thomas showed her to her desk on the ground floor which she would share with a couple of the other secretaries. The offices were very old but tastefully decorated in pale pastel colours that contrasted with the darkness of the original wood, which adorned the inside of the building. At the back of the office was an old Aga cooker which served as a sort of filing cabinet, and her desk was fashioned from a dark mahogany. The computers, however, were state of the art. Her new colleagues, Charlotte and Odette, welcomed her warmly.

Thomas left her to get to know the other girls and said he would see her at the morning meeting, which was arranged for 11am. He told her they would talk after the meeting about her new role and responsibilities. Charlotte spent some time with her explaining the logging on and email system. Both French girls quizzed Josie quite extensively. Odette was not as friendly as Charlotte, who confided in Josie that Odette had applied unsuccessfully for Josie's job. Charlotte told her that Odette's English hadn't been considered strong enough to fulfil the job requirement. Josie hoped this wouldn't prevent them working well together. She could obviously understand Odette's disappointment, but hoped they could become friends.

At eleven she accompanied Charlotte to the morning meeting. The management team provided everyone with an update on major projects and plans for the coming week. Thomas introduced Josie to everyone and suggested that she book an appointment with each of the account directors so that they could explain their roles and any support that may be required. Josie was a bit confused as she had been led to understand that she would be working for Thomas. She decided to wait until their one-to-one meeting to find out more. The meeting room also served as sort of canteen for the staff and it had a fully equipped kitchen in a small room at the back. It was where all the stationery and other supplies were kept along with the franking machine. The room was known as 'Routage' and Charlotte told her it was the hub of the agency. The staff hung out there to drink their coffee and eat their lunch. When it was a colleague's birthday they usually celebrated there with cake and champagne.

Josie loved the sound of the 'Routage' routines. It had been nothing like that at Chemfast as only the five of them worked there. She thought this was going to be much more fun. Once the meeting was over, she followed Thomas to his office where he outlined what support he expected of her. Like most modern managers, he dealt with his own emails but would be relying on her to keep his diary up to date, arrange appointments and generally manage his time. Thomas stressed that the most important task was helping him with his accounts, which mainly required communicating in English. He explained that she would be working with Daniel Bergerac, the Account Director for the Chemfast conference in Brussels. Thomas also explained that they rented office space to Mervyn Bradley, an independent American PR expert, and she would assist Mervyn on an ad-hoc basis when he was in the office.

This all sounded rather daunting to Josie and, seeing her expression, Thomas said, "Don't worry, it sounds worse that it is. We'll break you in very gently and Mervyn is away for the next few weeks so you'll have plenty of time to get used to Daniel and me first." He reeled off a list of tasks he wanted her to accomplish that day. The rest of the day sped by in a blur of activity. At lunchtime, everyone seemed to have something to do so Josie just popped out for half an hour to get a sandwich and have a look at some of the shops. When she returned to the office, she joined some of the others in the Routage to eat her sandwich and silently enjoyed the banter which was going on around her. Josie hoped that it wouldn't be long before she would be joining in. A pretty brunette introduced herself as Marguerite. She had been at the dentist that morning and had missed the earlier introductions. Marguerite told Josie she worked just next door in the accounts department. She was very formal and polite in welcoming Josie to the agency but there was a twinkle in her eye and Josie took to her immediately. Although Charlotte had been pleasant and helpful, she had seemed a bit haughty, looking down her nose at Josie, and had been a bit gossipy. Odette had been a lot less friendly and had spent part of the morning gossiping with the other secretaries, Pasquale and Christine, in the next room. Josie thought perhaps if she did need some help Claire or Marguerite would be the ones to ask. As if reading her mind, Marguerite said, "If you don't feel comfortable asking for help from those two harridans," she nodded in the direction of Charlotte and Odette, "then come and ask me. I know what they're like. They've been here forever, so they think they know it all."

"I will," Josie replied, thanking her, and planning to invite Marguerite to join her for lunch later that week. It would be a good way of getting to know her and an opportunity to learn a bit more about everyone else. At 3 pm she had a meeting with Daniel Bergerac to discuss the Chemfast conference in Brussels. Daniel, just like the other account directors she had met, was charming. He was in his early thirties and had a mop of blond hair with the springiness of natural curls cut short, and huge, baby blue eyes. On his desk was a photograph of a very pretty, petite blond woman and five gorgeous children, ranging in age from around ten years to twelve months. The children all looked adorable with masses of blond curls. Daniel noticed her looking at the picture.

"All mine, I'm afraid. All five of them," he said looking fondly at the photograph.

"They look lovely," Josie replied, meaning it.

They chatted politely for a few minutes about his children and where the family lived before Daniel changed the subject to the Chemfast conference. He had already had an initial meeting with JC a few weeks previously. They were now due to present their proposal for supporting the conference with PR opportunities, a meeting had been scheduled for that coming Friday.

"I think it would be useful for you to be involved at this early stage," he told Josie, "and then when we go to Brussels you will be up to speed on all the plans. Besides, you know JC better than me and will have a good idea of what he really wants."

"I'm not so sure," she replied, knowing how fickle JC could be sometimes. JC was notoriously vain and both she and Libby had learned pretty quickly how to play on this to get their own way. Daniel ran through some of his initial ideas and plans for the conference. Josie was incredibly impressed with just how professional the organization was. Daniel demonstrated a complete understanding of what JC was aiming to get out of the conference, which was essentially recognition for Chemfast in Europe, rather than its American parent company which often dominated such events. In his presentation, Daniel recommended that JC be the principle spokesperson to the media: the focus was to be on developments in the chemical industry across Southern Europe. Brussels rather than Paris had been chosen as the venue for the conference to ensure customers outside of France felt they were just as important.

Daniel also recommended that JC be entirely open with the media about the imminent move to London. JC had been adamant that he didn't want this mentioned at the conference, he wanted to keep the focus on Southern Europe. But Daniel felt that if news leaked out and it hadn't been included in the main briefing, then it would seem Chemfast had something to hide. Josie agreed with him and promised to support his arguments at the presentation with JC. The rest of the main presentation covered display panel concepts, supporting literature and the announcement of new strategies. Daniel told Josie he was almost finished writing the publications in French and they would soon be translated into English. He suggested that Josie take charge of the proof reading of the English versions of all publications and she happily agreed. Josie also pointed out that she might be able to help with the direct translation, particularly as she was so familiar with Chemfast's previous work and all the necessary jargon. Daniel was pleasantly surprised and gave her a beaming smile, "Josie, it's very unusual around here for someone to volunteer for extra work. I think we are going to get along just fine."

By 6 o'clock, the official finishing time at Renseignements, Josie was exhausted. There had been a lot to take in and it was obvious that Thomas expected her to be up to speed as quickly as possible. She had spent most of the day meeting the rest of the team, making appointments with those who were too busy and ensuring Thomas's diary was up to date. It was pretty obvious that the temp who had been covering before Josie's appointment had let things slide and the diary was in a right mess.

Charlotte and Odette were out of the door bang on 6 o'clock. But Josie wanted to finish inputting the data into the new electronic diary she had set up. They both gave her a strange look as they left, but she just ignored them. Marguerite popped her head around the door a few minutes later. "Don't stay too late," she said, "See you tomorrow."

"Will you have lunch with me tomorrow, Marguerite?" Josie asked the younger girl.

"I'd love to," she replied, smiling. "I'll come and get you around 12.30, OK?"

"OK." Josie smiled. Marguerite seemed so sweet and she really thought she might need an ally in the agency. Josie worked for another fifteen minutes and then went to the Routage to collect her jacket. She was surprised to see most of the management team in there, drinking coffee and just generally chatting.

"Hi Josephine," said Thomas with a surprised look on his face. "What are you still doing here?"

"I just wanted to finish some work ahead of tomorrow," she replied, feeling a bit uneasy at being the centre of attention. All of the senior managers were coolly appraising her.

"Well that's a first," said Véronique, one of the senior account managers. Véronique was a very tall, attractive woman with short cropped hair. Josie thought that hairstyle only suited people with pixie-like faces and high cheek bones. Her clothes were very masculine too but she had a very open manner and Josie had enjoyed the chat they had earlier that day.

"You'll have to watch out, Josie," added Daniel Bergerac, "the other girls won't be happy. They adhere strictly to working hours.

We have to bribe them to stay late with food and overtime pay. Even then they act like they are doing us a favour, well most of them, anyway!"

"Now, now Daniel, don't be so bitchy," said Véronique, laughing. "As true as it might be, you must let Josie judge the other girls for herself." The older woman winked at her, "It shouldn't take you very long." Josie smiled but was feeling increasingly uncomfortable. After all, this was her first day and she didn't want to get off on the wrong foot with anyone.

"How was your first day, Josephine?" asked Thomas, changing the subject and giving Véronique a reprimanding look.

"Good, really good, everyone has been incredibly helpful. I'm sure I'll enjoy working here with you all." Her reply was intentionally diplomatic, yet she noticed Daniel and Véronique exchanging glances.

By the time she reached home Josie was exhausted and just wanted to sink into a hot bath. As she opened the apartment door she could hear male voices in the sitting room. She put her coat and bag in her bedroom, checked out her appearance in the mirror and went to see who was visiting. Josie was pleasantly surprised to see Claude and Christian. But they became strangely quiet when she entered the room, almost as if they had been talking about her.

"Don't mind me," she said to the group which also surprisingly included Libby. "Hey Libby, what are you doing here? I thought you were back in the UK!"

"I just called around to see you all before I leave tomorrow," Libby replied. "It was very quiet without you at Chemfast. I missed you so I phoned here and Chrissie said to pop around. How was your first day, Josie? I bet Thomas is as gorgeous as ever?"

Ignoring the fact that she did feel as though they had been talking about her, Josie told them all about her first day, what was expected of her and her uneasiness about some of her new colleagues. "Maybe I'm being over sensitive but a couple of them really do seem to resent me," she told them.

"Don't worry," Chrissie said, "when I first joined my company the French people weren't very friendly at all, they seemed suspicious of my motives for working there. But they're all really fine now, providing I pull my weight of course," Chrissie smiled. "In fact I pull my weight a damn sight more than they do, but it's worth it to keep everyone happy."

"I hope you're right," Josie replied, "it was such a good atmosphere at Chemfast and I would hate to work somewhere where people didn't like me."

"Thomas and Jacques Fredet liked you enough to offer you the job," added Libby, "and from what you say both Daniel Bergerac and this Véronique woman seem to rate you too. So don't worry so much Josie, you'll soon sort out the others, just wait and see." Libby got up to leave and went around the group exchanging hugs and kisses. She got to Josie last and gave her a big hug. "Well I'm off now. I'll call you before I leave in the morning." Josie felt a little let down. "But I thought you came to see me." Josie was a bit hurt by her friend's sudden departure despite her tiredness.

"But you're back so late," replied Libby, "and I have loads to do at home." She gave Josie a peck on the cheek and said she'd call her the next day.

After a bit of discussion about food, the others all decided to go out for a pizza. Josie was so tired she declined the invitation, saying she was going to have a soak in the bath and just chill in front of the TV. She did ask them to bring her back a takeaway when they came home. Christian looked particularly disappointed, but even his comical impression of a desolate puppy couldn't persuade her to go with them. As the group left the flat, Josie sighed with relief and ran herself a bath. It was gone 8.30 pm by the time she finally sat down in her dressing gown to watch television. After a few minutes of watching a French film she dozed off, only to be awoken moments later by the intercom buzzing. She got up to answer it and was surprised to hear Christian. He had returned early with her pizza. Josie pushed the button to let him in. She was glad that he had made the effort to come back early, but she worried that she didn't have any makeup on and was wearing her scruffy old dressing gown.

"Tough," she thought, purposely not daring to look at herself in the mirror, as she went to let him in. Christian had two large pizza boxes, "I didn't like the thought of you sitting here on your own, Josie. I brought my pizza back too. I hope that's OK with you?" He looked so endearing with his huge dark eyes, and with a genuinely anxious look on his face, that she couldn't help but be pleased, despite her tiredness.

"Of course, Christian, and thanks for the gesture. You really didn't need to but I'm glad you did." His face lit up and again Josie thought what a sweet man he was. She told him to fetch plates and glasses from the kitchen while she changed. She quickly slipped into reasonably decent track suit bottoms and a t-shirt and made it back to the sitting room in just a few minutes. Christian had opened the pizza boxes along with two bottles of beer. "No need for plates or glasses," he said pointing to the food on the table, "boxes and bottles will do. And I remembered that you prefer beer with pizza rather than wine." Josie was touched that he remembered and sat down at the table next to him. They chatted easily as they tucked into their pizza and had a second beer each. When they'd had enough, Josie cleared the boxes and bottles away and made them both a coffee.

They sat side by side on the sofa in companionable silence, watching the news and sipping their coffees. Christian put his arm around Josie and pulled her closer to him. It felt so natural that she just snuggled up, resting her head on his shoulder. Neither of them spoke. He began gently stroking her hair and then kissed the top of her head. She smiled up at him and this time he reached over and kissed her very gently on the mouth. As he pulled away, Josie put her arm around his neck and kissed him herself, this time more passionately. After a few moments, Christian pulled away and, holding Josie gently by her shoulders, he looked at her and said, "Josie, I really like you but I gather from what I've picked up from Claude and Chrissie you've had a bit of a rough time lately. Well, as far as men and relationships are concerned. I don't want to rush you into anything new, especially if you're not ready. But I just want to say that I am not like those other guys. I really like you and I think we could have a good thing going, but only if you really want to. I could as easily be your friend but I would like to be far more," Christian caressed her cheek softly, "While I was away skiing, I just couldn't get you out of my mind. I knew you were going through a bad time so I've tried not to hassle you since I came back. But you looked so lovely tonight, especially when I came back with the pizzas….." He trailed off when he realized that Josie had tears in her eyes.

After all the traumas with Max, then splitting up with Paul, the uncertainties of finding a new job and now Christian being so adoring and lovely, the floodgates just opened. Josie could hardly keep the teardrops from falling. "I'm sorry Josie," he said, sounding really concerned and wiping away her tears with the tips of his fingers. "I really didn't mean to upset you. Shall I go?"

"No, please don't go," she replied, wiping away the tears with the back of her hand, "it's all just been so traumatic of late. I suppose I was more nervous than I let on about starting this new job. You have been so lovely to me, Christian." Josie kissed him gently on the lips. "I really like you too but I'm afraid of rushing into things. I always seem to get it all so wrong. I'm a little bit scared. But I do want to see you again. I just need to take things slowly." Christian pulled her gently into his arms and, laying her head on his shoulder, softly stroked her hair. "Josie, I promise I won't hurt you or treat you badly. Trust me, just a little bit, and I'll prove it to you." Josie was overwhelmed by a mix of elation and fatigue. They stayed cuddling and caressing each other, talking effortlessly about their respective likes and dislikes, their families and respective backgrounds. At 10.30 the others came back and exchanged knowing glances when they saw Christian and Josie cuddled up together on the sofa.

"Time to go," Claude told Christian. "Early start tomorrow so let's be off, I definitely need my beauty sleep!"

"Yes you do, my friend," replied Christian jokingly.

Claude smiled and said, "I guess you'll be walking home then?"

"Not on your life," he replied. "Just give me a few minutes with Josie."

Chrissie picked up on it straight away and ushered Claude out into the hallway on the pretext of showing him something from the balcony.

"Sorry, that wasn't very subtle," said Christian, taking Josie's face in his hands and kissing her again passionately.

"Can we meet tomorrow evening, Josie? We could go for a meal or the cinema?" he asked, "I finish work around four and I can pick you up straight from work," Christian smiled, "if that's not too presumptuous of me?"

"That would be great, Christian," she replied, thinking that it would be a pleasure to spend some more time with this handsome French man. It would also give her the opportunity to show him off to the girls in the office. Josie gave him the address of the new office and he promised to call her the next day to make arrangements. Once the boys had left, Chrissie couldn't wait to hear what had happened with Christian. She told Josie that he had been really disappointed that she hadn't come out with them earlier, "but when Claude suggested he take the pizza back, he said he didn't want to frighten you off. It was Claude who persuaded him to change his mind," said Chrissie.

"Well you obviously have him well trained," said Josie.

Chrissie tossed a cushion at her, "you cheeky mare."

Josie told her how sweet Christian had been and that they were meeting after work the following evening. "Great," said Chrissie, "he's a really lovely guy Josie, and I know Claude trusts him with his life. He's hot too... not as hot as Claude of course but then I'm so much hotter than you.... so fair's fair!" Josie couldn't help but laugh, "Dream on Chrissie, Claude's only after you for one thing." Chrissie raised her eyebrows and pouted, 'and what would that be exactly?"

"English lessons," said Josie, "and somewhere to kip when he goes out in Paris." Both girls burst into laughter.

"Oh yeah....well Christian's only interested in you because he's heard you're easy!" retaliated Chrissie, moving off the sofa quickly before Josie whacked her over the head with a cushion. The girls headed off to their bedrooms still teasing each other. As Josie was settling down under the duvet her mobile bleeped. It was a message from Christian: "Looking forward to seeing you tomorrow, sleep well. C xxx"

She sent a quick reply: "me too" and switched off her bedside lamp. As tired as she was, Josie couldn't get off to sleep. Her thoughts kept drifting back to her first day at Renseignements and the evening with Christian. His kisses had turned her on but she wasn't planning on jumping into bed with him straight away – well not yet at least. Too many of Josie's past relationships had, as with Max, been based just on sex, and she really didn't want to go through a repeat of that situation again. In her heart of hearts she knew that she'd behaved stupidly and should have realized that Max probably didn't have a faithful bone in his body.

The thought did make her a bit uncomfortable. She hadn't exactly been great girlfriend material herself over the years and really had no right to judge Max so harshly. Images from the past pushed their way into the forefront of her mind. Charles Francis. Handsome, educated, sexy and 20 years older than her! Josie smiled remembering the first time she met him. She'd managed to get a job in a local solicitor's practice the summer before she went to university, just doing some admin and reception work to cover staff holidays. Charles was one of the senior partners and from the first time they met he was very flirty with Josie, as he was with all the female employees.

On her first day, he'd stopped at the reception desk and introduced himself. When he shook her hand, he had seemed to hold it that fraction of a second longer than was necessary. He also looked directly into her eyes when he introduced himself and Josie could feel herself starting to blush. She'd never met anyone quite so 'suave' and who had made such an instant, physical impact on her. For the previous two years she had been going out with Jon, a boy from her school. Both were planning to go to different universities and though Jon was convinced their relationship would last, Josie wasn't so sure. She did care about him but wanted to have a good time at university, without feeling guilty. They had been sleeping together for almost eighteen months and, although Josie enjoyed sex with Jon, there was no way it could be described as 'wow'.

During her working day she didn't have much to do with Charles, but when their paths crossed she always felt a strong attraction to him, despite the age difference. After working at the office for a couple of weeks, Josie was invited out for Friday night drinks by Jayne, one of the legal secretaries. They went to a local wine bar a few streets away from the office and Josie noticed that several of the partners from the office were also there, including Charles. When he saw Josie standing at the bar waiting to be served, he raised his glass and winked at her. She smiled back, a frisson running through her body and an unexpected dampness in her pants!

"Whoa!" she said to herself. "What's that all about?" She glanced back at Charles. He was still looking directly at her, as if he knew just what sort of reaction he'd had on her. She turned away quickly, blushing and accepting the glass of wine that Jayne passed her. The two girls moved away from the busy bar but didn't join the group of partners. Jayne had worked at the office for nearly a year and was quite a chatterbox. So Josie probed her about the people who worked there, without mentioning any names. Jayne seemed to know all the office gossip but didn't mention Charles once. Josie was aching to ask about him but didn't dare in case it sounded like she was interested in him. Eventually, when Jayne had exhausted her repertoire of office gossip, Josie, trying to be subtle, asked "What about the partners?"

"Well the two senior partners, Matthew Bannister and Charles Francis, have been in business together forever. Matthew's married with three children but Charles is a self-confessed bachelor. He does have an awful lot of female friends, most of them absolutely gorgeous. He wheels them out from time to time for functions but I don't think any of them are serious. Charles is lovely. He's a right flirt but that's as far as it goes. Everyone likes him. He's incredibly well respected in Bristol legal circles. He does quite a bit for charity too. I can't believe someone hasn't snapped him up yet! I wouldn't mind, even if he is a bit old."

Josie didn't say anything. Jayne's revelations were very interesting. Charles Francis was even more interesting. She made her way back to the bar to buy another round and couldn't resist glancing over at where Charles and the other partners had been standing. There was only him and another man whom she didn't recognize. The other partners had left. They were deep in conversation and Josie took the opportunity to observe him from across the bar. He was extremely handsome in a classic, Burton shop window way. Dark brown, well cut hair with a very slight tinge of grey at the temples, piercing, clear blue eyes, a Roman nose and thin but sensitive lips. He looked in good shape too. He'd taken off his suit jacket and she could see the muscles in his back straining against the cotton material of his shirt. As if sensing her gaze, Charles turned to stare at her. Embarrassed to be caught eyeing him up, Josie blushed but didn't look away. Charles smiled at her knowingly and then turned back to his conversation.

Josie took the drinks back to Jayne and they continued chatting about the office and their plans for the weekend. They finished their drinks and left the wine bar. Josie didn't look in Charles's direction again. The girls lived on opposite sides of Bristol so went their separate ways at the end of the road. Rather than phone for a taxi, Josie decided to enjoy the warm, summer evening and walk down Park Street towards the city centre and pick up a cab from there. As she made her way through the tree lined streets of Clifton towards White Ladies Road, she couldn't help but think about Charles and the way her body had reacted to him. Her thoughts elsewhere, she stepped out onto the road without looking and was nearly knocked over by a sleek, dark green sports car. The car swerved to avoid her and then pulled up a few feet away. The roof of the car was down and as the driver turned his head, Josie was mortified to see that it was Charles.

"I'm so sorry," Josie said, realizing she had no option other than to approach the car. "I was in a world of my own!"

"No harm done," he replied with a twinkle in his eye. "Can I give you a lift somewhere?"

The thought of sitting next to Charles in the close confines of his sports car made Josie feel very jittery indeed.

"I was heading to the centre to pick up a taxi," she said, "I don't want to take you out of your way."

Charles opened the car door without saying a word. Josie slipped into the cream leather seat trying to look as elegant as possible. Conscious that her skirt was maybe exposing a bit too much leg, she tried discretely to pull it down. Charles raised his eyebrows and grinned. He put the car into gear and drove off towards the city centre.

"Where do you live, Josie?" he asked.

"Frampton Cotterell" she said.

"I'm heading to Iron Acton; I can drop you home if you like?"

"Are you sure?" she replied. "I can easily get a cab."

"My pleasure," said Charles.

The way he said it made Josie's insides turn to jelly.

"So how are you enjoying your summer job," he asked her.

"It's great," she replied. "Well, it's not very challenging but it's a job and the people are really lovely."

"Really, so how do you like to be challenged then, Josie?"

She wished she hadn't said it now.

"I'm not sure really. I like learning new languages. I'm going to study languages at university."

"Interesting! You don't fancy a career in law then?"

"No" she replied, "it's not my thing. I really want to travel and work abroad, my best subject is French, so studying languages seems like a good idea."

"Is your boyfriend going to university with you?"

"How do you know I've got a boyfriend?" she replied sharply.

"Just a hunch," he laughed.

"Jon, my boyfriend, is going to Durham. I'm going to Cardiff. So not exactly close."

"You don't want to be tied down, Josie. You're far too young. You should enjoy yourself at university. There will be loads of young men, away from home for the first time. You should make the most of it!"

Josie was surprised at Charles's comments.

"What do you mean?" she asked him, knowing that she was pushing her luck.

"You know exactly what I mean!"

"So you're talking about sex?" she said. Josie couldn't believe she was being so bold.

"Of course I am," Charles laughed.

"I'm not planning on sleeping around when I go to university," said Josie haughtily.

"Really? What about experimenting?"

"Experimenting?"

"Yes, experimenting with different partners. Safely of course!"

The tremors running through Josie's groin were becoming uncontrollable.

"Do you understand what I mean, Josie?" he continued.

"Of course," she said with a confidence that she didn't quite feel.

"So how many sexual partners have you had then?"

Josie didn't want to get caught in a lie.

"Just the one, just Jon, I'm almost eighteen and we've been together for almost two years."

"And how is sex with Jon?" asked Charles. "Does he make it good for you?"

"Sex with Jon is good, thanks for asking! But then I have nothing to compare it to."

She couldn't believe she was having such a frank conversation with Charles. The whole car journey was becoming rather surreal.

"True, but that can be sorted!"

"Can it?"

"Well if you want it to?"

By now Josie's knickers were soaking wet and her clitoris was throbbing alarmingly. She definitely wanted to know a bit more of what Charles had in mind.

"Well, in the name of experimentation, I guess it would be wrong not to!"

Charles pulled the car into a lay-by. Josie snuck a quick peek at his crotch and could see from the outline of his penis that he was as turned on as she was. He undid his seat belt and turned to face her. Looking directly into her eyes he said, "Do you really want to, Josie? I'm not into playing games but I would very much like to be your 'experiment'."

Looking him directly in the eyes, Josie placed her hand on his leg. She could feel the taught muscles under the soft fabric of his trousers tightening.

"As I said, it would be quite wrong not to!"

He leaned forward and ran his finger gently over her lower lip. "It would indeed. Do you have to be anywhere this evening?" he asked.

"No but I will need to call home to let them know I'm going to be late."

"You do that!"

Josie was excited and scared at the same time. What on earth was she doing? Essentially she was agreeing to sex with a partner in a solicitor's office, and one which her Dad used for business. But despite her reservations, Josie had never felt so sexually excited before.

"OK," she said, reinforcing the concept in her own mind.

Charles snapped his seat belt back on and pulled out sharply from the lay-by. After a few minutes of driving in silence, he turned onto the main road into Iron Acton. The sexual tension in the car was palpable; you could cut it with a knife.

"How long have you lived in Frampton?" Charles asked, breaking the silence.

"Since I was eleven," she replied. "We moved to be in the school catchment area."

"Of course, I mustn't forget that you are, in fact, still a school girl! Now there's a thought!"

Josie squirmed. Compared to many of her classmates she thought she was actually quite sophisticated. But obviously not in the eyes of this man. He turned the car into a side road and then into the driveway of a large Edwardian house. He switched off the engine and turned to stare at Josie.

"What's going through that pretty head of yours, Josie?" he asked, looking directly into her eyes.

Taking a deep breath, she decided to tell him the truth.

"I'm very nervous Charles, but very excited too. But I do have one question."

"Fire away."

"OK, why me? You can have the pick of any beautiful women. Why an ordinary little school girl like me?"

Charles laughed. "I like your directness. Basically Josie, there's nothing better in life than sex. But it needs to be great sex. If it's not great it's a waste of time. I don't make a habit of luring schoolgirls into my home, if that's what you're thinking. But once in a while, you meet someone and the chemistry is so strong that you simply have to do something about it."

Josie was completely taken aback. She'd felt attraction from the outset but hadn't realized that Charles had felt it too. He leaned towards her and kissed her very gently on the lips. Josie closed her eyes in anticipation of more but it seemed that was it for now. Patting her on the knee, he opened the driver's door and stepped out of the car. As she scrambled for her handbag on the floor, he opened her car door and extended his hand to help her out. Again, Josie was conscious of the length of her skirt, as she stepped out of the sports car. He closed the door and, placing his hand on the small of her back, guided her towards the front door. As they stepped inside Josie looked around with interest. The decor was as she expected, very smart and sophisticated. The walls were decorated a plain white and adorned with a selection of abstract paintings, the furniture was modern and minimalist. Charles opened a door directly off the hallway and gently ushered her into a light and spacious sitting room. He dropped his suit jacket onto the back of a chair and pulled her into his arms.

"This is where the fun starts, Josie," he said, bending to kiss her. His lips caressed hers, gently at first, and then harder, as his tongue gently probed until their tongues finally met. His hands grasped her buttocks, pulling her close, so that she could feel the hardness of his erection against her leg. His hands ran up and down her body, making her tingle. Her arms automatically wrapped themselves around his neck, pulling his body even closer. He wedged his knee between her legs and she couldn't stop herself from rubbing her crotch hard against him. Charles lifted her skirt and slipped his fingers inside the elastic of her pants and then into her soaking vagina. She groaned with pleasure as his fingers slipped inside her and his thumb found the swollen nub of her clitoris. She could feel herself climaxing, her need for release was overwhelming. Josie pushed herself harder against him. The whole process had only taken a few short minutes but Josie was reeling from the aftermath of her orgasm. He continued kissing her, whilst fingering her vagina, bringing her to the brink once again. Sliding his fingers out from between her swollen lips, he licked each one like a child with a lollypop.

"Enough for now," he said, cupping her chin in his hands. "I need to take a shower and make a quick phone call. It's probably best if you make the call you need to make too. You won't have much time later."

He left the room, returning a few moments later with a glass of white wine which he placed on the large, dark mahogany coffee table in the centre of the room.

"Where's the bathroom?" she asked him, conscious that she needed to freshen up herself.

"There's a cloakroom across the hallway but I don't want you to shower just yet, Josie. I want to taste every inch of you, exactly as you are."

She didn't reply. She couldn't. Once Charles left the room, she took a big gulp of the wine and then headed for the loo. She wiped herself dry and ran a sink of warm water to wash herself. She was conscious of Charles's words but she didn't feel clean and needed to freshen up a bit. Catching a glimpse of her face in the mirror, she thought she looked different. More confident, more self assured, and her eyes were sparkling from a mix of wine and desire. She emptied the sink and made her way back to the sitting room. Charles hadn't reappeared so she phoned home, trying to sound as nonchalant as possible. Her mother answered and Josie explained that everyone was going back to Jayne's house and she was going too.

"Have fun sweetheart," her mother replied.

Josie hated deceiving her mother. They had a great relationship and both her parents were pretty open-minded. But she knew they wouldn't approve of what she was up to with Charles. At that moment, Charles walked back into the room with a bottle of wine and another glass in his hand.

"Bye Mum."

"All OK?" Charles asked her, the hint of a smile tugging at his lips. He was wearing a khaki t-shirt, loose, beige chinos and his feet were bare.

21

"Sure, all's good. I just need to send a text."

"To the boyfriend?" he asked and she nodded.

Josie keyed in a quick message to Jon, "Having a night out with the girls from work. Catch you tomorrow. J xxx."

She immediately switched her phone off in case Jon, or her mother, called her back.

"So now that's all settled," said Charles, sitting next to her and draping his arm over her shoulders, "what would you like to eat, Josie?"

She hadn't thought about food. She wasn't at all hungry. In fact, she was so churned up in anticipation that she didn't think she could eat a thing.

"I really don't mind," she said, sipping her wine and looking directly at Charles.

Taking the glass from her hand, he placed it on the coffee table and pulled her gently onto his lap. He grasped her hair, pulling her head back gently, and ran his tongue along the length of her neck. Josie could feel his erection rubbing against her thighs and tentatively slipped her hand down to stroke the length of his cock. He was obviously wearing no underwear and she was turned on by the feel of his hard penis through the fabric of his trousers. The illicit sensation of his kisses on her neck was sending ripples of pleasure throughout her entire body.

With a quick movement, Charles moved Josie from a sitting position on his lap, so that she was spread across his knees. He continued to caress her buttocks. Again he slipped his fingers inside her knickers and into her hot, wet hole. Then he lifted her skirt and pulled down her lacy pants, revealing her bum cheeks. As he fingered her deeply, he gave her a gentle slap on her bottom. Josie was shocked and then even more surprised at her body's reaction. Sensing her pleasure, Charles slapped her buttocks a bit harder and Josie groaned, unable to control her reaction to his firm hands. Then he slapped her really hard. Josie thought that she would totally explode. The combined manipulation of his fingers deep inside her with the slaps on her bottom became unbearably erotic. She could feel herself coming again and simply let her body go with the flow. With his fingers still inside her, he began to rub her clitoris with his thumb. Josie felt raw but couldn't resist moving against his hand until she could bear it no longer and felt the release of an orgasm for the third time in less than an hour. He removed his fingers and this time offered them to Josie to suck. She slipped his fingers into her mouth, tasting herself for the first time ever. Charles watched her intently. She did feel a bit self-conscious but continued to suck his fingers nevertheless. He removed his fingers and kissed her deeply. Then he stood up, his erection visible, pulling Josie to her feet too.

"Come on, I'm starving. Let's see what we can rustle up in the kitchen."

She followed him down the hallway and into a large open plan kitchen-dining room that overlooked a pretty courtyard at the back of the house. There was a breakfast bar island in the middle of the room and Charles indicated that Josie sit on one of the tall stools. He topped up their glasses and started taking food out of the fridge.

"Feta salad OK with you?" he asked.

"Lovely," she replied.

"I like to eat light in the evenings," he told her as he began to prepare the salad.

"Can I help?" Josie was enjoying watching a domesticated Charles at work.

"I can manage thanks." He looked up from his task of chopping black olives, smiling at her.

"Is there anything you don't like?" he asked, quite suggestively.

"No, I'll eat anything," Josie said in an equally suggestive tone.

Charles laughed and carried on with his task. Within a few minutes, the salad was ready and he put out a couple of plates with cutlery. From the fridge he found a pre-prepared dressing and then quickly warmed some flat bread in the microwave.

The food made Josie realize just how hungry she was.

"Tuck in," he said, piling her plate with at least half of the salad. Josie picked up her fork and tasted the refreshing plate of cheese, olives and mixed salad. It needed a little dressing so she helped herself and tore off a piece of flat bread to soak up the sauce. There was no point in standing on ceremony, she thought to herself. She wanted to seem confident and self assured even though she didn't really feel it. In fact, this all felt very grown up indeed and Josie wasn't sure if she wasn't a bit out of her depth. They ate silently for a few moments before Josie broke the ice.

"So how long have you lived here," she asked. It sounded like small talk but she was genuinely interested.

"Around five years now," Charles replied, stabbing a piece of lettuce and feta cheese with his fork. "I bought the house as in investment originally. I used to live in a flat in Clifton, close to the office. I had this place done up by a friend who's an architect and when it was finished I loved it so much that I couldn't bring myself to rent it out. Also, I found living so close to the office made it quite hard to switch off at times. So now I rent out the flat and live here instead."

"Sounds ideal," Josie said. "It's a great house for a party."

"A student type party, you mean?"

"No, I mean a sort of dinner party. The kitchen is lovely and I always think an open plan dining room is better. It means the 'chef' can be involved with the guests without disappearing off all the time."

"What about your home?" he asked.

"It's lovely too," she replied. "My mum has good taste and we also have an open plan kitchen-dining room. Family or friends are popping in and out all the time and if it's supper time, well there's always plenty of food for everyone. I really like that. It's how I want my home to be. Whenever I get one of my own, of course."

Charles just nodded and continued to devour his salad. He topped up their wine glasses again but Josie only took a few small sips of hers. She wanted to be clear headed for whatever he had planned for the rest of the evening. Once they'd finished the salad, Charles stood up and pulled Josie to her feet. He then led her back into the sitting room, carrying their wine glasses. He placed them on the coffee table and sat down on the sofa, pulling Josie down next to him.

"Don't be frightened, Josie," he said gently, his finger caressing her jaw. "I won't do anything that you feel uncomfortable with and I'll take things gently this evening. I just want you to enjoy yourself and to learn – learn about how great, how really great sex can be!"

Josie just nodded, she couldn't trust herself to speak and her body had once again developed a life of its own. Her nipples and clitoris throbbed in anticipation and she was so wet that she was worried that she'd leave a damp patch on the sofa. Taking a sip of her wine, she leaned into Charles and offered up her mouth for a kiss. She wasn't disappointed. He kissed her parted lips, gently and then harder with more urgency, so that their tongues were intertwined deep within each other's mouths. He caressed her face, her arms, the nape of her back, every part of her, apart from the areas where she most desperately wanted to be touched. With a swift, sudden movement, Charles pulled her onto his lap again but this time stood up with her in his arms.

"Time to adjourn to somewhere more appropriate, I think," he said, carrying her upstairs.

Josie wrapped her arms around his neck and gently nipped his chin and neck as he headed toward one of the bedrooms. Charles unceremoniously dropped her onto the bed. It was still light outside so he closed the curtains of the bay window. The room was now in semi darkness but they could still see each other quite easily. Charles pulled off his t-shirt and lay down next to her on the king size double bed. Josie lay on her back, looking at the older man with anticipation. Leaning over her, he ran his fingers from her knee, up her thigh and to the edge of her knickers. This time, he didn't slip his finger inside her but cupped the whole of her vagina with his hand, massaging her with his palm. She pushed her pelvis against his hand, lifting herself to meet him. She placed her hands gently on his shoulders, steadying herself as she moved her body faster against his hand.

Charles quickly moved his hand from her pelvis and pushed her back onto the bed. He moved his leg between hers, lifting her top over her head. He then gently pulled her bra straps off her shoulders and pushed her bra down, exposing her large, full breasts. He ran his fingers around the aureole of her right breast before gently pinching her nipple. He then bent his head and sucked on her left nipple. Josie was by now dripping wet and the whole of her lower body felt like liquid. She pushed her soaking crotch hard against his leg that was nestling between hers and pinning her down. Charles continued to pinch and lick her nipples until Josie thought she'd explode. She wanted him inside her but didn't want to rush him. Sensing her impatience, Charles moved his leg, then unzipped her skirt and pulled it down past her ankles. He moved down her body, placing his mouth over her mound, still covered by her fine, lace panties. He breathed heavily onto her clitoris and Josie almost hit the ceiling. The sensation was like nothing she'd ever experienced before. His tongue teased her through the thin material and she felt a rush of hot warmth course through her body. Charles gently teased her panties off her body and then, kneeling before her, put his hands under her buttocks and lifted her wet and gleaming clitoris towards his mouth. As his tongue licked and probed her lips and nub, slipping in and out of her in rhythm with her thrusts, he slipped one of his fingers into her, wetting it before he pulled it out and slipped the tip gently into her anus.

Josie had never experienced any form of anal penetration before. She tensed at first but as the tip of his finger slipped slowly into her, she couldn't believe what the combination of his tongue and fingers were doing to her. Again, she could feel herself starting to orgasm and as she pushed herself harder into his face, she had the biggest, wettest orgasm of her life. In fact, it felt like she'd wet herself. As Charles moved up her body, he kissed her deeply and passionately. His face and lips were soaking and for the second time that night she tasted her own juices.

"A gusher!" Charles said, smiling proudly down at her. Josie didn't know whether to be pleased or embarrassed. She guessed that he was referring to her very wet and intense orgasm. So far, Charles had taken full control of her body but she didn't want him to think she was a selfish lover. She moved up onto her elbow and gently placed her hand on his chest, gradually moving her fingers down his torso until they slipped into the top of his chinos. She found the tip of his penis and moved her index finger gently around the tip. He grabbed her wrist and pulled her hand out of his trousers.

"Not yet," he said. "I haven't finished with you."

Turning her over onto her stomach, he undid her bra and slipped it off her arms. He gently lay on top of her, bearing his weight on his elbows, kissing the back of her neck. He then sat back on his haunches and, placing his hands on her buttocks, spread her so that her backside was completely open. He gently rimmed the outside of her anus and then probed with little caressing darts of his tongue. At the same time, he moved is hand under her, cupping the whole of her mound. He slipped his thumb inside her vagina and then his index finger, hooking his finger towards her anus.

This time, Josie lifted her whole lower body up towards him, wanting more and more. Before she reached the point of no return, Charles flipped her over onto her back, lay alongside and pulled her on top. He told her to kneel up and to grab her own heels. Josie obeyed and he moved his body down the bed, until his mouth was once again in line with her labia. Gently holding her buttocks, he pulled her clitoris closer to his mouth and licked her all over again, moving from clitoris to perineum and back again. Within a few seconds, Josie could feel the rush of warm liquid drip down from her melting hole into his mouth.

"My God," she exclaimed, moving herself away from his mouth, the intensity too much to stand any longer.

Charles moved back up the bed, grinning. Josie collapsed onto her back, completely spent. He kept grinning at her, as he ran his fingertips over her belly and the tops of her legs. She couldn't move or respond to his caresses, her lower body had turned to mush. He swung his legs over the side of the bed and stood up. Very slowly, he unzipped his trousers and elegantly stepped out of them. His erection was impressive and Josie literally gasped as it sprung out proudly in front of her. As he moved to the side of the bed, Josie instinctively turned her mouth towards the head of his penis and licked the tip gently.

"You're going to do exactly as I tell you Josie."

She looked up at him, her tongue still teasing the swollen head of his cock and nodded.

"I want you to lick the length of my shaft, making me as wet as possible. And then I want you take each of my balls in your mouth and roll them around."

Josie obliged, glad that he was telling her what to do. She and Jon had experimented a bit with oral sex but neither was very experienced, and it hadn't been great. Charles definitely knew how to push all her buttons and she hoped that if she followed his instructions she'd do the same for him.

As she slipped his testicles into her mouth, sucking gently on each one, being careful to cover her teeth with her lips, Charles let out a low, groan.

"Now I want you to lick the head of my cock and slip your tongue into the slit at the top."

Josie did as she was told, warming to the task. A slither of pre-cum escaped from the tip of his phallus and Josie licked it up and swirled the white fluid around her mouth, before flicking her tongue over the slit again. Charles let out a low, animal groan. Instinctively, Josie moved her mouth over the full head of his penis, sucking it like a lollipop. She pushed her tongue around the rim as she sucked his length, moving her hands to gently squeeze his balls. She could feel the telltale movement of his approaching orgasm. Charles pulled suddenly from her mouth as if steeling himself not to come.

"Not yet, young lady," he said, steadying himself against the bed.

He lay down next to her, his erection at a right angle to his taught, tanned belly.

"I think it's time I fucked you?" he said, a hoarseness creeping into his voice.

"Yes please," Josie replied, opening her legs so he could see her swollen, open womanhood.

He lay on his back and pulled her on top of him. Reaching into the drawer of the bedside cabinet, he reached for a condom.

"I'm on the pill," Josie told him, hoping that this would impress him.

"Even so, you should always be careful, Josie."

He slipped the condom easily over his steel hard penis and placed his hands on her hips.

"I want you to lift your pussy above my cock and then lower yourself gently onto me," he told her.

Once again Josie obliged and, putting her hands on his shoulders, lifted her hot, open and ready hole over the head of his penis. She teased the tip with her lips before she pushed herself slowly down the length of his shaft. He filled her completely and it felt as if he was going to split her in two. She moved her body back up his length and back down again, her vaginal muscles gripping him.

"Push your legs along mine," Charles said.

Josie moved her shoulders forward, and her legs down the length of the bed, until she was literally on top of him but with his cock still deep inside her. She moved herself slowly at first and then faster as the red, hard tip of her clitoris came into direct contact with the taut muscles of his stomach. He placed his hands on her waist to control the pace and then on her buttocks so that he could penetrate her even more deeply. Her breasts dangled tantalizingly over his mouth and he lifted his head upwards to suck on them, moving from one to the other, nipping her tender, swollen nipples with his teeth. Josie moved faster and faster, her climax approaching as her clitoris repeatedly brushed against his torso. Charles moved his hands back to her waist to steady her thrusts. As her muscles contracted around him, her juices finally flowed all over him, he thrust his hips deeply into her as his body released in an intense and shuddering orgasm. Josie kept clenching her muscles, drawing every last drop of sperm out, until she could hold on no more. He was still semi-hard and stayed inside her as they lay together.

Charles began to run his fingers along her spine, from between her shoulder blades down to the top of her buttocks. He then began to caress her cheeks, patting them gently at first and then landing some slightly harder slaps. Josie could feel his cock hardening inside her again and despite feeling sore and swollen, couldn't stop herself from moving along the length of him. Their movements were slower, gentler. Josie was so tender and swollen that the friction of her clitoris against his stomach was almost unbearable. She changed her position, still on top, but leaned back and gripped his ankles. He seemed to move even deeper inside her. She moved along his shaft from tip to core, building up a faster pace to meet his urgent thrusts. With one final thrust, Charles came again and Josie felt a huge sense of satisfaction at having given him pleasure too. She leaned back over him so that her face was close to his. Charles put his hand on the back of her head and pulled her mouth toward him. He kissed her softly on the mouth and gently eased her off his body. Standing up, his penis was still semi-hard in the aftermath of sex. Grinning at her he headed for the bathroom to flush away the condom. Josie lay back on the pillows, tingling from head to toe. She couldn't believe how many orgasms she had just experienced. She genuinely didn't realize it was possible. With Jon it was usually a bit of foreplay and then a quick fuck. Many times afterwards Josie would masturbate to finish off what Jon had started. She didn't have the heart, or the experience, to tell him what to do.

"How are you feeling, Josie?" Charles asked, returning to the bedroom, a towel around his waist and one in his hand for her.

"Amazing," she said.

"Good," he replied grinning. "Fancy joining me for a shower?"

"I'd love to," she replied, taking the towel from his hand. Her instinct was to wrap it around herself but she simply flung it over her shoulder and made her way across the bedroom to the bathroom, wiggling her bottom in the process. Charles burst out laughing, but there was a hint of admiration in his eyes too. Josie knew she had a good figure and was prepared to flaunt it.

The shower was behind an oval shaped wall of black and white tiles, like some sort of sports changing room. There was a huge, round shower head and jets coming out of the walls. Josie dropped the towel on the floor and let the hot water cascade over her body. Charles joined her, and taking the shower gel, rubbed it all over her body, massaging her breasts and buttocks. She took the bottle out of his hands and returned the favour, rubbing the soap into his chest and torso, moving slowly down to his genitals. His cock sprang to life once again. She continued massaging the soap along the length of his cock and around his balls. Josie then cupped water in her hands to rinse him. Ensuring there was no trace of soap, she fell to her knees and took his cock in her mouth. As the hot shower cascaded over her head, she licked and sucked him just as he'd instructed her earlier. He came in her mouth, fast, hard, a hot rush, his hands holding her head in place so she didn't lose a drop of his sperm. Standing up, Josie kissed him deeply, sharing the liquid she had saved in her mouth. He kissed her back, sucking her mouth dry of his semen. Pushing her gently away, he reached for the shampoo bottle and gently washed and rinsed her hair. He switched off the shower, stepped out and then wrapped her in the towel she had dropped on the floor.

"There's a hair dryer in the drawer next to the bed," he said wrapping his towel around his waist.

Josie dried her hair quickly, sitting on the side of the bed. Charles picked his clothes up off the floor and dressed quickly. Glancing at the clock next to his bed, Josie was surprised to see that it was only ten o'clock. She felt a bit awkward. She didn't know what she was supposed to do next. Charles had already left the bedroom so she retrieved her clothes from the floor and began to dress. Her knickers were still damp and so, feeling brazen, she slipped them under the covers of Charles's bed.

Josie found Charles in the kitchen clearing away the dishes.

"You OK?" he asked her.

"Fine thanks", she replied.

"Just fine?" he asked, cupping her chin in his hand.

Josie smiled, "Absolutely great!"

"That's more like it." He bent and kissed her gently. "Would you like another glass of wine?"

"Yes please." She was glad that he wasn't pushing her out the door straightaway. Josie sat on one of the high kitchen stools and sipped her drink whilst he carried on clearing up.

"I'll call a cab if that's OK," she said.

"Sure, use the phone in the hall, the number's on a card in the drawer."

"What's the address?" she asked.

He told her and she made her way into the hall to call the taxi company. Josie returned to the kitchen. She felt as if she was walking on air.

"Fifteen minutes," she said, picking up her glass to finish her wine.

Charles nodded.

Josie wanted to ask 'what now' but didn't want to seem too keen.

"Any plans for the weekend?" she asked instead.

Charles raised a quizzical eyebrow. Josie realized that he may have misinterpreted her question.

"I'm going to London tomorrow," she continued not wanting him to think that she was pushing to see him again. "My mum and I are going shopping and then to see a show in the West End."

"Sounds fun," he said.

Josie smiled at him and Charles pulled her into his arms. His piercing blue eyes held hers.

"I know you're thinking - what next?"

She blushed, embarrassed that she'd been so transparent.

"I'd really like to carry on with our 'experiment', but only if you really want to."

She nodded.

"Good," he replied, kissing her gently on the forehead. "Monday night then, as you have such a busy weekend ahead of you!"

Josie had the distinct feeling that he was mocking her plans but she let it go.

"Monday it is," she replied. The anticipation was almost unbearable. They exchanged mobile numbers and Charles told her he'd text her on Monday to finalize the arrangements. The taxi tooted its horn outside and Josie picked up her bag, ready to leave.

"See you Monday then," she said.

"Looking forward to it," he replied winking at her.

During the taxi ride home, Josie thought about her evening with Charles and could feel herself getting damp once again. Her parents were in the sitting room watching TV as she stuck her head around the door.

"Hi honey, did you have good evening?" her mother asked.

"Yes, lovely," she replied. "I'm off to bed Mum, we have such an early start in the morning."

Lying in bed, she couldn't get the thoughts of Charles and what he'd done to her body out of her mind. She was soaking wet again and, with a will of its own, her hand moved down the bed towards her throbbing clitoris. She came quickly and, as Charles had taught her, licked her fingers, enjoying the taste of her own juices.

For the rest of that summer, Josie visited Charles's house as often as she could. The sex was amazing and he taught her well. He introduced her to gentle bondage and porn, amongst other things. The week after her first evening with Charles, Josie ended her relationship with Jon. He was really upset and couldn't understand what had changed. She used the excuse of university and how she didn't feel it was fair for either of them to be tied. Her mother was surprised too but didn't interfere. Although her parents were pretty broad-minded, Josie knew they wouldn't approve of what she was up to with Charles. As far as her family was concerned, Jayne from the office was her new best friend and that's where she was spending so much of her time. The summer passed quickly and before she knew it Josie was packing, ready to go to university. She knew she was in love with Charles but she also knew that if she told him that, then that would be the end of it. He'd made that very clear from the start. On their last night together, Josie was tearful. She pretended that it was because she was nervous about going to university but he didn't believe her.

"You are going to have an amazing time," he told her, "don't be sad, Josie. Here, I've got something for you."

Charles handed her a small, flat package. It was a book, "50 Ways to Please a Man."

She laughed. "I thought you'd taught me everything I needed to know."

"Nearly everything," he replied. "Go on, pick a number."

Josie picked number eighteen and Charles insisted that she carry out the act of pleasure corresponding to the number.

On her way home later that evening, Josie sobbed her heart out. She had really fallen for him and wasn't looking forward to starting university. But when she arrived at her hall of residence the following Monday, she couldn't help but get carried away with all the excitement of freshers' week.

Josie did visit Charles when she came home from university during her first term, but it didn't take long for her to start 'experimenting' with the young men she met in Cardiff. The visits dwindled, and by the end of her first year Josie was so caught up in university life that she stopped contacting him when she came home. Josie didn't regret a single moment that she spent with Charles Francis. He taught her so much, and five years later she still had the book he gave her, which she dipped into now and again, just to refresh her memory.

Ellis Rose

CHAPTER 2

Josie awoke with a smile on her face the next morning. Fond memories of Charles combined with anticipation of her date with Christian. She took extra care dressing. She had taken note that the secretaries at Renseignements wore quite informal clothes, with the exception of Charlotte who was a bit frumpy. Josie decided on a more formal appearance in line with the account directors and senior managers, she thought it might mark her out as a serious player. She said goodbye to Chrissie and headed for the Métro with a real skip in her step. Even though it was only early March, the sky was bright blue with the promise of a warm spring. She popped into the bakery opposite the office and bought a mix of croissants to offer her colleagues for breakfast. Josie didn't know how this would go down with the people at the agency, but thought it was a nice gesture.

Josie put her coat in the Routage and left the croissants on a plate next to the coffee machine. When passing Claire's desk, she told the receptionist that she had bought some croissants for people to share. The look on Claire's face was a picture. "I guess that's a first then," Josie chuckled to herself as she took a bite of the croissant she had set aside for herself. Her morning was filled with meetings with the rest of the team and she finally managed to bring Thomas's diary up to speed. Thomas was out that morning but had told her he would be in after lunch. He wanted her to send out a press release to the agricultural list on behalf of a client who manufactured tractors and other farming machinery. Josie decided to take the initiative and, after questioning Charlotte, established that all current media contacts were stored on a shared drive on the agency network. Josie printed off a list of agricultural media (including TV and radio reporters) ready for her meeting with Thomas. Throughout the morning a few people stopped by to thank her for bringing in the croissants. When she went to get herself a coffee mid-morning all the croissants were gone.

At lunchtime, Marguerite came to pick her up and the two left for one of the local cafés. They ordered light snacks and water. Josie would have loved a glass of wine but thought better of it. She didn't want to give the wrong impression. Once their food arrived, she noticed Marguerite paying for hers with vouchers. "What are they?" she asked the younger girl.

"Food vouchers," she replied. "You can buy them from Madame Raymonde in accounts. The agency subsidizes them. You can use them anywhere local, most people use them to purchase take-away sandwiches in the delis. Didn't the other girls tell you about them?"

"No," replied Josie, "I'm surprised no one thought to mention it. But I do feel there's a bit of resentment towards me from the other secretaries, especially Odette."

This was Marguerite's cue to give Josie the lowdown on the girls as well as the management. Marguerite explained that until recently all the secretaries had worked for a dedicated director but it was felt that this was not the most effective use of their time. One director and his team might be really busy and need the help of two girls rather than just one. The new system meant each secretary looked after the diary of at least two of the managers, but that they had to be flexible in providing support to other directors when called upon. The only exceptions were Monsieur Fredet (who was supported solely by Claire who also covered reception) and Thomas, who had a number of English speaking clients and so needed the support of someone who spoke fluent English.

All of the girls, with the exception of Pasquale and Marguerite, had applied for Josie's job, but had been disappointed when they were informed that someone new was coming in. Odette had been particularly frustrated. She had been with the agency for a very long time and assumed that she would be offered the new post. Charlotte had been quite upset too as she believed, and quite rightly, that her English was far better than that of the other girls.

However, she was not renowned for using her initiative and could be quite spiteful at times. This trait had not gone unnoticed by the senior management. Marguerite explained that she provided secretarial support in the accounts department, but like the others was not immune from being asked to help out when the agency was really busy.

Marguerite was a wealth of information on all the agency politics and personalities. She told Josie about the big boss Jacques Fredet, who was a self-made man. Jacques had set up the agency back in the 1980s when PR and advertising agencies were booming. The agency was privately owned but there were a number of investors who came along to regular board meetings. Thomas and Jean Paul were also shareholders and attended board meetings. They were both being groomed to take over from Jacques when he retired, although Jacques seemed to have no plans to retire any time soon. Jean Paul was a bit staid and direct, but very straight and professional. Philippe was great fun and he had a lovely wife who was expecting their first baby. Véronique was unashamedly gay and very popular among all the staff as she had a great sense of humour. Marguerite blushed a little as she told Josie all about Daniel. She obviously had a little crush on him. Daniel was a real family man, but also a heart throb for most of the female employees. Marguerite had a far-away look in her eyes as she described how sweet he was to everyone and so cute with his blonde curls and big blue eyes.

"You haven't mentioned Thomas," said Josie.

"You must be very careful of Thomas," Marguerite replied. "He has a terrible reputation. He can be charming one moment, distant the next, and he has much higher expectations than the other directors. Thomas is married to a woman called Valérie. She was once a top Parisian model and very famous. This has not stopped Thomas from having a fling of some sorts with nearly all the female account managers," Marguerite paused for effect enjoying the shocked look on Josie's face, "and of course secretaries and admin staff. He is slowly working his way through the entire agency. His affair with Christine has lasted by far the longest. They have been seeing each other a couple of years. There are some in the office who swear that Thomas is the father of Christine's little boy and not her husband."

"How do you know all this?" asked Josie, really shocked that her new boss had such a reputation. Josie remembered Libby identifying him as a bit of a flirt from their very first meeting. But she certainly hadn't realized that he was such a serial womanizer. Even though Thomas had been nothing other than courteous and professional in all their dealings to date, he rapidly went down in her estimation.

"If you ever want to know what's going on in the office just listen to Madame Raymonde and Monsieuer Renard in the accounts department. They've both been here forever and are real gossips. I just listen to them and pick things up that way. You can also pick up all the latest gossip in Routage, particularly as the managers spend time there as well as the secretaries." Marguerite realised that Josie was in complete and utter shock. "Despite what I've told you Josie, they really are a great bunch of people, even the other girls. They just need to get used to you, that's all."

"Sure, I guess I would feel the same if I was them," said Josie, "I'll do my best to be as open minded as I can. I think there's only a few I haven't met yet. I've been told I'll be working for Mervyn Bradley too, what's he like?"

"I don't really know him that well," replied Marguerite, "he comes and goes quite frequently and doesn't really mingle with the rest of the management team. I guess that's not surprising as he is completely independent from the agency and just pays for rent and admin support. He seems pleasant enough though. Have you met Sally Marsden-Lloyd yet?"

"No, who's she? It's the first I've heard of her," said Josie.

"Sally's the daughter of a good friend of Monsieur Fredet's. She's Canadian and here for work experience," Marguerite rolled her eyes. "Another one to watch out for, she really has a very high opinion of herself. Sally is forever bossing us all around. She works on one-off projects and is supposed to do most of the admin herself, but she's incredibly lazy. None of us like her very much, but we have to be careful because of her connections. I'm not sure the managers are that keen on her either, Véronique definitely isn't. But they also have to put up with her. Be careful of her, Josie."

They headed back to the office and Josie thanked Marguerite for joining her for lunch. It had been a real eye opener. She felt like she now had a real insight into the people at the agency. Undoubtedly there would be more to learn as time went by.

Josie met with Thomas promptly at 2.00 pm. He was pleased

that Josie had researched the relevant media for the press release ahead of the meeting. Thomas went through the list indicating who should receive the release and in what language. He emailed her a copy of the press release in French and English, asking her to check the translation, and told her to ask one of the girls where she could find the relevant headed paper and envelopes. Josie asked Claire who as usual was very helpful. Within an hour she had made some very slight amendments to the English text, checking the meaning carefully against the original French version, printed off the press release, stuffed them into envelopes and franked them.

Later, Thomas came to check how she was getting on. He was surprised to see that Josie had already finished and was reading Daniel Bergerac's revised presentation for JC.

"Are you sure you've done it properly?" he asked her. "It certainly didn't take you very long."

"Well it's not exactly rocket science," Josie replied sharply. She regretted her words almost immediately. "Sorry Thomas, I didn't mean to be rude but it's not such a difficult job and you helped enormously by indicating which press should receive it." Josie smiled sweetly, hoping her soothing words would defuse the sting of her original comment.

Thomas laughed, "Honestly Josephine, if I had given that job to Charlotte or Pasquale they would be moaning and groaning and getting the other girls to help them out. You are a real breath of fresh air around here, keep up the good work."

Josie was glad neither Charlotte nor Odette were in the office to hear what Thomas had said. "Just doing my job," she replied to him in English but with an American drawl. Thomas laughed and asked, "What are you doing after work this evening? Some of us are going to a drinks reception with a big client, the Four Seasons Hotel Group. They are entertaining some key potential investors and basically need bums on seats to make the event seem buzzy. You are more than welcome to come along," Thomas smiled roguishly, "it might provide a good insight into some of the less mundane work we do here."

"Well I was meant to have a date but it's not confirmed as yet, so I guess I could come along for a short time," said Josie.

"He is a very lucky man," replied Thomas, "we have taxis ordered for 6.00 pm to take us to the Georges V. I'll see you then."

"Am I dressed OK?" she enquired, a bit embarrassed to ask

but the need to ensure she was appropriately dressed outweighed her reluctance.

"Oh yes, you're fine. See you at 6.00 pm."

As soon as Thomas left, she quickly stuck her head around the door of Marguerite's office and asked if she had a few minutes. When she told her new friend about Thomas's offer, Marguerite was really surprised. "Well you really must have made an impression. Secretaries don't normally get invited to those sorts of events. Sally has been angling for an invitation forever, but has yet to receive one," Marguerite looked suddenly concerned, "Josie, I wouldn't broadcast this to the others if I was you. It's not going to win you any friends." Josie nodded and thanked her for the advice; as she turned to leave Marguerite stopped her.

"Be careful of Thomas, I've told you what he's like."

"I will, don't you worry" replied Josie, who couldn't decide whether to be elated or anxious about the invitation. She also needed to tell Christian and tried calling him but his mobile was switched off. Josie sent him a text saying that she had to work late but would love to see him later on, and could he give her a call?

It was gone 5.30 before he finally called her back. Christian seemed disappointed that they couldn't meet straight from work and explained he had an early start the next day. Josie told him that she would be going to the Georges V. When Christian found out it was a social event he was quite off with her. Josie apologized and told him that she really did want to see him, but couldn't confirm a time. They both mutually agreed to postpone the date. When the call ended Josie felt really bad and was in two minds about phoning him right back. Instead she phoned Chrissie to tell her about her change of plan and asked her to mention to Claude that she wasn't messing Christian about, it was a work social and might be of benefit to her career. Chrissie promised to mention it to Claude who would be sure to smooth things over with Christian.

Just as the other girls were leaving she popped into the cloakroom to check her makeup and hair and waited for the rest of the team in the reception area. Thomas and Véronique were the first to arrive, followed by one of the account managers, a lady called Cécile. They all hopped into the first taxi, with Jacques and Jean Paul following closely behind in the second. No one seemed too surprised that Josie was accompanying them, but she still kept quiet and listened to the banter amongst them. It took nearly thirty minutes to get to the hotel on the Avenue Georges V, due to the early evening traffic. Josie had never been inside the hotel before and wasn't disappointed. The huge reception area was beautifully decorated, with high vaulted ceilings and huge twinkling chandeliers. They walked past the famous Galerie Lounge into one of the prestigious banqueting suites. There were a number of people standing around mingling and chatting. In the taxi, Cécile had told Josie that the previous year the hotel chain had been voted second best in the world. They were now trying to take over the number one spot, and were flying in potential investors to the flagship hotel in Paris to showcase their facilities. They then planned to replicate the event at all their other hotels worldwide.

Cécile also informed her that it was most unusual for Renseignements to ask staff to participate directly in these kinds of events. Renseignements wasn't the type of agency that encouraged its staff to act as hosts and hostesses. The Four Seasons Hotel Group however, was one of the agency's biggest clients. The Managing Director had asked Jacques Fredet personally, if the Senior Account team could come along. They knew so much about the chain and could talk knowledgeably to all the guests.

Josie felt a little uncomfortable. She knew next to nothing about the hotel and wondered why she had been invited. Just then a poker faced waiter thrust a glass of champagne into her hand. She decided to keep a low profile and stood at the back of the room, sipping her champagne and watching the rest of the team mingling easily with the guests. After a few minutes Véronique joined her. "God I do so hate events like this. The room is full of jumped up, terribly self-important business men who think they are masters of the universe," Véronique smiled conspiratorially. "Most of these little boys have only succeeded in business due to their rich daddies' help,"

Josie was surprised at the bitterness in Véronique's tone. "Well, these guys do pay our bills at the end of the day, don't they?" replied the younger woman.

"I know, but I just sometimes find it all so terribly false. I hate pretending to be interested in what such boring people have to say. I would rather be tucked up at home, relaxing in front of the TV with my adorable cats." Véronique was distracted by the arrival of a beautifully groomed middle-aged woman. "Well look what the cat dragged in, Madame Pretentious herself."

Véronique explained that the woman was Hélène Du Tilly, wife of the Managing Director of the Four Seasons Hotel Group. She was constantly interfering in all PR events and was renowned throughout Renseignements for being a royal pain in the backside. Hélène spent most of her time in Paris, even though her husband's main offices were in Toronto. Véronique had a lascivious glint in her eye when she confided that Hélène was notorious for having numerous affaires with both men and women. Hélène Du Tilly scanned the room haughtily and, spying Véronique and Josie, headed towards them, shooing away a waiter who approached her with a tray of drinks.

"Véronique, darling," she said, air kissing the space either side of her head.

"Hélène, you look marvellous," replied Véronique.

"So do you, darling," she replied, letting her finger gently caress Véronique's high cheek bones, "and that haircut really suits you, simply divine. We must get together for lunch soon, for old times' sake." Josie noticed Véronique was blushing. "Some history there," thought Josie to herself.

"Who is this gorgeous girl?" asked Hélène, turning towards Josie and smiling. Véronique introduced Josie as the agency's recent international recruit, not bothering to mention she was a secretary. Josie was grateful for that. Hélène asked her a number of probing questions about her background. Josie embellished her work experience, exaggerating the time she had spent in Switzerland and Italy before eventually moving to Paris. Hélène switched effortlessly to Italian and Josie was able to respond reasonably fluently to the older lady's questions.

"We could do with a bright young thing like you working for us," said Hélène looking pointedly at Josie who began to feel a bit uneasy under her hard stare.

"Now, now," replied Véronique, sensing Josie's unease, "no poaching our staff, Hélène. Jacques Fredet would be livid. Besides I'm sure we have some sort of agreement in our contract which prohibits Josie leaving the agency for our biggest client." Hélène laughed but the emotion didn't quite reach her eyes. Josie felt that she was probably the sort of woman who always managed to get her own way.

"I hope you can both stay for dinner," Hélène said, "I've arranged a table in the restaurant for twenty-five guests, but I'm informed that some of the investors won't be arriving until tomorrow. I hate empty places, please say you'll join us?"

Josie took her cue from Véronique who reluctantly agreed to stay. As soon as Hélène had left to greet the other guests, Thomas and Jean Paul came over to join them.

"Looks like we have to stay for dinner," Thomas said to Véronique, who rolled her eyes. "You don't have to Josephine, especially if you're going to make that date." Before she could answer Véronique told them that Hélène had personally invited them both to stay and they had agreed.

"How are you finding it all so far?" Thomas asked Josie.

"Actually I feel a bit out of my depth," she replied, "but it's all very interesting."

He smiled and patted her shoulder a bit like a benevolent father.

A few minutes later they were ushered into an adjoining room for dinner, which wasn't as formal as Josie had feared. Ever the perfect hostess, Hélène, conscious that all of the guests might not make it on time, had arranged a buffet and a number of large round tables without place names. The buffet looked superb with cold meats, salads, seafood, fresh fish, and ten different types of bread and pates. In pride of place were generous helpings of lobster and caviar. Josie thought she had died and gone to heaven. She was careful not to load up her plate in case she showed herself and her colleagues up. She was also careful not to drink too much wine for the same reason, particularly as the champagne she had drunk at the reception had gone straight to her head.

Josie ended up seated next to Cécile and a quiet, shy Frenchman in his early twenties who told her he worked for the hotel chain. Conversation with the young man wasn't that easy but the meal soon passed with no formalities or speeches. The guests then started to drift off to the hotel bar or their rooms and Véronique came to find Josie.

"I'm going home, Josie," she told her, "but the others are staying for a little while longer. You can come with me and share my taxi or stay here, it's up to you."

At that very moment, Thomas joined them and told Josie the same thing. It was quite late and Josie was feeling the effects of a long day and too much alcohol. She didn't want to outstay her welcome so she told Véronique she would go with her. Thomas gave her a strange look and leaning towards her said quietly, "Be careful Josie, Véronique is bit of 'lady killer'. I love her to death but...just be careful."

As the women were leaving, Hélène approached them again. She gave Véronique a strange look and told her to give her a call soon. Turning to Josie, she told her that if ever she decided to leave Renseignements, she should give her a call. There would always be an opening for her at the Four Seasons Group. Josie thanked her but felt a bit uncomfortable as the older lady delivered the ritual three farewell kisses. In the taxi, Véronique asked her what she thought of Hélène. Josie didn't know what to say. She found Hélène intriguing even though she came over as the typically spoiled wife of a successful businessman, who thought she could get or do whatever she wanted.

"I can't really judge," she replied, "I've only just met her. She seems very together, but I guess that comes with all the money and, of course, status."

"She was François du Tilly's secretary many years ago," Véronique confided. "He took over the company at quite a young age as his father suffered serious ill health. The family didn't approve of him marrying her but she arranged a meeting with François's parents and convinced them that she would be a good wife. She obviously really impressed them because they gave their blessing."

Josie viewed Hélène in a new light and was about to say as much when Véronique added, "What she didn't tell them was that she could never have children. When they found out they were livid but it was too late, the couple were married and François was besotted with Hélène. Their marriage has lasted over thirty years and although they both have their dalliances, they are still devoted to each other. She even encouraged François to have children with another woman so that the Four Seasons 'Dynasty' survives. That young man you were sitting next to is his son by an ex-mistress and he looks after them both financially. Hélène is friendly with the ex-mistress and very supportive of everything her husband does for them." This was all too bizarre for Josie who came from a normal, British, middle class background.

"How do you know all this?" she asked Véronique.

"Well, we were quite friendly once, a few years ago," she replied, a faint blush rising to her defined cheek bones, "but it started to get a bit difficult, what with me working on the account and Hélène thinking she could tell us how to run things. Jacques Fredet wasn't best pleased. That's putting it rather mildly," she sighed. "Jacques didn't encourage the friendship to continue. We still meet occasionally at events like tonight but we are by no means as close as we once were."

Josie nodded in contemplation. Reading between the lines she guessed that Véronique and Hélène had been lovers, but she felt it was none of her business. A few minutes later they arrived outside Josie's flat and she thanked Véronique for the lift home. The older woman gave Josie the three ritual goodbye kisses and thanked her for coming along that evening.

"No, thank you for inviting me and for spending time with me," she replied, even though it was really Thomas who had invited her. "I really enjoyed myself."

Josie waved off the taxi and headed up the five flights to the flat, completely exhausted. Chrissie was already in bed and she just hit the sack herself, amazed at the whirl of events that had engulfed her over the past two days. It felt as if she had already spent a lifetime at Renseignements.

At work the following day, news had somehow leaked out. It was the talk of the office that Josie had attended the event with the senior managers. Odette was particularly cold with her and the others were a bit off too. Josie suspected that this was Odette's doing. She managed to catch a few quiet minutes with Marguerite mid-morning and asked her friend what everyone was saying about her. Marguerite told her that it was really only Odette who was miffed but was stirring it up amongst the others. They also knew that Josie had left in a taxi with Véronique and were putting two and two together and making five.

"Oh let them," said Josie angrily. It wasn't her fault that Thomas had invited her to the function and that Véronique had been so genuinely kind to her. She spent the rest of the day with her head down, getting on with some work for Thomas. Josie worked through her lunch hour, not wanting to talk to her colleagues. That afternoon she met Daniel Bergerac and they went through the Chemfast presentation. Daniel was very happy with Josie's input. He commended her and thought her inside knowledge of the company had been of immense help.

"Are you okay Josie?" he asked, "You seem a bit quiet today."

Not wanting to sound bitchy or catty she told him that she was tired from the late night.

"As long as that's all it is," he replied, as though he could read her mind.

She smiled weakly, and headed back to her desk. That evening she left at 6.00 pm along with all the other girls. Josie was surprised to find that Charlotte took the same Métro line home. They made polite conversation and Josie found out that Charlotte lived with her elderly mother not far from the Place de Clichy. Charlotte mentioned that she was going to a talk on Italian art at one of the local schools. Josie told her that she had studied the History of Italian Art as part of her language degree and Charlotte invited her to join her that evening. Josie was grateful for the invitation but there was no way she wanted to go to a boring lecture, especially with the rather strange Charlotte. She told her that she had other plans but would be delighted to meet some other time. Charlotte seemed genuinely pleased and told Josie she would let her know the date of the next talk.

"Can hardly wait," said Josie to herself.

Back at the flat, Chrissie was home and in the middle of cooking supper.

"Chrissie, you're a star," said Josie. "I just want to eat, have a bath and chill out. I'm so tired. This job is much more demanding than Chemfast," Josie frowned, "I think it's more the people than the actual job which make it such hard work."

Over supper she told Chrissie about the previous evening and the atmosphere in the office that day.

"Don't worry," her friend told her, "it's just that you are the new girl and so they're giving you a hard time. It's perfectly natural, it will all blow over in no time, just you wait and see," Chrissie sighed, "I spoke with Claude last night. He was supposed to call and let me know how his talk with Christian went. But he sent me a text saying he had to go home to Provence. There's a family matter he has to deal with."

"OK," replied Josie, "I don't want to make a big fuss. I just didn't want Christian to think I was intentionally messing him about. He's working two night shifts now so I guess I won't see him until Saturday night. It's a shame Claude can't come with us."

"Oh I don't mind really," replied Chrissie, "as long as I get the chance to have a bop at this club I'll be happy. Anyway Claude might cramp my style."

Chrissie's words were brave, but Josie could see that her friend was obviously a bit miffed at Claude's hasty trip home.

"Don't get me wrong, I'm not planning on picking anyone up," Chrissie continued, "I just think it would be more fun if it was just us girls. It's been ages since we had a girls' night out."

"Too late for that now," added Josie, "we've already invited the guys and they seem to be looking forward to it. I think I'll invite my new friend from work, Marguerite. She's a real sweetie, you'll like her. She lives at home and I get the impression she doesn't have much of a social life. I don't think she's ever had a boyfriend."

Chrissie agreed and said she looked forward to meeting Marguerite. At work the next day, Marguerite was delighted to be invited, but declined the invitation to stay overnight as she felt her mother wouldn't let her. The atmosphere in the office was better too as Charlotte was very friendly and told Josie that the next talk was in a month's time. Charlotte had already booked two places. Josie put the date in her diary and thought that it would be worth giving up one evening of her time, especially if it meant less resentment towards her at the office. On Friday, Josie and Daniel Bergerac met with JC. They went through the proposals for the Brussels conference in great detail. JC was in a really good mood and accepted their recommendations without hesitation, even agreeing to announce the office move. He then told Josie he was taking her to lunch. "Oh, OK," she replied, a little surprised, "but I only have an hour, JC."

"Oh don't worry about that," said Daniel, "it's only your birthday once a year, take as long as you want. We all wind down a bit on Friday afternoons anyway."

"Are you sure?" Josie asked, not wanting to take advantage of the situation.

"You carry on, I'll clear it with Thomas, don't worry, have a great time."

Josie had a very pleasant lunch with JC and told him all about her first week at Renseignements. She decided to leave out how horrible some of the girls had been, though.

"I thought the place would suit you," he told her, "I really think you'll do well there. Josie, you are exceptional with people at all levels, you're diplomatic when necessary and you have excellent organizational skills. They are very lucky to have you."

"Thanks JC," Josie said, blushing. She was quite taken aback as JC was not normally very complimentary.

"How's Libby getting on?" she asked, "I haven't heard from her at all in over a week."

"She's been really busy Josie, perhaps she just didn't have time. She'll probably call you tomorrow."

Josie arrived back at the office having been out for nearly two hours with JC. They had shared a bottle of wine so she was feeling quite tipsy but managed to cover it up well. A few minutes later, Claire called her from reception and asked her if she could come into the Routage for a moment. When she entered, everyone was there with birthday cards, champagne and chocolates and their best wishes. Josie was quite overwhelmed and had to struggle to stop the tears welling up in her eyes. Even Jacques Fredet made an appearance. He popped the champagne and gave her the cork for good luck. Everyone raised their glasses and wished her happy birthday.

There was no more work accomplished that day and everyone left work early. Josie was feeling really merry. The long lunch with JC, followed by champagne at the office, had gone straight to her head. She headed for the Metro with Charlotte and even considered inviting her out the next night, but thought better of it. Charlotte didn't seem the type to want to go clubbing. At home, she crashed out on her bed and didn't wake up until gone 9 pm when her mobile started beeping. It was a text from Libby apologizing for not calling before now but promising to call the next day.

Josie went into the kitchen and was surprised that Chrissie wasn't at home. Then she spotted a note on the table, telling her that Chrissie and Daniel had gone to the cinema and would be back later. Josie felt a bit guilty; she hadn't thought to invite Daniel out with them the following evening. Daniel was a bit too 'fuddy-duddy' for a nightclub; it wouldn't be his scene at all. A thought struck, "Perhaps I should arrange for Daniel and Charlotte to meet. They seemed ideally suited, and might well hit it off!"

Josie was sitting down in front of the TV with a sandwich and a glass of mineral water when she realised that Christian hadn't been in touch once since Tuesday. To be fair to him, she hadn't contacted him either, but he had said he would call her. Josie dropped off and only woke when Chrissie finally returned home with Daniel, who presented her with a card and bottle of champagne.

"Thank you Daniel," Josie said, feeling even guiltier than before.

"I gather you're having a girls' night out tomorrow, then," he commented. Josie caught Chrissie's eye and understood that her friend had covered for her.

"That's right, shame Libby can't be here though, particularly as it's her birthday too!"

"But I thought….." Daniel started to say, only to be abruptly interrupted by Chrissie asking him if he wanted a coffee and giving him a knowing look.

"There's something going on with Libby," thought Josie to herself. It was out of character for Libby not to phone her but she knew she'd get to the bottom of it eventually.

Ellis Rose

CHAPTER 3

The next day Josie was woken by the sound of someone trying to open her bedroom door. She sat up, startled, and the door burst open. Chrissie appeared with breakfast on a tray – pain au chocolat, fresh orange juice, coffee and a single red rose.

"Very romantic!" she said. "Thanks, what a perfect start to the day."

Chrissie sat on her bed while they shared breakfast and opened her presents. Throughout the week Chrissie had hidden all the post from the UK. There were gifts and cards from all her friends and family. There was even a card from Paul, but needless to say not one from Max. Josie was disappointed that there was no card from Libby. Chrissie had bought her a stunning handbag which she had admired a while ago in a small boutique off the Boulevard Haussman. After breakfast, the girls hit the supermarket to stock up on nibbles for the evening ahead. They also picked up something for breakfast the next morning, as they guessed the air traffic controllers would crash at their place that evening. Then they spent the afternoon deciding what to wear, washing their hair and getting ready to go out.

Marguerite was the first to arrive and she presented Josie with a photo frame from her mother's antique shop and a beautiful silk scarf. Josie was overjoyed and gave her a big hug. Christian, Yves and Joel arrived, laden with flowers, cards and champagne. Christian gave her a quick peck on the cheek and wished her Happy Birthday but didn't give a separate card or gift. As they were all enjoying their first glass of champagne, the intercom buzzer rang again.

"We're not expecting anyone else are we?" said Josie to Chrissie. Her friend just shrugged her shoulders as she answered the intercom and waited in the hallway. A few moments later the new guest entered the room. It was Libby.

"Lib, what are you doing here?" screamed a delighted Josie, who was overjoyed to see her friend.

"Well I couldn't miss our birthday celebrations, could I," she replied, "so I came over this afternoon. I'm flying back on Monday morning."

"But why haven't you called me? I've been quite fed up with you, I must admit."

"Because you always ask too many questions and I'm no good at lying to you. Anyway, here's your present Josie. Happy birthday!"

"Thanks, Libby. I'll just go and get yours from the bedroom."

The girls exchanged gifts while the champagne continued to flow. Looking around their sitting room, Josie noticed that Marguerite seemed to be getting on very well with Yves and that Christian was hovering around Chrissie like a bee around honey. Josie was quite hurt at Christian's coldness towards her. He was obviously flirting with Chrissie to get back at her for standing him up the other night. She didn't expect her friend to flirt back so openly though, and was equally hurt by this.

"Are you okay?" Libby asked Josie, seeing her friend standing in the corner of the room looking miserable.

"Look at them," she said referring to Chrissie and Christian. "It seems that while the cat's away Chrissie will play!"

"Oh pay no attention," replied Libby. "I know Chrissie is besotted with Claude. She's probably just flattered by Christian's attentions. If what you say is true, he's probably trying to teach you a lesson. You know how insecure men can be! Come on, just enjoy yourself. Don't let him upset your birthday celebrations."

"You're right, Libby. Sod Christian. If he is so immature and childish then let him play his silly games, I'm not biting."

With that, she replenished her and Libby's glasses and made a bee-line for Joel, the new Air Traffic Controller they had brought along. He was quite good looking but tall, gangly and blonde, not Josie's type at all. But she flirted with him outrageously, with a lot of teasing and touching, which seemed to please the young man no end. As they were all leaving for the nightclub, she completely ignored Christian whom she had caught watching her whilst she was talking to Joel. They needed two taxis and Josie deliberately got into the first one with Joel and Yves. Josie asked Marguerite to join them. Christian's face was a picture as they drove away in the taxi.

La Scala was spectacular. The place was huge with a massive circular bar on the ground floor with spiral staircases either side of the room leading down to another bar and a large dance floor. They quickly installed themselves at a long, low table surrounded by comfortable sofas, and the guys went to order drinks. Once they returned, the girls headed straight for the dance floor and Josie spent virtually the next two hours dancing non-stop. She danced with her friends, with the air traffic controllers, with strangers and on her own. She was quite tipsy but having a really good time. Christian continued to avoid her completely but she didn't care. She was buzzing with the atmosphere of the place. Eventually, as her feet were killing her, she returned to their table where Marguerite and Yves were all over each other, snogging like their lives depended on it. She sat down and picked up a nearly full glass of champagne, not caring whose it was. She leaned over the balcony and watched her friends on the dance floor, unaware of Christian coming up behind her.

"Are you having a good time, Josie?" he asked her a bit sheepishly.

"Wonderful, thanks Christian. And you?"

He just shrugged. Josie really couldn't be bothered to play games with him so just turned back to watch her friends on the dance floor.

"Do you want to dance?" Christian asked.

"Maybe later, my feet are killing me in these new shoes," she said.

Christian nodded, it seemed he didn't know what else to say and so sat down on the sofa close to where Josie was leaning over the balcony. Tired of watching the dancing, she turned around and slipped into the seat next to him. "Where's Chrissie?" she asked him pointedly. Again he shrugged. Josie knew exactly where Chrissie was. She was having a drink at the downstairs bar with a guy with whom she had been dancing for the past hour or so. They sat there in an uncomfortable silence for a few minutes, sipping their drinks. Totally fed up with the strained situation, she turned to him and said, "Look Christian, I know you were a bit upset that I had to cancel our date on Tuesday but it was a genuine last minute work commitment. I really want to make an impression at the new agency; it's a great opportunity for me. If I want to get on, it sometimes means putting work first. If you can't understand that, then you're not the man I thought you were."

"But you didn't even bother calling me," said Christian, frowning.

"You said you'd call me," said Josie incredulously, "and I knew you were working nights so I didn't want to disturb you, in case you were sleeping." Josie stood and reached down to collect her handbag, "flirting with my best friend to make me jealous doesn't make it any better." She quickly slipped on her shoes and turned to head for the ladies, but too many glasses of champagne and extremely high heels made her giddy and she fell awkwardly, landing in Christian's lap. The shock of the fall completely silenced her and the next thing she knew, Christian was kissing her. She started to resist but his kisses were very insistent and so she found herself responding, against her better judgment. Eventually, when they both came up for air, Christian said, "Well, there was really no need to throw yourself at me quite so dramatically, Josie!"

Josie playfully pretended to slap him around the head and he grabbed her wrist, holding it away. "Let's go outside for a minute, it's really hot in here and I want to talk to you somewhere a bit quieter." Josie nodded in agreement. Christian helped her up so she wouldn't fall again and led her to the entrance. They had their wrists stamped to allow them entry back in. There were a few people milling about outside, enjoying the crisp night air, and he led her down the steps to a low wall. They sat down, Josie was shivering a little and Christian put his arm around her shoulders. "I've been stupid," he said to her, pulling her closer. "I totally overreacted when you cancelled our date and I apologize for that. But I was more upset not to hear from you during the rest of the week and thought either you didn't want to see me or you'd met someone else," Christian looked sheepish. "The thing with Chrissie was just that Claude told me to make sure she was okay during the evening. I guess I took it a bit too far. Chrissie did tell me off in the nightclub. She told me she didn't need a guardian and that I'd better grow up if I wanted any sort of relationship with you. That's why I came to ask you to dance. And then of course you threw yourself at me and here we are."

Josie had been watching him whilst he was talking to her and noticed the smile tugging at the corner of his mouth as he delivered his final words. Again she tried to swat him with her hand and he caught her again. This time he kissed her open palm, moving up her arm and then to her neck. As he neared her mouth, she could hear his faint whisper, "Forgive me Josie, I really am sorry". And with that he started kissing her again. Eventually she pulled away, shivering from the effect of the cold night air. Christian released her and suggested they go back inside. As they walked back into the club hand in hand, she was relieved that their differences were now settled. They joined the others on the dance floor and she noticed Chrissie giving Christian a thumbs-up sign and a big smile.

After a few tracks, the music slowed down and Josie found herself swaying gently in Christian's arms to the sounds of Lionel Ritchie. He pulled her closer towards him. "I am so sorry," he again whispered in her ear, "I want you so much, Josie." He gently moved her head with his hand so that it was resting on his shoulder. Josie put her right arm around his neck and pulled his mouth to hers. This time Christian pulled away. "We'd better stop that, Josie," he said holding her away from him by the shoulders, "or we'll be kicked out for indecent behaviour." Josie just smiled and they continued to dance closely but without kissing. Eventually the music came to an end and the nightclub lights went up. They all met back at their table and gathered their belongings. Outside there was a horrendous queue for taxis but Josie suggested they walk a little way towards the Gare du Nord where they would find some taxis more easily. Within half an hour they were back at the girls' apartment. They were all pretty drunk, although Josie had sobered up considerably as she hadn't had another drink since going outside with Christian. Some of the group continued to drink champagne; Josie, with Christian's help, made a tray of coffee.

The taxi had dropped Marguerite home en route, much to Yves's chagrin, but the couple had exchanged phone numbers. It was well into the early hours of the morning when Libby called a taxi to take her home and both Joel and Yves decided to leave too, sharing the taxi with her. Josie had been sitting on Christian's lap at the dining table sipping her coffee. He whispered to her, "Can I stay?" She was virtually sober now and had been wondering what Christian would want to do, particularly as he lived further out in the suburbs than the others. She wanted him to stay but she didn't want him to think she was a pushover, particularly as they hadn't even been talking at the start of the evening.

"Sure you can, but you'll have to sleep on the sofa," she said with a wicked glint in her eye. He looked disappointed but nodded in agreement. As the others left, winking and grinning at Christian, Chrissie took Josie to one side.

"I hope things are okay with you and Christian now," she asked her friend. "I know he was flirting with me horrendously at the start of the evening but I had quite strong words with him and hopefully he listened to what I said. He really does like you Josie, but, like most men, he can't always understand us 'independent career minded Brits'. A bit chauvinistic I know, but endearing none the less."

"I really like him Chrissie, but he did cheese me off earlier this evening. He told me you'd spoken to him, and thanks for that. I've told him he can stay over but he'll have to sleep on the sofa. Poor man, he looked so disappointed. I haven't told him yet that I've changed my mind."

"Oh go on, put him out of his misery. I'm off to bed now anyway so I'll leave you to it."

Christian was in the kitchen where he had carried all the cups and glasses which he left on a tray by the sink.

"Thanks for doing that," Josie said putting her arms around his neck and moving her body in close to his. He leant forward and kissed her very gently.

"You're very welcome," he replied. "Are you sure there isn't anything else I can do for you?"

Josie took his hand and led him back through the sitting room and into her bedroom. She urgently pulled him down onto the bed. They lay next to each other, just kissing and caressing very gently, for what seemed like ages. She loved the fact that he didn't immediately rip her clothes off, even though she was extremely excited by his kisses. Christian propped himself up on his elbow and stared wistfully into her eyes. He ran his fingers very gently over her chin and down her neck, caressing her softly. "Beautiful Josephine," he whispered, "are you sure about this? I really don't want to rush you."

Josie responded by pulling his face down to her waiting lips, kissing him forcefully and passionately. He responded with equal passion and moved his hands slowly up inside her shirt until he reached her breasts. Christian circled his fingers around her erect nipples and then, reaching behind her, undid her bra and lifted her shirt over her head. He buried his face between her breasts and started kissing her nipple whilst gently caressing the other with the open palm of his hand. Josie pushed him away and slowly undid the buttons of his shirt before pushing it off his shoulders. His torso was barely visible in the dark bedroom. The faint glow from a street lamp filtered through the blinds. His body felt hard but his skin was soft, with just a smattering of dark hairs on his chest. Josie moved her mouth down his neck, kissing the little indent below his Adam's apple, down to his shoulders and then his nipples, all the time gently caressing his shoulders with her fingertips. As she gently teased his nipples with her fingers and tongue, he let out a low, animal groan and pulled her face back close to his. They were now both kneeling on the bed, face to face, the tops of their bodies bare and glowing in the feint light. Christian continued to caress her, holding her eyes with his urgent gaze. His hands then began to move down her body towards her navel. He undid her belt, buttons and zip and slipped his hand inside her trousers. His fingers found her now throbbing and erect clitoris and it was Josie's turn to let out a moan of pleasure.

Josie brushed her hand over the front of his trousers and felt his powerful erection. She purposely caressed the tip of his penis without undoing his trousers until she could tell he could stand it no longer. Then when he could barely suppress his moans of pleasure she undid his trousers and without words they both stood up at the same time, ripping off their clothes as fast as they could. Christian laid Josie back on the bed so that her legs were still over the side. He knelt on the floor in front of her and, opening her knees, very gently kissing her pussy lips. He then slowly licked her clitoris from the tip all the way down and back again. He licked, sucked, probed and bit, bringing her to the brink of release. Even after she had reached climax, he kept on with his task until she came again. Her whole head and body felt like they were exploding. Josie was raw from his attentions and had to tell him to stop.

To give herself time to recover, she indicated that he should sit on the edge of the bed. Following his lead, she then opened his knees and began to tease his thighs, belly button, hip bones, everywhere with her tongue, intentionally avoiding his throbbing penis until his groans told her he could stand it no longer. Taking his shaft in her hands, she ran her tongue over the tip and down the sides before taking as much of him in her mouth as she could manage. Just like Charles had taught her. After a few minutes of this intense attention, Christian lifted her from the floor onto his lap. She wrapped her legs around his waist and he slipped easily inside her. Holding onto her hips, he moved her up and down and then in circular movements so that her whole body seemed to be bonded with his. He held back until she came again, allowing himself his own exquisite release only when he felt her shuddering on top of him.

They remained panting in that position as they tried to catch their breath. He held her gently against him so that she wouldn't fall. Suddenly Josie shivered and Christian released her, rolling her over onto the bed. He kissed her again on the mouth and pulled the quilt over them both. As Josie snuggled up close to her new lover, she caught a glimpse of her alarm clock. It was already 4 am and all of a sudden she felt really shattered. She could tell by his steady breathing that Christian had fallen asleep immediately and she wasn't far behind him.

Josie awoke the next morning still snuggled up in Christian's arms. She could hear Chrissie bustling around the kitchen preparing breakfast. She gently tried to untangle herself from Christian's embrace, but his arms tightened around her, as if he never wanted to let her go.

"Are you awake?" she whispered in his ear.

"Mmm, just a little," he replied, pulling her even closer to him. Josie could feel his erection stirring and pressing against her thigh.

"Christian, I have to go to the loo," she told him. "I promise I'll come straight back. Do you want tea or coffee?"

"Coffee and hurry back!"

She smiled back at him, remembering how great their love making had been the night before. Chrissie was sitting at the dining table drinking tea and eating toast. "Morning, lazy bones," she said, pouring her a cup of tea from the pot.

"I'll be right back," she told her. On her way back from the loo she put the kettle on to make Christian a coffee and drank her tea while she waited for it to boil.

"Everything all right?" Chrissie asked her, barely concealing a smirk.

"Lovely, thank you very much for asking!" said Josie, raising an eyebrow.

"Come on Josie, how was it? Spill the beans!"

"As I said," she replied, grinning, "lovely, thank you. What are you up to today?"

"Not sure," said Chrissie. "I thought I'd make us a chilli or something easy for supper. Libby's coming over. I'll pop out and pick up some stuff," Chrissie smiled, "I fancy a bit of fresh air anyway."

"Well I'm going back to bed, and to sleep, before you say anything. Chilli sounds great Chrissie," Josie tossed over her shoulder. "Can I ask Christian to stay?"

Chrissie gave her a flat look. "Sure, the more the merrier, sounds like he'll need a good meal to keep his energy up!"

Josie made Christian a coffee and headed back to the bedroom. He was fast asleep. She put the coffee on the table next to him and slipped in beside him as quietly as possible so as not to wake him. She drifted off to sleep but awoke suddenly as the front door slammed. She guessed it was her flat mate leaving for her walk and shopping. Josie was wide-awake now but happy to lie next to Christian. She couldn't help but scrutinize him as he slept. He was a good-looking man with very dark hair and rich dark brown eyes. He had a tiny scar on the corner of his left eye and Josie had to stop herself from reaching up and just touching it, just to feel his skin beneath her fingers. The duvet didn't cover his upper body and as she recognized from the night before he was in good shape, with dark skin and just the right amount of muscle in the right places.

"Are you staring at me," said Christian, opening one eye, making her jump as if she had been caught doing something wrong.

"Just checking you out, that's all," she replied grinning at him.

"And do you like what you see?" he asked, rolling onto his side and pulling her closer to him.

"So far, but I think there's more on offer."

"You wicked woman! Just wait there…. don't go anywhere!" He jumped out of bed and was about to head out of the door for the bathroom. "I'd better put something on," he said, "I forgot you have a flat-mate."

"Don't worry, Chrissie's gone out. I heard her leave a few minutes ago."

He poked his head around the door and called out, "Chrissie?" There was no answer. He turned and grinned, "You're right, she's out."

"Didn't you believe me?" asked Josie raising a quizzical eyebrow.

"Just making sure, I don't want to create an embarrassing situation. Claude has a very short temper and he might get the wrong idea."

Christian was back within a few minutes and again Josie had the opportunity to admire his body as he walked back into the bedroom. Josie was lying naked on the bed and Christian began to get erect.

"So do you like what you see?" he asked her as he climbed onto the bed.

"A great deal of further inspection is required before I can answer that," she replied, putting her arms around him. His skin was cold and his touch made her shiver.

"I can see I am going to have to warm you up," he told her, running his hand down her back, over her buttocks and then gently back up her spine.

"Yes please," she replied, moving her body against his.

They kissed passionately and he moved his leg between hers as he kept gently caressing her back and buttocks. Josie moved her hand down to his penis which was rock hard against her stomach and moved her hand gently up and down him, slowly and teasingly. Taking his cue from her, he too moved his hand down, gently pulling her pubic hair before letting his fingers slide inside her, whilst his thumb massaged her clitoris. They moved apart except for their hands and watched themselves masturbate each other, in the most intimate way. Josie could feel herself reaching an orgasm and whispered quietly, "Don't stop, please don't stop."

Christian looked deeply into her eyes as she came, soaking his hand with the juices that flowed from her. As her orgasm subsided, he licked the juices off his fingers and bent to kiss her. She was still moving her hand gently up and down his penis and she could tell by his breathing that he too was nearing orgasm. He moved her hand away, telling her that he wasn't ready yet, and pushed Josie gently onto her back. He moved on top and began an onslaught of kisses from her face and neck to her breasts, navel and then again down to her most secret sexual parts. He licked her very gently, sensing that she wouldn't be able to stand too much pressure after her first orgasm. His gentleness had the required effect and Josie came again with a much slower but longer orgasm, extended by the persistent pressure of his tongue while she came.

He rested his head on her stomach, running his fingers up and down her inner thighs as her body recovered again from the intense pleasure he had given her. As he felt her relaxing beneath him, he rose above her, letting his penis move very gently over her stomach and back down to her vagina lips. He was so hard that he slipped easily inside her and in a complete reversal of the usual missionary position, opened his legs outside of hers. The feeling was sensational and, like the night before, they moved together as one. Christian began thrusting harder and harder until it felt like he was so deep inside her he would snap. Josie came quickly with a short sharp orgasm, while Christian's was prolonged and intense. His eyes bored into hers as he pumped himself into her and she was surprised at the intensity of his look, almost as if he had won a major prize.

Spent, he stayed inside her for a few minutes until his now limp member began to slip out of her. Neither of them spoke as he held her in his arms, both lost for words due to the intensity and intimacy of the moment. Josie felt herself drifting off to sleep again and hugged him closely. Christian suggested they take a shower. Josie passed him a towel to wrap around his waist in case Chrissie came back, and they showered. They soaped and sponged each other playfully. Christian was raring to go again but Josie pushed him away, she could barely walk as it was. He pretended to be hurt but she knew he was just messing about, and they both broke into fits of laughter. By the time they had dried each other and fooled around it was already early afternoon and they were both starving. Josie offered to make Christian some lunch. But he insisted on taking Josie and Chrissie to the local café for a late lunch; it was the least he could do, he insisted, particularly as they were feeding him that evening.

After lunch, Chrissie returned home to prepare supper, allowing Christian and Josie time to go for a walk, under the proviso that they did the dishes later. The couple walked companionably along the river Seine, hand in hand. It was a lovely day, but with an early spring chill in the air. They stopped at the Jardin des Tuileries for a hot chocolate and sat under a tree, watching the Sunday afternoon crowds stroll by. Josie sat between Christian's legs and he wrapped his arms around her. He was such good company, easy to talk to and a caring and thoughtful lover, perfect. Yet her mind kept going back to Max and how things had been with him at the beginning. "Stop it, you stupid woman," she thought to herself. "He's not worth it, and you have a gem of a man here, who seems to think a lot of you."

Sensing a change in her mood, Christian asked her if she was okay.

"I'm fine thanks, just a fleeting memory of the past, that's all. Shall we make a move?"

She stood and pulled Christian up so they were standing face to face. He put his hand under her chin and tilted her face up to his. "Don't dwell on the past, Josie. Think of the future. You have an exciting new job and we're getting on okay, aren't we? Well, more than okay, I think. I just hope you think so too?"

"Of course I do, Christian. And I am sorry if sometimes I seem a bit hesitant but it's been an eventful few months for me. I'm a bit wary about rushing things. We've had a lovely time and I'm sure we'll have loads more. I don't know how much Claude has told you but none of it is secret and I'm happy to tell all myself. Perhaps then you'll understand my need for a bit of caution."

"I know about that guy Max, if that's what you mean," he replied.

"Yes, that's exactly what I mean. Also, when I thought it was all over with Max, I started seeing a friend of his called Paul, but that didn't work out for a number of reasons. Mainly because he rushed me into a relationship I wasn't really ready for, but also he knew all about Max and never really trusted me completely. So you see, I am cautious because I've been hurt, though as far as Paul was concerned, I think he was hurt more than me."

"I do understand Josie, and I don't want to rush either. I just want to get to know you better. I don't mean just sleeping with you, although I have to admit that was marvellous. I'd like to get to know the real you. I'd like to discover what lies beneath that confident, bubbly exterior you put on for everyone."

Josie was quite taken aback. "What do you mean, put on? I don't put anything on. What you see is what you get."

"Sorry, I used the wrong words. I don't mean 'put on' in that way, I mean your defence to stop people seeing the real you. The caring, compassionate friend you can be and I am sure, one day, a loving partner and wife."

"Is that a proposal?" she coyly asked him, trying to make light of the moment. Christian had hit a chord and she needed to think about what he had said.

"No it's not. Well not yet, anyway. Now don't take that the wrong way. I really do like you. I also respect your need to take things slowly. So I'm not going to pressure you into anything. All I ask is that we spend time together, get to know each other and then see what happens, OK?"

"OK," she replied meekly.

He gave her a quick kiss on the lips and, tucking her arm through his, they set off on the long walk back to the flat.

"Dan called," Chrissie told Josie, "he wants to come over, but I managed to put him off. I told him we were all knackered from last night. I couldn't bear the thought of having to pretend it was just us girls out last night."

"Good decision," Josie replied.

Watching him absorbed in the motor racing on the TV, she kept thinking about what Christian had said to her earlier. He was really sensitive and caring, good looking too with a great body and a good job. Prospects, her parents would say. "I'm turning into my mother," she said to herself. Libby arrived a few minutes later, regaling them with hilarious tales of JC and the office move. Over supper there was a lot of teasing and banter among the four of them, with Christian in particular taking the brunt of it, having admitted that he paid to have his cleaning, laundry and even ironing done.

"Gives me more time for partying," he explained defensively.

They all had work the next day and Christian had an early shift so he made his apologies and left, promising to call Josie. The girls cleared the supper things away, and while they washed up Josie told Chrissie what Christian had said earlier.

"Well he's right, isn't he? I mean, look how fabulous you were over the Thierry thing, coming with me to the office and everything. And you always have lots of friends calling from the UK. All you need is a decent man and your life would be perfect!"

"Now you sound like my mother," Josie replied, "I don't

necessarily need a man in my life to make it perfect."

"We were all really concerned about the 'Max' thing, Jose. We could see he was using you but, well, you were so besotted you couldn't see it. Still that's over now and you can get on with your life."

"I guess so Chrissie, it's just that so much seems to have happened this year. I sometimes feel like I'm on a roller coaster and can't get off. I mean, first there was Max and then fleetingly Paul, and now there's Christian."

"Oh for goodness sake, yes a lot has happened, but now you should just try and enjoy your new job and your new man, and maybe life will settle down."

Josie knew her friend's advice was sound but somehow she just didn't think she was the settling down type. Part of her enjoyed the uncertainty of her lifestyle since she had moved to Paris, and yet part of her also wanted the security of a strong relationship. Josie felt more confused than ever and she had to cope with a new job too.

CHAPTER 4

At work the next day, Marguerite thanked Josie for inviting her and explained all about Yves. He had called and they were going out on a date later that week. Josie was pleased for the younger girl, who seemed a bit shy and quiet. She put this partly down to the fact that she still lived at home with her parents and partly her timid nature.

"My mother would like to meet you," Marguerite said, "I've told her all about you, and she says you remind her of herself during her younger days. Would you like to come for supper?"

Josie was quite taken aback; she wasn't used to friends' parents taking an interest in her. Marguerite lived above an antique shop owned by her parents in the 16th arrondissement, and it would be interesting to see that as well as meeting the parents.

"I'd love to," she replied.

Later that morning she headed for the Routage to make coffee for herself and the other secretaries and bumped into a tall, young, blonde woman in the corridor.

"And you are?" said the blonde woman abruptly in French.

Josie explained who she was and that she had joined the company the previous week. Switching to English, the woman said, "Ah, so you're the one Thomas was talking about at this morning's meeting. Well, I'm Sally Marsden-Lloyd," she examined Josie condescendingly, "I'm sure everyone's told you about me already. I'm very important here. I was away on holiday last week, skiing in Switzerland."

Sally Marsden-Lloyd had a strong Canadian accent and her

voice was very high pitched and nasal. Josie couldn't resist baiting the woman, who was already rubbing her up the wrong way.

"Sorry, what did you say your name was?"

"Sally, Sally Marsden-Lloyd. I work here as…well as an Account Manager of sorts. But I'm far more important than that." She looked really miffed that Josie hadn't recognised her instantly.

"Well, I'm very pleased to meet you, Sally. Which accounts do you work on exactly?" Josie asked, knowing full well that Sally was not an account manager at all.

"I work on the home interest and pet food accounts with Jean Paul, the automotive account with Philippe and I will be working with Daniel on the Chemfast Conference, which takes place in Brussels next month," she replied haughtily.

"I'm working on that account with Daniel as well. We recently gave a presentation to JC." Sally looked completely confused. "You know, the European President, Jean Carrère. Of course he loved all our ideas and then took me to lunch afterwards. Daniel seems to think that my inside knowledge of the company is pure gold, it gives us an extra edge." Sally was quite speechless and the expression on her face was a real picture.

"See you around," Josie tossed over her shoulder as she headed for the Routage. She could barely contain herself and once inside the Routage burst into a fit of giggles.

"What's so funny?"

She hadn't noticed Véronique in the kitchen at the far end of the room. Remembering what Marguerite had said about Véronique's 'not so high opinion' of Sally, Josie told her all about their short encounter.

"Good for you," said the older woman. "I can't stand her. She's a jumped up little madam who thinks she's really special. Her French isn't terribly good either. Thank goodness she's only with us for a year. Most of us are counting down the days until she leaves in the summer. I know for a fact that poor Fredet only puts up with her for the sake of her father. They are old friends apparently. Make sure you watch out for her, Josie, she has a knack of making it look as if she's done all the hard work, when in fact everyone else has."

Sally chose just that moment to burst into the room. She looked really cross when she caught sight of Josie and Véronique laughing and joking together.

"Have either of you seen Daniel?" she asked, obviously desperate to find out if what Josie had said was true.

"He's on holiday this week," Véronique informed her, "but if you want to get up to speed on the Chemfast Conference, I'm sure Josie can brief you," Véronique turned to Josie with a smile tugging at the corner of her mouth, "that's of course if you have the time, Josie? I know how terribly busy you are." It was all Josie could do to stop herself from laughing.

Véronique smiled thinly, "Actually it will have to be later in the week, Sally. I've just remembered that Josie is coming with me to the Four Seasons meeting and we need to prepare for that."

This was the first Josie had heard about any meeting. "But what about Cécile?" she asked.

"Oh, Cécile will come too, but as you know Hélène was very impressed by you the other evening at the reception." Véronique looked pointedly at Sally when she said, "Hélène suggested you would be an invaluable member of the team, particularly with your exceptional language skills."

"Does Thomas know?" enquired Josie, still surprised at Véronique's proposal.

"Thomas will be fine with it. I just hope you can manage everything when Mervyn gets back, that's all. I'm sure if you're struggling with too much work we can get you some help." Véronique smiled sweetly at Sally, "What exactly are you working on at the moment, Sally?" The young women turned bright red at the implication that she would be supporting Josie and looked fit to burst a blood vessel. She turned abruptly on her heels and stormed out of the room, slamming the door behind her.

Véronique and Josie both burst out laughing, "You're terrible, you know. You shouldn't wind her up like that," said Josie between fits of giggles.

"Well you did the same and it's not terribly difficult," said Véronqiue. "I'll go and let Thomas know about the Four Seasons. I'm sure it will be okay. Hélène was very insistent that you join the team, even though she doesn't actually attend all the meetings, thank goodness."

Josie returned to her office but couldn't help smiling to herself about the recent turn of events. Charlotte and Odette noticed her mood and were desperate to find out the latest office gossip. "Come on then, what's so funny?" asked Odette, who was always the more direct of the two, "Nothing really," replied Josie, "it's just that I've finally met Sally Marsden-Lloyd and I'm not sure we're going to get on."

"You, me and everyone else," said Odette, smiling at Josie for the first time since she joined the agency. "I thought you two would get along as you both speak English. But I guess I'm wrong."

"You sure are! Please don't confuse the English with the Americans and Canadians, we all take it very badly indeed. We are very different beings," said Josie.

"Look out, here she comes with Thomas," whispered Charlotte, pretending to be occupied with her work.

"Josie," said Thomas, calling her by the shortened version of her name for the first time since she had joined the agency, "we have a bit of a delicate situation vis à vis the Four Seasons account. I gather Véronique has asked you to join the team without checking with me first," Thomas cast an eye at a clearly triumphant Sally Marsden-Lloyd, "Sally has been showing an interest in that account for quite some time now and I did tell her that she would be first in line should the team require additional support." Thomas looked a bit sheepish and found it difficult to hold Josie's gaze. "I am going to have to insist that Sally joins the account team and goes along to tomorrow's meeting, and we'll see how things go from there. If the requirement for additional support is on-going, then we'll review it when Sally leaves later this year. By then you will have more experience with the agency." Josie was livid and Thomas obviously picked up on her mood. "Maybe then you'll be in a better position to take on more work, Josie. Is that OK with you?"

Josie was incredibly angry but she wasn't going to give Sally the satisfaction of seeing her disappointment. "Thanks for letting me know, Thomas. What with the Chemfast Conference, your pending briefs and of course Mervyn's too, I'm sure I've enough to keep me busy."

"Good girl," he said patting her shoulder. As they left, Sally smiled thinly at Josie with a look of absolute self-satisfaction.

"Perhaps I should call Véronique and warn her?" Josie asked Charlotte and Odette. Charlotte just shrugged, but Odette thought it a good idea. So Josie called Véronique and explained what Thomas had said.

"Shit, I really don't want that stupid, arrogant Canadian bitch working with me," she said, "but I know Thomas and he is a very stubborn, but fair man. Well, I'll be so vile to her that she won't want to work on the account and then you can. Just you wait and see. Thanks for the tip off, Josie."

Josie managed to avoid Sally for the rest of that day and the day after. Travelling home with Marguerite on the underground the following evening, the girls discussed the situation with Sally and what, if anything, Josie could do to avoid working with her.

"She only likes to get involved in the high profile stuff," Marguerite said, "you know, press launches and conferences and stuff. She's rubbish at organising them but comes over as looking really good as she gets everyone else to do the work for her. We've learned the hard way now, and so every time she asks us to do something we check with one of the Account Managers or Account Directors first. That way they know indirectly that we're doing the work and not her."

"It's unusual for me to take such an instant dislike to someone," replied Josie, "but her whole demeanour is one of such condescending superiority. She's absolutely no better than any of us. I wonder how the Four Seasons meeting went?"

"We'll find out soon enough tomorrow. Come on, this is our stop," said Marguerite.

The girls emerged from the Métro into an impressive tree lined boulevard in the 16th arrondissement of the city. They walked for about five minutes and turned into a smaller, but equally impressive, side street. The area was considered to be one of the most affluent of the Paris suburbs. Josie spotted the antique shop, nestling between a prestigious looking apartment block and a very expensive clothes shop. "Wow!" she said under her breath. The window of the antique shop was very simple, featuring only a cream ottoman draped with a deep red silk. The ornate sign above the door announced: "Antiquités Exclusives - Jean Pierre de la Fontaine".

Looking into the shop, Josie could see that the simplicity of the window dressing was carried on throughout the interior. There were just a few large pieces of furniture and a display of china and old clocks. Josie could also see a sign which read 'Showroom'. "Come on Josie," Marguerite said to her friend, grabbing Josie's arm. They entered the shop and an old-fashioned bell rang above the door. A very distinguished man in his late forties emerged from the back room. Josie assumed he was Marguerite's father. He was talking on his mobile phone. He waved to the girls distractedly and indicated he wouldn't be long. Josie continued her perusal of the shop, which was even more impressive inside. The main room obviously had a theme, as all the furniture was a rich creamy colour with very ornate legs and handles and gold fleur de lys designs. She had no idea how old any of it was but it looked very expensive. She turned over one of the price tags on a small chest of drawers and it read 6000 euros. "My god," she thought to herself, "this is the real stuff."

Josie followed Marguerite through to the second showroom, which was very different to the front of the shop. The back room was much larger, but every wall, corner and metre of floor space was covered with pieces of furniture, all priced and tagged with a date. There were hundreds of items of what Josie thought of as 'bric-a-brac,' but again based on the prices displayed they were obviously collectors' items. Marguerite began to explain to Josie the different types of furniture, and spoke with great knowledge about the antiques business.

"Gosh Marguerite, you're a real expert," Josie told her, fascinated by the facts and figures her friend was reeling out, "you should work here, not at the agency."

Josie turned to be greeted by an extremely elegant woman, dressed in a smart, dark brown trouser suit, with a green silk blouse, and a velvet scarf thrown casually around her shoulders. She was immaculately coiffed and manicured and would have looked extremely daunting, if it wasn't for her wide smile and the sparkle in her green eyes. The woman was incredibly beautiful and sophisticated and Josie felt very dowdy by comparison.

"Maman, this is Josie," said Marguerite, kissing her mother on both cheeks.

"I guessed that, my darling." Her words were razor sharp and the older woman smiled benignly at her daughter. "Delighted to meet you, Josie, I've heard so much about you. I am Françoise de la Fontaine, Marguerite's mother."

"Enchantée," replied Josie, who was completely mesmerised by her surroundings and by the stern figure of Françoise de la Fontaine. The woman's handshake was firm but warm.

"We've always encouraged Marguerite and her brother, Luc,

to take an interest in the business. It's very rewarding. Luc loves it but Marguerite wants to do her own thing and earn a pittance working for others instead of for us," said Françoise de la Fontaine, rolling her eyes theatrically. "We all think it's a very sad state of affairs," she continued, a small smile hovering over her frosty countenance.

Josie could see that the older woman was not being totally serious and Marguerite was smiling too, "Now stop it Maman, don't be so wicked. You know you love the fact that I want to be a bit independent. I just take after you!" Marguerite explained, "Antiques are in my blood, they have always been a part of me, and one day I will support the business. But for the moment I want a bit of independence."

"Have it your own way, my dear. But you will forgive your dear Maman for wanting what's best for you," Françoise turned her attention to Josie. "Perhaps when she finally gets bored of the agency she will come and take over our PR and Marketing, you must help me persuade her, Josie."

"We've had this conversation before, Maman," said Marguerite, "and as I've explained, I am merely a secretary in the accounts department. I have very little involvement in the account handling side of things. Josie does more of that work, isn't that so?"

"Well I wouldn't go that far Marguerite, not yet anyway. I'm doing a little of the work because of my previous links with my last company. I'm basically a secretary too, although I have my own ambitions. The work is interesting and I'd like to do more on the accounts side."

At that moment, Marguerite's father came into the back room and briefly introduced himself. He then launched into a breathless and long explanation of a deal he was trying to complete. Françoise offered her advice, where she could get a word in. Marguerite indicated that Josie should follow her and leave her parents to their business. There was a large set of double doors at the back of the showroom and Josie followed her friend through these and up a wide flight of stairs to the next floor. Opening another set of double doors, Josie found herself in a huge, airy sitting room. The room was elegantly decorated and all the furniture looked expensive. "Probably more collectors' items," thought Josie, looking around and thinking how humble her apartment seemed by comparison.

The girls headed for the kitchen where Marguerite made a tray of coffee and biscuits. Josie was dying for a glass of wine but didn't like to ask. The kitchen by contrast was very modern with a lot of marble and chrome. The girls sat at a breakfast bar and sipped their coffee, chatting about the shop and how Marguerite's parents breathed and lived their business. After a while they were joined by Françoise who began preparing supper. "We'll eat around 7.30 pm if that's okay with you?" Both girls nodded in agreement. "Luc should be back by then and no doubt he'll be starving as usual!"

Josie asked if she could help with the preparations. "Thanks Josie, but Marthe, our housekeeper, has already completed most of the preparations. I just have to put it in the oven. Why don't you girls go and watch television and I'll call you when it's ready?"

They went back into the sitting room and Marguerite put the news on the TV. She offered Josie a glass of wine, which she readily accepted. By 7.30 pm, supper was ready but there was no sign of Luc. "I've tried calling him," said Jean Pierre, Marguerite's father, "but there's no answer. I assume he's on his way back. I haven't heard from him all day."

"Let's start without him then," said Marguerite's mother curtly. Françoise found it difficult to mask the look of evident concern. She was clearly disturbed by her son's absence.

"My brother is a bit of a tearaway," whispered Marguerite to Josie when her mother left to fetch the food from the kitchen. "Knowing Luc he's probably stopped off at a bar on the way home. He's only just had his licence back after a drink-driving offence. I do hope he's being sensible. We all love him to death but he's the most irresponsible person alive. Maman worries herself sick. Although he has a great flair for the business and that makes both my parents happy."

They had just finished their starter, a whole Camembert cheese baked in cranberries and served with salad and hot French bread, when Luc finally burst into the room, breathless from obviously having run up the stairs from the showroom.

"Bon soir everyone," he said, "I'm so sorry I'm late. The traffic was truly awful. Whoever built the Periphérique around Paris should be shot. It's just a glorified car park at this time of night."

Both parents smiled indulgently, Marguerite just rolled her

eyes and gave a little snort. Josie had quickly picked up that Luc was the golden boy as far as her parents were concerned. He was in his early twenties, tall and slender with reddish blond hair, which looked like it would be curly if it hadn't been cut so short. Even though he was wearing a suit and tie, Josie could tell he was incredibly toned and tanned.

"Luc, this is my friend Josie from work," said Marguerite to her brother. Luc turned to look directly at Josie for the first time. She found herself gazing into the most piercing and intriguing green eyes. They were almond shaped, with the longest and darkest eyelashes Josie had ever seen on a man.

"So this is the infamous Josie who is completely leading my little sister astray," said Luc, smirking, "I am delighted to finally meet you." He took her hand and kissed it dramatically. Josie could feel the heat rising to her face. The touch of his lips on the back of her hand was electric. She quickly pulled her hand away. Josie was lost for words, but managed a smile in acknowledgement. Luc caught her eye and gave her a devilish wink, making her blush even more. He sat down next to her and Josie couldn't help but hold her stomach in and stick her chest out. She barely ate a morsel of the delicious main course, which was some kind of boeuf bourguignon – her favourite. She also declined dessert but had another few glasses of the red wine which was flowing freely. Josie listened to family banter among the de la Fontaines. But all the while she was very conscious of the physical presence of the young man sitting beside her.

After dinner, the girls helped Madame de la Fontaine to clear up and then they joined the men for coffee in the sitting room. It would have seemed very formal to Josie if the family hadn't been so welcoming and lively. Josie needed the coffee to help sober up. She had drunk far too much wine. The coffee helped a great deal and she quietly observed the warm interaction between family members. Realising Josie might be feeling a little left out, Françoise asked her about her family. Josie told them all about her upbringing and was conscious that it all sounded rather dull. She skipped over her university years, fearful that it might prove a bit too racy for present company. Josie concluded by explaining just how much she was enjoying living and working in Paris.

"Tell them about Sally," Marguerite told her friend, and Josie explained about her confrontation with the rude Canadian girl the previous day.

"So you're not usually as quiet as you are this evening?" asked Luc, making Josie blush once more.

"Josie's not quiet at all," objected Marguerite, "it's just that with you around, dear brother, nobody else can get a word in edgeways." Marguerite had a twinkle in her eye; she clearly enjoyed sparring with her brother. Luc held up his hands, admitting his guilt. "I know I'm monopolizing the conversation, you know how fired up I get when talking about the business," Luc smiled at Josie, "I love attending the auctions, it's a real thrill, you should come along some time."

Both parents, brimming with pride, explained how wonderful Luc was at seeking out bargains. Josie could hardly believe the effect this handsome man was having on her. It was just like Max, all over again. She resolved not to get caught up again in another hopeless contretemps.

"Well Josie?" prompted Luc, "would you like to see me in action?"

"It sounds wonderful," Josie stammered. She realised that Luc was fully aware of the effect he was having on her. Checking her watch in order to avoid his penetrating gaze, she realized it was late. "I've been having such fun I hardly realized the time, you'll have to forgive me but I'd better make a move." Josie stood and shook hands with Monsieur and Madame de la Fontaine. "Thank you so much for your kind hospitality. It's been a pleasure to meet you." Despite her protestations, Marguerite and Luc insisted on accompanying her to the Métro. When they reached the station Luc enquired if she would rather they ordered a taxi. "Thanks anyway, but I'll be fine. It's only a few stops and a short walk home," said Josie. She gave Marguerite a hug and thanked her again. She went to shake Luc's hand but he leaned over and gave her the ritual three kisses on the cheek. Again her skin burned at his touch. "I hope we meet again very soon, Josie." She hardly dared to reply in case her voice croaked, so she just smiled. "See you tomorrow," said Marguerite, linking arms with her brother and setting off back towards their apartment. Josie could hear them laughing together as she headed down the steps and into the Métro. Fortunately she didn't have to wait too long for a train and sat with her head against the cool window, thinking about how gorgeous Luc was and the startling effect he had had on her.

"Stop it," she scolded herself. "He is a typical, rich, spoilt lad about town and anyway you've got Christian." Thinking about Christian, she remembered she had switched her phone off earlier. Josie switched it back on but had no signal until she finally emerged from the station at the other end. As she approached the apartment, her phone started to beep. It was a text message and a voicemail message too. Josie checked the voicemail which had been left earlier in the evening. Christian wanted her to call him right away. She let herself into the flat and called him straight back. He was delighted to hear from her and asked, in a very non-possessive way, if she had enjoyed her evening. Josie replied positively, omitting any mention of Luc. They arranged to meet on the Thursday evening. "I thought I'd cook you a meal," Christian said, "and perhaps you can stay over at my place. I'm on a late shift on Friday." Josie replied quickly, "But I've work the next day," realising too late that her response had been quite abrupt.

"OK," he sounded hurt, "I was going to offer to drive you into work in the morning but if you really don't want to…"

"I'm sorry Christian. I didn't mean to sound so sharp. I'm just tired I guess. I'd love to stay over as long as you don't mind getting up early on your morning off."

"For you Josephine, it is no trouble at all," he replied humorously, shrugging off her previous abruptness.

"Excellent! Well I'll get the train over to you after work then. It will save you coming over all this way twice."

"I really don't mind coming to pick you up, Josie," replied Christian.

"No honestly, I'll get the train and you can meet me at the station. I'll call you to let you know what time I'm arriving. I imagine it will be a little after 6.30."

"OK, that's great, it's a date. I'll see you then," Christian whispered. "Goodnight gorgeous, sleep tight and dream of me, as I will of you."

"Goodnight Christian. I'm sure I will," she replied, smiling.

Chrissie was still out with some of her friends from work so after a large glass of water Josie showered and went to bed. She didn't sleep very well that night as images of Luc, Christian and Max kept passing through her mind, getting all jumbled together. She slept fitfully and felt dreadful when her alarm went off the next morning. Josie was tempted to stay in bed for an extra 30 minutes and forgo washing her hair. But she remembered the scheduled agency review meeting that morning. With glamorous managers like Véronqiue and Cécile around, she wanted to look her very best. More importantly, she didn't want to offer Sally any opportunity to outshine her.

CHAPTER 5

Once Josie had showered she took a cup of tea into Chrissie and gently roused her. Chrissie groaned and sat up in bed, peering through bleary eyes. "Thanks Josie, I really need this. I had one too many last night. "How about you?"

"It was a really lovely evening. Marguerite's family are great, very wealthy and she doesn't really need to work at the agency at all. It's her bid for independence, naturally her parents would rather she came and worked for them. But I can understand her decision. Have you heard from Claude?"

"No I haven't," said Chrissie angrily. "I really don't know what's going on. He was full on early last week and we had such a fabulous time with his friends in Normandy. I just don't know what I've done wrong! I feel as if I've really met my soul mate. But he seems to have backed off the second we started to get really close. I just don't get it. He's gone from very hot to very cold in the blink of an eye. I desperately want to call him, but I don't want to scare him off. I just don't know what to do for the best!"

Josie was completely surprised. It had seemed that Claude was incredibly keen on Chrissie. In fact it was Chrissie, or so it seemed to her, that had held back, at least at first. "Look, stop mooching around, why don't you send him a text saying something like 'hope you're having a good week, speak soon'. I'm seeing Christian tomorrow evening and I'll discretely see if he knows what's going on?"

"Thanks Josie, that's good advice," Chrissie decided to wait until lunchtime before sending the text. She explained that she didn't want Claude to feel harassed. Josie thought this was a bit daft but didn't say anything as her friend was clearly upset about the whole situation.

The agency review meeting was at 11am and, as Daniel Bergerac was on holiday, Thomas had asked Josie for feedback on the plans for the Chemfast conference. She had been working on it all week and had pressured the design agency to get the mock-ups for the display panels and literature over in time for the meeting. They had been sent over by courier earlier that morning and she had checked them ahead of the meeting. They were perfect apart from one slight error which she intended to highlight during the meeting. Josie wanted to demonstrate that she was on the ball and knew what she was talking about.

The previous meeting had been quite informal and held in the Routage room. Today's meeting was in Jacques Fredet's room with a proper screen, laptop and projector. Josie had copied her work onto a memory stick as well as sending it by email to the laptop computer used for presentations. When she entered the room, she noticed Sally was fiddling with the laptop. Sally almost jumped out of her skin when she saw Josie, as if caught doing something she shouldn't. The room soon filled up with the other managers and Josie began to feel pretty nervous. Marguerite, Charlotte and Odette had all wished her the best of luck. Josie was really pleased that the girls in the office seemed to be warming to her.

Jacques Fredet began with an overview of the agency in terms of clients and financial input. Jacques then announced that he would be putting together a special project team to look at a sporting sponsorship event. He didn't go into too much detail and informed them that for the moment it all needed to remain highly confidential. Josie caught sight of Sally looking pretty smug. Her title was Special Project Administrator and she no doubt automatically assumed she would be working on the new account. Thomas and Jean Paul each gave an overview of their different sectors and then Josie was invited to present the plans for the conference. She tried to look confident as she stood in front of the assembled managers and administrators. There had been no time at the start of the meeting to detach her presentation from the email. Josie opened the inbox to retrieve the document but her email wasn't there. With calmness, she didn't really feel, Josie apologised to her colleagues in the room and extricated the memory stick from her trouser pocket. After a few seconds, the presentation she and Daniel had given to JC flashed up on screen. Josie handed around the mock-ups from the designers. Before anyone had an opportunity to pick up on it, she highlighted the amendment which needed to be made to the copy on one of the leaflets. Then Josie ran through the presentation nervously. She knew she was talking far too fast and the thought of not being able to answer difficult questions at the end was making her even more nervous. When she'd finished she asked her colleagues if anyone had any questions and, winking at her, Véronique asked, "How did you persuade JC to agree to announce the office move? I know Daniel was having problems on that front."

"Well to be quite honest, I knew JC wouldn't be able to resist the personal publicity so we changed the slant slightly. I suggested JC focus on the fact that it was his decision, as head of the European Office, to move to London, rather than the Americans'. That helped, plus the fact that there will be a TV crew covering the conference. We know we can't guarantee TV coverage for Chemfast, but as they are there covering the global warming summit anyway, we might well be able to elicit some favourable TV interest. Also JC knows the Chief Executive of TF1 and is planning to use his influence there to sway it."

"But what about my idea, the history of Chemfast?" blurted Sally, obviously put out by Josie's contribution to the meeting.

"Oh, we thought it would be far more interesting to focus on the future of Chemfast as a key player within the industry, rather than looking backwards," said Josie innocently, "also, there was that scandal a few years ago with one of the big oil companies. Chemfast was taken to court as the result of some sort of confidentiality issue. The company obviously didn't want all that raked up again. We will, of course, have a response ready should anyone ask the question but again we will be putting a positive spin on it."

"Spoken like a true PR girl," said Véronique, "Well done Josie."

Everyone else, with the exception of Sally, congratulated her. Josie blushed but inside felt wonderful. She couldn't believe that in such a short space of time she had started to make a small, positive impression on her colleagues. The meeting continued with reviews by the rest of the management team. Finally, it was over to Véronique and Cécile for the Four Seasons review. Véronique referred to the reception, which the company viewed as being very successful, and then asked Sally to provide an overview of the meeting held the previous day. Both Cécile and Sally looked completely surprised.

"But I haven't prepared anything," said Sally in her whining, nasally twang, "I thought Cécile or you would do the review, Véronique."

"But you were at the meeting too Sally, I seem to recall you were most insistent that you attend." Véronique looked around the room and managed to catch the eye of Fredet, "I'm still not entirely clear what role you can play in developing this client, I would think the least you could do is to review the meeting and make a small contribution towards this morning's update?"

Josie almost felt sorry for Sally, but not quite, as she was convinced the Canadian had deleted her email with the Chemfast presentation. Put on the spot, Sally blustered her way through an overview of the meeting but everyone could see she was struggling to remember anything of importance at all. After a few moments, she admitted defeat and Véronqiue took over, sharing a look and a sigh of exasperation with the other people in the room. Josie made a mental note not to get on the wrong side of Véronique. She liked her very much but also recognised that there was a hard side to her which she didn't much care for. Josie wasn't sure if she had the temperament to develop such a hard-nosed approach. Although she had to admit it was pretty effective.

"And what Sally has omitted to say in her overview is that, next month, the Four Seasons are planning to open four new hotels across Europe and want us to handle the launch events. We will need to work closely with their in-house team to ensure a consistency in themes, etc... What's more the hotels are not new-builds, so there are no environmental issues to be dealt with. They have bought up existing, independent hotels and refurbished these to the Four Seasons' very high standard." Véronique paused for effect. Everyone was incredibly pleased with the extra agency work. "That's the good news. The bad news is that Hélène du Tilly will be the principle contact at the Four Seasons, with Jean-François as her second in command."

Josie remembered that Jean-François was the son of the Four

Seasons Managing Director, Hélène's husband, but by another woman.

"Oh dear, I can see fireworks," said Philippe McKay. Philippe and Véronique were very friendly and Josie assumed that he more than anyone else would know if there had been anything going on between the two women in the past.

"Who will you have on your team, Véronique?" asked Monsieur Fredet, with some concern evident in his voice. "The current team are pretty stretched with all our day to day PR activities. I suggest you pull in one Account Manager and one Administrative Secretary to support you. If you need more people, then I will of course step in to help."

Josie knew that Véronique had a lot of time for Jacques Fredet who, despite his age, was still very well respected within the PR industry, not just in France but throughout the whole of Europe. He was considered to be very forward thinking. But as a general rule he didn't tend to interfere with the day-to-day running of the accounts, acting more as a figurehead for the agency and the PR industry in general.

"Thanks Jacques," she said, "that would be great. I'm planning to arrange a brainstorm session to start things rolling. I think it's important that the brainstorm is open to volunteers, fresh blood so to speak. I can draw the team together after that. Will you chair the session?"

"Of course, great idea," Jacques looked around the room. "Any more volunteers?"

A number of Account Directors and Managers agreed to join the session and Josie was expecting Sally to do so too. But Sally, in this instance, just kept quiet. Véronique managed to catch Josie's eye and her look seemed to say, 'go on, you volunteer too!' Hesitantly she said, "I know I'm still very new to the agency but perhaps I can join the meeting? It will be a great opportunity for me. But also I might be able to make some sort of objective contribution."

"Great," replied Véronique quickly before anyone else had an opportunity to say anything, "Let's all meet the same time tomorrow and I'll circulate a brief in advance."

As people began leaving the meeting, Josie found herself walking just ahead of Sally. "A real jumped up little madam, aren't you," Sally said viciously, "Well don't get too big for your boots.

They really know how to cut you down to size here, even for the slightest little thing. If I were you I'd watch your back." Sally rudely pushed past Josie and made her way upstairs to her office. Josie was completely taken aback at the nastiness of Sally's words. She was beginning to think maybe she should keep her head down, just for an easy life, but that simply wasn't in her nature. Also, she really wanted to get on in the agency and, although it was early days, she believed she was already making a bit of an impression, mainly through her enthusiasm and commitment.

Later that day, she caught up with Véronique in the Routage. "Can I have a word please, Véronique?" she asked, "In private?"

"Sure," replied Véronique, "come up to my office."

They made their way up the two flights of stairs to Véronique's office, which took up the entire length of the top floor. The office was light and spacious and displayed a number of awards, gained through her work for Renseignements over the years. "What's up Josie, you look really concerned about something?" Josie had always found it difficult to conceal her feelings.

"It's about Sally. I really don't want to upset her any more than I already have. She seems to be really angry with me. Perhaps it would be better if you invited her to join the new team and I'll drop out."

"Over my dead body," replied the older woman, "Sally had the same opportunity to volunteer today as did you, but she chose not to. Anyway Hélène specifically asked for you to join the team, so I would have invited you later if you hadn't volunteered. Hélène doesn't rate Sally at all. None of us do. Not even Jacques, but his hands are tied because of his friendship with her father."

"If you're entirely sure, I'd be happy to be a part of the team" replied Josie, not entirely certain whether to be thrilled or scared by Hélène's sudden interest in her.

"As you know, Thomas insisted Sally be part of the day-to-day team and I want a separate team working on the new project."

"OK," Josie smiled rather weakly. She was beginning to wonder if she wasn't taking on too much. Mervyn Bradley was due back the following week. Josie had no idea what her role was supposed to be in supporting him but she'd soon find out.

Later that day Véronique sent out an email explaining the new brief. Josie printed it off to read and absorb at home. After supper, she sent a quick text to Christian confirming the arrangements for the following evening and settled down to read the brief and make some notes. She'd told Chrissie all about the episode with Sally, who agreed entirely with Véronique's view of the whole situation. Chrissie reported that she had sent the text message to Claude. But there had been no reply. Josie knew, from Christian, that the controllers were working the late afternoon shift and told her friend, "I'm sure he'll call as soon as he finishes work."

"But Josie, you know as well as I do that they have lots of breaks and it's never stopped Claude texting me before. I don't even know if he's back at work. I just wish I knew what the hell is going on with him."

"Well, if you haven't heard anything by tomorrow evening I'll subtly find out from Christian just what's got into him. Those two are very close, I'm sure he'll say something."

"Thanks, you're a good mate. It's bloody typical though. The one guy I was really getting to care about goes cold on me. I guess it's retribution for all the times I've been the same way in the past."

For the first time since she had known her, Josie saw that there was a vulnerable side to Chrissie. Her friend's eyes had welled up with tears and she looked very down and despondent.

"Come on," she said, "read this brief with me and let's see if we can come up with some great ideas for tomorrow's meeting. I'm starting to feel a bit out of my depth."

The girls read the brief together. "This sounds like a lot of fun," said Chrissie, "Will it involve you travelling to all these wonderful places?"

"I don't know yet. I would guess the more senior members of the team would be responsible for that. I'll probably just provide support from the office. It does sound exciting, though. I'm not sure what's really expected of me at tomorrow's meeting but, reading the brief, one idea does spring to mind. Listen, what do you think?" Josie explained her idea to Chrissie. Among the usual need for high profile launch events with corresponding media coverage and VIP attendees, the main aim was to promote the uniqueness of the Four Seasons. It was important to demonstrate that at every Four Seasons hotel in the world, the quality of accommodation, food and service was second to none. Although some of the premises were smaller and allowed for less flexibility in terms of additional facilities like gyms or swimming pools, the high standard of service and food would be the same throughout each hotel. The challenge was to create a solid and easily identifiable link to demonstrate this fact.

The report stated that it was anticipated that the refurbishment work would be completed at all the new premises, more or less at the same time. Josie's idea was to have four consecutive opening events, all held on the same day and linked together via video conference technology: a grand launch party that spanned four different countries. It would be difficult to plan but incredibly effective in promoting the international credentials of the luxury hotel chain. There could be a single theme for all the events, which would support the message of consistency in quality and standards, and each could be officially opened by the same celebrity, city-hopping by private jet to each site. Josie wasn't entirely sure if the logistics would all work out. But the idea sounded suitably ambitious and completely different to any other launch before. Chrissie congratulated Josie and thought it was a marvellous idea.

"Thanks Chrissie, I just don't know. I think I'll wait and see what everyone else says tomorrow. I'll only put this idea forward if it seems right at the time."

"I think you underestimate yourself, Josie," said Chrissie encouragingly, "I don't recall ever seeing anything like this in the press before."

"Yes maybe you're right, let's think of a common theme that may work."

"Well," replied Chrissie, "it may seem a bit obvious, but how about the Four Seasons? There are four hotels, aren't there, so each opening could correspond with one of the seasons. Madrid would be ideal for summer, Geneva should be winter, maybe London for autumn and that leaves Amsterdam for spring. I'd imagine various backdrops of autumn leaves, tulips, snow peaked mountains, citrus groves…"

"Chrissie, you are a genius! That does sound like a wonderful idea. I'll add it to the list. We could get the key national food and drink journalists along and then maybe also invite a celebrity chef from each city to prepare the reception. Although from past experience I know just how celebrity chefs can be such drama queens, and that might upset the staff at the Four Seasons."

"You could do it the other way round, maybe," said Chrissie thoughtfully, "and get the Four Seasons chef to prepare the reception but invite a celebrity chef and the national food and wine journalists to the event for the 'tastings'."

"Brilliant, Chrissie, that's two great ideas you've given me. I think I'll get into work early tomorrow and type this lot up ahead of our meeting. I wish I had a laptop, I'd do it now if I did."

"Can't you ask for one?"

"I wouldn't dare. None of the other secretaries has one. I don't want to rock the boat any further. The girls in the office are just about beginning to accept me. I'll manage though. I'll get up really early and make a start," said Josie.

"Don't forget to let me know how you get on, call me lunchtime, promise?"

"OK, I promise. I'd better go and get my bag ready for tomorrow night. I won't have time in the morning. Chrissie, I'm more excited about the meeting tomorrow than I am about seeing Christian, do you think that's normal?"

"Who wants to be normal? It's vastly overrated. You are looking forward to seeing him though, aren't you?"

Josie hesitated before replying, "Yes I am. I really am. But I simply don't get that churning feeling in my stomach, like I did with Max."

"Look Josie, you have to forget about Max," said Chrissie crossly, "it's over, he's a shit and you know he's a shit. Christian is a good guy and no pushover either. Don't ruin what could be a really good thing for the sake of a complete bastard like Max."

"I know you're right. But bastard or not, he really got under my skin." Josie paused, wondering whether to confide in Chrissie further, "I met someone else the other evening. Luc, Marguerite's brother. He's absolutely gorgeous and there was clearly a spark between us. I really shouldn't be having these thoughts when I'm supposed to be going out with Christian."

"Josie, you really are on your own," said a clearly exasperated Chrissie, "You do like your life complicated, don't you?" Josie just shrugged her shoulders, "I don't try to make it complicated, all this stuff just keeps happening to me. It's not like I'm willing it to happen or anything."

"Look, all I can suggest is that you just go with the flow," said Chrissie. "You'll have a lovely time with Christian tomorrow evening. Forget all about Max and this Luc guy. You're just acting crazy at the moment, probably because of all this pressure at work."

"I suppose you're right. I'm off to pack my bag and go to bed. See you in the morning, and thanks again, Chrissie, for all your help," said Josie.

Josie didn't sleep very well again that night and by the time her alarm went off she'd already been awake for at least an hour. She showered and dressed and headed for the Métro. Josie reached the office early. The front door was locked but there were lights on in several of the offices upstairs. She rang the doorbell and a few moments later Jean Pierre Benet let her in.

"Morning Josie, you're bright and early this morning!" He seemed surprised.

"Morning Jean Pierre, I just wanted to do some preparation for the Four Seasons brainstorm and I don't want to get behind with my other work, so I've come in a bit earlier, that's all."

Jean Pierre raised an eyebrow. "Right, fine, very conscientious I must say! Why not ask Claire for a key? Just in case you decide to come in early again?"

"Thanks, I'll do that," said Josie and headed for her desk to begin work on the presentation, "Thank goodness for Google," she thought as she copied her presentation onto a memory stick. Josie had managed to download some images from the internet depicting seasonal changes in different countries, and researched a number of celebrity chefs. She managed to get most of her normal work done ahead of the meeting. Her two colleagues wished her good luck again. There were about eight volunteers in the meeting room, including Josie. Jacques Fredet was there along with Philippe and Jean Pierre. Thomas was at a client review meeting so he couldn't attend, and Cécile had also been called away to another meeting. Véronqiue welcomed everyone and opened the meeting by running quickly through the brief. She then invited people to put forward suggestions, on post-it notes, which were stuck to a flip chart, prepared in advance with a number of different headings. The headings covered team make up, opening event, theme linking the hotels, brand amplification and media. Josie hadn't participated in a brainstorm like this before and was reluctant to put her ideas on to the 'post-its'. She really wanted to present her ideas properly and decided to just give a few hints. Then, hopefully, she might get the opportunity to say more as the meeting progressed.

Once everyone had posted their ideas, Véronique grouped the sticky notes together under the different headings. Then, selecting suggestions, she asked the person who put forward the idea to elaborate. Josie noticed that her suggestions: Seasons, Celebrity Chefs and Video Link weren't grouped with the other ideas but stood out on their own. One account manager suggested a sponsored sportathon at each hotel. But Veronique explained that it wouldn't work as not all the hotels had the same leisure facilities. Another manager suggested a newspaper promotion in all the leading daily newspapers for each city. The group discussed the idea that the promotion might be a competition to win a weekend break at each of the four luxury hotels. Véronique thought this might work as a follow up but it wasn't sufficiently strong for the launch. After discussing one or two other ideas, Véronique picked up the post-it with the word 'seasons' on it and asked what that meant.

"That's my idea," said Josie nervously, "most of mine are linked, sort of. I've prepared a quick presentation giving an overview of my ideas, if that's okay, Véronique?"

"Sure," replied Véronique, clearly surprised. They set up the laptop and Josie, for the second day running, found herself nervously facing her colleagues. But it was different this time. The day before she was presenting on behalf of Daniel Bergerac who had done most of the work, today she was presenting her own ideas. Josie ran through her ideas confidently and swiftly and then passed out the hand-outs she had prepared earlier. "Any questions?" she asked, not sure if their silence meant approval or disapproval.

"I love it, it's a magnificent idea," said Véronique, jumping up from her seat and giving Josie a hug. "It will obviously need working up a bit and we need to really look at the logistics of the four simultaneous events. But its novel, unique, a fantastic idea. Well done, Josie!"

The meeting progressed with the focus now on Josie's idea and at the end of the session, as everyone started to leave the room, Jacques Fredet approached Josie who was helping Véronique to gather up the flip chart. "Well, young lady," he said, putting a fatherly arm around her shoulder, "that's two days on the trot you've managed to impress me. I think you may prove to be quite a find. Keep up the good work."

"Absolutely terrific," interrupted Véronique. "Josie will definitely be involved with the team, provided Thomas is happy with that."

"Don't worry about Thomas, leave that to me," said Jacques Fredet. "Will you be able to manage this extra work as well as working for Thomas and Mervyn?" he asked Josie, who was trying her best not to look too pleased with herself.

"Well, I'm sure I can manage this and working for Thomas," said Josie, "but I don't know what's expected of me from Mervyn so it's hard to say yet. Plus there's the Chemfast conference coming up. But that's just a one-off and most of the prep for that is done now."

"Well, give it a go and if it gets too much come and talk with me or Thomas," he said. "I'm sure we can sort something out. Perhaps one of the other girls could help Mervyn. He's not here that often anyway. Well done Josie. That was a very good and creative piece of work. I'm very pleased."

"Thank you, I really enjoyed working it up," said Josie. Once Jacques Fredet had left, it was Véronique's turn to praise Josie. "You really do show great potential, Josie," she said, "I think if we can make this launch work really well it could mean an early promotion for you, and well deserved."

"Thanks, Véronique. I just hope I don't end up making the other girls resent me."

"Oh, don't worry about them. They're a nice bunch really, except for Sally of course. Most of them just work because they have to, not because they want to. There are very few who are even remotely interested in getting on. With the exception of Charlotte, of course, who has been here forever. Sadly she doesn't have the interpersonal skills to get on. Don't get me wrong, she is quite intelligent for a secretary…I'm sorry, forgive me, I didn't mean that as a personal slight."

"Don't worry, no offense taken. I certainly don't want to be a secretary forever. It's just a means to an end. If I'm entirely honest I'm not sure what that end is as yet. I really don't know."

"Well, maybe you've found your niche. Now which of our unsuspecting heroines shall I get to type this lot up?"

"I'll do it, Véronique," said Josie, "I was here after all so it will be easier for me. I'll get it to you by the end of the day, how's that?"

"If you're sure, but don't neglect any of Thomas's work. I can easily get someone to transcribe our notes from the session."

"I'll be fine, really," said Josie and worked through her lunch break to get the typing done. When it was all complete, she felt a surge of satisfaction as she hit 'send' and sent the email to Véronique. Josie had an instant reply: 'You Star!' which made her feel appreciated by the older woman, who was becoming such an important mentor.

Thomas came back not long after she'd finished the Four Seasons work. He asked her for the press releases and the English translations.

"What press releases?" she replied.

"The press releases that I emailed you this morning, Josie."

She looked through her in-box but there was no email from Thomas. She checked her junk mail, nothing. She could sense his impatience.

"I'm sorry Thomas, but I haven't received an email from you this morning!"

"Well I definitely sent it," he said, checking his Blackberry, "Look!"

She could see that the email had been sent but had no explanation as to why she hadn't received it.

"This is really urgent. I'll send it again and you need to do the translations straight away."

He hurried off leaving Josie feeling awful. She looked again at her inbox, waiting for his email to appear.

"What's up, Josie," asked Charlotte, returning to her desk.

"Thomas sent me an email earlier but I didn't get it. So now he's pissed off with me. But it's not my fault."

Charlotte just shrugged her shoulders. Josie had the distinct impression that her mishap with Thomas had pleased her.

"Ah well," she thought to herself. "That'll teach me!"

As she waited for Thomas's email to come through, she checked her other email folders just in case. She clicked onto her 'deleted' box and there it was, unopened but deleted. Had she done that herself accidentally or had someone deleted it for her, and if so, who?

"Has Sally been around this morning?" she asked Charlotte.

"She's been in and out, why?"

"No reason." She didn't want to make any false accusations.

Her phone rang and Thomas asked her to come to his office. He didn't sound too happy.

She entered his office in trepidation. Both Sally and Véronique were there too.

"Josie, I understand that you offered to do some typing for Véronique earlier instead of doing my work?"

Josie was bewildered, it all seemed a bit of a kangaroo court.

"I'm sorry Thomas. I stayed in over my lunch hour to do Véronique's typing. And I really didn't receive your email earlier. I don't know what to say."

"Josie, it's also been brought to my attention that you've been talking about Sally to the other girls behind her back. In this agency, we don't tolerate 'tittle tattle'. I'm really disappointed in you."

Now she was even more taken aback.

"What do you have to say for yourself?"

Josie looked at Véronique, who just shrugged her shoulders.

"I really don't know what you mean," she responded. She wasn't going to let Sally get away with this.

"Are you sure, Josie?"

"Of course I'm sure," she replied angrily. Josie had listened to the other girls' opinions of Sally, which she'd shared. But the only person she'd spoken with directly was Véronique, who apparently hated the Canadian. Josie was more confused than ever.

"I really don't know what you mean, Thomas. I don't know where this rumour came from but I can assure you it is totally unfounded."

Josie sounded more confident than she felt. She knew that Thomas had no proof, and that Sally was stirring things up for her. Finally, Véronique spoke up, "Josie came up with some great ideas at today's brainstorming and then offered to work over her lunch hour to get the details typed up. If I had known there was outstanding work for you, Thomas, I wouldn't have let Josie do the work. But she assured me that she was up to date."

Josie was mortified. They were all turning on her.

"I was up to date. I genuinely didn't receive the email, Thomas. I would never have neglected your work. I hope you know that?"

"Maybe you deleted it," interjected Sally before Thomas could respond.

"Why would I do that?"

"So you can steal all the limelight again!"

Josie couldn't believe what she was hearing. Sally must have deleted the email. Surely Thomas and Véronique could see what she was doing.

"Right, that's enough," said Thomas looking at Véronique as if for an explanation.

"Josie, Sally, we run a harmonious agency here and I want it to stay that way. So any personal differences that you two may have need to be put aside. I don't expect to hear any more of this. We'll leave it at that for now but any more of this competitive nonsense and there will be serious repercussions. Right, off you both go!"

Josie left the room ahead of Sally. She made her way quickly downstairs. She couldn't bring herself to speak to the Canadian bitch. She headed straight for the ladies, not ready to face anyone. She splashed her face and looked at herself in the mirror. Everything had been going so well and now she felt a complete idiot. She realised that she couldn't trust anyone. Not Charlotte or Véronique and definitely not Sally. Her only ally seemed to be Marguerite. She had gossiped a bit about Sally, but she was sure that the Canadian was responsible for deleting the email for her Chemfast presentation and the email that Thomas sent that morning. But she couldn't prove it, and if she accused her then it would only make the situation worse. What upset her most was that Thomas now thought badly of her. Josie was also confused about why Véronique hadn't stood up for her.

"I am going to have to watch my back very carefully," she said to herself. She felt that her bubble had truly burst, and she'd learned a hard lesson.

Back at her desk, there was the email forwarded from Thomas with the documents to be translated and another one from Véronique. She opened it straight away, it read: "Hi Josie, so sorry about that. Thomas caught me on the hop. Are you free to meet for a drink after work tonight? Véronique."

"What is going on?" Josie thought.

Josie didn't reply straight away. She needed to gather her thoughts. She opened Thomas's email and worked through the documents carefully, making sure that the translations were spot on. Only when she'd finally finished and sent them back did she reply to Véronique.

Josie wrote, "Hi Véronique. Sorry, can't make it tonight, another time maybe. Josie."

She didn't want to give her the satisfaction of acknowledging that she felt badly let down.

"Claire was looking for you earlier," said Charlotte.

"I'll go and see what she wants," Josie replied.

Claire was on the phone when Josie arrived at reception, but she indicated that she wouldn't be long.

"Here's an office key for you," she said when she got off the phone. "Try it out to make sure it works before you go."

Josie thanked her and tested the key in the lock. It worked perfectly. She hadn't noticed Sally, walking behind her on her way out.

"Don't think you're getting away with it that easily," she said her nasal twang even more pronounced than usual, "I'd watch my step if I were you. In case you hadn't noticed, Véronique is a queen bitch and Thomas wouldn't dare take your side against me. He knows how much Jacques values my father's friendship."

Josie was not going to let herself be intimidated.

"Thanks for the kind and encouraging words of support," Josie replied, "I'll bear your advice in mind." Josie brushed past Sally, thanked Claire for the key and headed back to her desk.

As Josie packed up for the evening, she sent a text to Christian to let him know she was on her way. He replied straight away saying how much he was looking forward to seeing her. The train left the Gar du Nord, and Josie remembered she had promised to call Chrissie.

"Hi Josie, how did it go with the Four Seasons thing?" her friend asked.

"Fab, Chrissie, they loved my ideas - well, our ideas - and I'm definitely on the team," said Josie, "But that bitch Sally really has it in for me." She briefly explained what had happened.

"You can't let her get away with it," said Chrissie.

"I know, but I don't know what to do about it. At least not yet. Hey, enough about work, did you hear from Claude?"

"Yes I did, actually. A very short text saying he had been mega busy but that he'd call on the weekend to arrange to meet up. What do you think?"

"I really don't know," replied Josie thoughtfully, "It sounds genuine enough. But it seems strange that he hasn't been in touch before now. I'm heading on over to Christian's. I'll test the waters and find out what's going on."

"OK, and thanks Josie. Have a great evening."

"I'm sure I will," she replied, hanging up and wondering what Claude was playing at. He had been so interested in Chrissie at the start and they hadn't argued or fallen out over anything. What on earth had caused the sudden rift in the relationship?

Christian met her at the station in his car even though it was only a short walk to his apartment. Josie was glad, it was raining heavily and she was very tired after the traumas at work. Christian gave her a big hug and took her bag, holding her hand as they walked to the car park.

"Good day?" he asked.

"Not too bad," she lied and told him all about the Four Seasons account and her ideas, but didn't want to put a dampener on the evening by telling him about the Sally situation.

When they arrived at the flat, Christian immediately put her bags on the floor and silenced her with a passionate kiss. Josie responded by putting her arms around his neck and kissing him back with equal passion. She could feel her body responding to his. She pulled back to allow him to unbutton her coat. Christian's hands found their way eagerly under her jumper.

"Stop it," she told him, laughing. "I need a bath and a drink, preferably together, before I can contemplate anything more passionate than a peck on the cheek. It's been a long day."

"OK," he said, putting his hands up, "the bathroom is off the bedroom, which is through there." He pointed her in the right direction and caressed her bottom. "I'll bring you a cold glass of dry white wine."

Josie smiled and made her way into the bedroom, taking in her surroundings as she did so. The apartment was very smart with a lot of dark wooden beams and tiled floors. The bedroom was decorated in caramels and creams, with a dark brown suede cover on a huge king size bed. She took off her clothes and folded them neatly onto the back of a leather chair in the corner of the room. Josie slipped into the skimpy, silk dressing gown she always used when travelling. The bathroom was completely white with just a few dark blue diamond shapes in the floor and wall tiles. There was a very large bath in the middle of the room – one of the old fashioned types with claw feet and a brass shower mixer. The bathroom also boasted an enormous shower, the cubicle fashioned out of very thick glass tiles. It was all very masculine and Josie felt quite dwarfed by her surroundings. She ran the bath, added some bath gel to create bubbles and sank into the enveloping warmth of the water. Josie could almost feel her eyes closing, but was interrupted by Christian with a chilled glass of wine.

"Thanks," she said, taking a sip of the wine before placing the glass on the floor next to the bath. "This is a fabulous bathroom, Christian, did you have it done yourself?"

"No, it was like this when I bought the apartment. But it was one of the major selling points, that and the location of course, being so close to the station. I'll show you around later. I love living here in the banlieue. Paris is great but it's good to get away from the hubbub, especially after a hard day in work. The banlieue has the best of both worlds. There is a beautiful park just around the corner with a lake and some excellent tennis courts. I love it in the summer."

"I didn't know you played tennis," she said, surprised, "we'll have to have a game one day. I absolutely love it. I haven't had a chance to play much since I moved to Paris."

"Sure, that would be great. Now I'm going to have to love you and leave you, there's some major cooking to be done." Christian leaned over and kissed her gently on the mouth before putting his hand into the bathwater and dabbing her nose with a bubble. When he left the bathroom Josie topped up the bath with hot water and sank further into its depths, thinking what a lovely guy Christian was. If only she could let herself fall in love with him.

A good half an hour later she emerged from the bedroom, feeling relaxed and refreshed. She had put on a pair of jeans and a casual shirt. Christian had suggested they spend the evening in. Josie followed the aroma of cooking into the kitchen, which was small but very well equipped with all the latest modern appliances. She peered into the saucepan which Christian was stirring vigorously - it looked like a casserole of some sort, but with lots of haricot beans - it smelled delicious. Josie attempted to stick her finger into the succulent mixture but he knocked her hand away.

"It's not quite ready yet," he said, raising an eyebrow.

"What is it?" she asked, her stomach rumbling in anticipation.

"It's Cassoulet, a very old family recipe. My grandmother is from Toulouse. She always makes this dish on special occasions. I prepared and made it last night, it always tastes better the next day. I'm adding the final ingredient, dry white wine, which makes it smooth and not too thick."

"What's in it?" asked Josie

"Loads of different cuts of meat, like belly pork, duck legs and, of course, Toulouse sausages. I also add lots of different vegetables, herbs and spices and white haricot beans."

"It smells wonderful! But you've made enough for an army, are you expecting anyone else?"

"Not likely," he replied offering her a taste with a wooden spoon, "I want you all to myself tonight. But it takes so many ingredients and such a long time to cook. I always make loads and then freeze it in smaller portions."

"Very practical of you," said Josie approvingly, "and it tastes absolutely delicious."

Topping up her glass of wine, Christian said, "Why not go and sit down next door, put some music on. There are some nibbles in there too. I haven't bothered with a starter. The Cassoulet is always so filling."

The sitting room, like the rest of the apartment, was very simply decorated in brown and creams, with two large brown leather sofas surrounding a low ash coffee table. The dining area boasted French windows leading onto a balcony overlooking the park. It was probably a wonderful sight when the flowers bloomed. Josie decided to look through Christian's selection of CDs. There was a real mix of modern and classical. She put on Dionne Warwick's greatest hits selection and settled back into one of the comfortable brown sofas. Josie felt so relaxed she had practically drifted off to sleep when Christian entered the sitting room. "You're really tired, aren't you?" he said, sitting next to her and caressing her arm.

"Yes, I suppose I am. Chrissie and I were up for hours last night working out the ideas for the Four Seasons and then I was up really early to get a head start. I'll get my second wind once I've eaten, though, don't you worry," she said, smiling seductively.

"Well, we can have an early night. In fact, I was counting on it," he replied, giving her a wicked smile.

"Christian, can I ask you something?" she said.

Josie suddenly remembered that she had promised Chrissie

she would find out about Claude and his distant behaviour. Christian frowned slightly and nodded.

"What's going on with Claude? I mean, when we all first met he was really full on with Chrissie and she's not an 'easy egg to crack'. But over the last few weeks…" Josie waited for Christian to step in, but he obviously hadn't taken the hint, "well, just as she's getting really interested, he's backed right off. Claude's not one of these guys who just likes the chase, is he?"

Christian looked distinctly uncomfortable and shifted awkwardly.

"Look, if you don't want to tell me, fine," said Josie forcefully, "but Chrissie is a good friend and I hate to see her hurting so much. If he's just not interested any more, then he needs to tell her. Chrissie deserves that at least."

"Claude is my friend too, Josie and it's not really up to me to say anything," Christian said solemnly, "just be assured that he does not want to hurt Chrissie, in fact I've never seen him so love struck. Well, not since…his previous girlfriend, anyway. Claude is just very confused at the moment. But he knows he has to speak to Chrissie. I think he's arranged to meet her."

Josie was intrigued and couldn't let it go. Something Christian said made her recall something Chrissie had alluded to. "I guess his ex is back on the scene, then?" It was a shot in the dark, but her instincts told her this could be the reason.

"How do you know that?" Christian asked her incredulously.

"It's pretty typical male behaviour in my experience. I'm sure Claude is very flattered to have two women interested in him." Josie scolded.

"That's unfair, Josie. Claude isn't like that at all. In fact, he's terribly unhappy. Come on, let's sit down and I'll tell you all about it." Christian snuggled up close to Josie on the sofa. "I may as well as you've guessed some of it anyway. But promise me you won't say anything to Chrissie. It's up to Claude to tell her, whatever decision he makes."

"I promise," she replied, crossing her fingers behind her back. Girlfriends are girlfriends after all.

Christian explained, "Claude is from a very wealthy background. His family own a great deal of land and local businesses throughout Provence. Claude's older brother is being groomed to take over the estate and his parents also wanted Claude to be involved in running their business interests. But Claude is very much his own man. He didn't want to become involved in the family business. Because of this he is considered a bit of a black sheep. His family don't approve of his job but respect his independence. I think they assume that one day he will finally see sense and be welcomed back into the fold. Claude assures me and all his friends that it's never going to happen."

Whilst he was talking, Josie helped Christian prepare the table and they tucked into the gorgeous Cassoulet. The meal was divine and she meant to compliment Christian but was far too enthralled by the story.

"His ex-girlfriend, Dominique, is the daughter of an old family friend," Christian continued. "I met her once a long time ago and I must admit she is stunningly beautiful." Josie pouted and Christian said, "Of course not as beautiful as you." Josie blew him a kiss and smiled, encouraging him to continue. "Dominique is also from an incredibly wealthy background, but like Claude she wanted some independence. I believe she used to work for a fashion chain in Paris. As you can imagine, Claude's parents were delighted with the match and encouraged the couple to become engaged. It was not long after that Dominique began behaving strangely. Poor Claude had a really rough time of it. Eventually he discovered she was having an affair with her boss and was pregnant by him. Dominique's boss was twenty years older and had the most dreadful reputation. Claude was naturally devastated. The boss left his wife and kids and set up home with Dominique. Unfortunately, a few weeks later, Dominique was involved in a serious car accident. It was touch and go for a while and she spent several months in hospital with a severe back injury. The doctors informed Claude that she might never make a full recovery. Naturally, what with the trauma, she lost the baby."

Josie reached across the table and stoked the back of Christian's hand, then entwined her fingers with his. "Poor Claude, such a tragic story. What happened next?"

Christian shrugged, "Well, despite feeling hurt and betrayed Claude spent every waking hour at the hospital. He is a good man, Josie." She nodded. "It was Claude that encouraged her not to give up hope and apply herself to physiotherapy. Of course the boss soon scurried back to his wife. He obviously didn't want a potential cripple on his hands, the dirty rat."

"Did Dominique make a full recovery?" asked Josie.

"Yes, but once discharged from hospital, she disappeared off the face of the earth. Claude and her family did all they could to find her, but had no luck. Three months later she sent Claude a letter apologising for leaving so abruptly and explaining that she needed time to sort her life out. Dominique asked him to forgive her for all the pain and grief she had caused. She told him she was safe and well and to forget about her," Christian poured them both more wine. "Claude found it difficult to give her up. He continued trying to track her down but she had covered her tracks well. The letter she sent him was posted from the South of France but it turns out she was working in the US for a fashion magazine. Claude was distraught. All of his friends rallied around, but we call it his lost year. Poor Claude was often off sick, we all covered for him to stop him losing his job. We couldn't get him to leave his flat, he was anti-social and impossible to talk too. Finally at the end of summer he seemed to snap out of it, and lately he has been his old charming and fun loving self."

"That's more the Claude we know and love. I'm shocked by his tragic past and Chrissie will be too," Christian raised an eyebrow disapprovingly. "That is of course when he decides to tell her."

"This year, when we met you, Libby and Chrissie...well, it was great for Claude, it was great to see him smiling again, the light back in his eyes."

"I hope it was great for you too," said Josie.

"Of course!" Christian raised her hand to his lips and gently kissed it. "We have christened you les Anglaises, and we are all crazy about you."

"But why is Dominique back on the scene?" asked Josie.

Christian shrugged. "A few weeks ago, Claude received another letter from Dominique informing him of where she had been. She was coming home and wanted to see him. Claude didn't know what to think. He confided that he still had strong feelings for Dominique, probably always would. But how do you forgive such a past? Not just the affair, but disappearing and not even trusting him with where she was. We discussed it at length and Claude decided it was best he meet with her, to lay the ghosts to rest." Christian began clearing away the dishes. "When did they meet?" asked Josie.

"Last week," Christian tossed over his shoulder, carrying the dishes into the kitchen.

"Just when he broke off contact with Chrissie," said Josie.

Christian came back with a fresh bottle of wine. "After the meeting, Claude told me that Dominique wanted him back. She admitted to being very foolish, but she had been far too young when they became engaged and felt tied down. She also told him that she missed him terribly and that was her reason for returning home."

"But he could never trust her again, surely?" said Josie

Christian's classic Gallic shrug partly answered Josie's question. "Exactly. Whilst she was away, and Claude was beside himself with worry, searching everywhere, he visited the boss. Claude thought he might have some idea about where Dominique might be. There was a blazing row and he found out a few home truths about Dominique. Apparently, she told everyone that being with Claude was like having a little puppy dog hanging around her neck. She needed a real man to fulfil her needs. Claude didn't believe it at first. But the boss threw some love letters and photographs in his face."

"What kind of photographs?" asked Josie?

"Pretty sordid stuff, Dominique in bed with her boss and other women, other men, you know the type of thing. Naturally Claude was really upset. That was the incident that finally helped him to move on and get over her."

"And now she's back," scowled Josie. She was incredibly moved by Claude's tragic past. It was like the plot from a romantic novel and not something you would think could happen to people you knew.

"Promise me you won't say anything to Chrissie, at least not yet," said Christian, "Claude is seeing Dominique again this evening. He told me he knows exactly what he's going to do and has promised to see Chrissie soon after."

"I won't say anything yet, but if he doesn't see Chrissie this weekend and explain," Josie looked imploringly into Christians bottomless eyes, "then I will say something. Chrissie is my best friend, after all."

"I know. Claude is my best friend too and he'd kill me if he thought I'd told you everything. But to be honest it's such a relief to tell someone else, Josie. I feel really sorry for Claude and I hope he does the right thing."

"What's the right thing?" Josie asked him.

"The right thing is what's best for all of them, I guess. Though I sincerely hope he doesn't decide to give Dominique a second chance. After everything she put him through he could never trust her again. I believe she is the sort who would get bored with him again after a while. It's almost as though she needs a 'Claude fix' for a few weeks and then moves on until she needs her fix again."

Josie thought Christian's words were very perceptive and showed once again what a caring, sensitive man he was. She reached for his hand across the table.

"Claude is very lucky to have you as a friend, and I am very lucky to have you in my life too," she said, meaning every word.

"You won't be saying that when I've made you do the dishes," he replied, getting up from the table and clearing the last of the plates."

"Oh yes I will, and I'm more than happy to do the dishes. That meal was wonderful!"

They cleared the table in companionable silence and, when Josie started to wash the dishes, Christian pulled her away and said they could wait until tomorrow. He made a pot of coffee and carried it through to the sitting room along with a huge bowl of strawberries. They shared the fruit and drank the coffee whilst watching the news on the television. Again Josie could feel herself falling asleep.

"Come on, sleepy head," said Christian, "let's get you to bed."

She followed him into the bedroom and slowly began to undress while he used the bathroom. Suddenly she felt self-conscious. She didn't know whether to take all her clothes off and get into bed naked or to put on the flimsy, silk negligee she had brought with her. She opted for the negligee as she also needed to use the bathroom. Christian came out of the bathroom wearing just a towel around his waist. "I had a quick shower," he explained, rubbing his head with a spare towel, "the bathroom's all yours."

Josie smiled at him, retrieved her toiletries bag and shut the bathroom door behind her. She still felt a bit awkward but Christian was so relaxed it did help her feel a bit more at ease. Josie washed her makeup off, cleaned her teeth, used the loo and re-emerged into the bedroom. Christian was already in bed, propped up on one arm watching her. She slipped into the other side of the bed still wearing her nightdress and Christian laughed, "You are very coy tonight, Josie. I don't remember you being so shy when I stayed over at your place."

"Well, a girl has standards, you know," she said, snuggling up close to him, "and my mother would be horrified if she thought I went for a sleepover without any decent nightwear."

Her mother would be horrified if she knew half of what she got up to, thought Josie.

Christian began to run his mouth down her neck and onto her shoulders, slipping off the fine straps and revealing her breasts. Even though she was incredibly tired, Josie responded to his kisses. Christian needed no further encouragement and within minutes had slipped off her nightdress and very slowly and sensually kissed and caressed her until she could stand it no longer. Sensing her increasing urgency, he rose, supporting himself with his arms, and began to make love to her, gently at first and then increasing his pace as he sensed their oncoming orgasms. As Josie began to climax she held onto his shoulders and stared deeply into his eyes. He stared back with equal intensity and also began to climax. Josie felt a closeness they hadn't experienced before. These feelings, together with the intensity of her orgasm, caused tears to form in her eyes.

"Are you okay, darling?" he asked her, holding her even closer and stroking her hair.

"Mmm," was all she could manage. Christian continued holding her in his arms until her breathing slowed and he could tell she was drifting off to sleep. "I love you, Josie," he whispered, kissing the top of her head. Although she was half asleep, Josie heard Christian's words and finally drifted off with a smile on her face.

Josie awoke early the next morning feeling completely relaxed and refreshed for the first time in days. Christian was still fast asleep, so she edged carefully out of bed and headed for the kitchen to make coffee. He was still asleep when she returned and for a few moments she enjoyed watching him sleep, snoring gently. You're staring at me again," he said, eyes still closed.

"I know," she retorted, "it never fails to surprise me how men can snore so loudly without waking themselves up." He grabbed her around the waist and pulled her down next to him on the bed.

"Snoring, was I? Well, young lady, you should have heard yourself in the night, and you were dribbling too!"

"I was not!" she yelled, trying to struggle out of his arms.

"Oh yes you were. And you talk in your sleep."

"No way," said a shocked Josie, "What did I say?"

"Oh something about what a hunk Christian was and how you must be so good to him at all times."

"Liar," she laughed, managing to free her hands and lob a pillow at his head. Christian caught her arms again and pushed her down onto the bed, kissing her hard on the mouth. She couldn't help but kiss him back.

He pinned her arms above her head with one hand and ran the other one up her leg and along the inside of her thigh. She could feel a rush of dampness in her groin and shifted her body so that her mound met his hand. He rubbed her clitoris with the base of his hand, touching every part of her. Sucking on her nipples, he kept her hands above her head while his fingers moved in and out of her hot, wet hole. Josie could feel her orgasm mounting uncontrollably and came over Christian's hand with a gush. With his fingers still deep inside her, he moved his body up the bed and kissed her hard on the mouth. Lying on his back, he pulled her on top of him, her back against him. He rubbed his cock against her wet pussy lips and guided his shaft deep inside her. Taking her hand, he moved it to her clitoris, encouraging her to touch herself. She moved her fingers over her swollen nub, rubbing the base of his penis with slow, rhythmic movements. Christian pulled out to the edge of her lips and then thrust himself deeply inside her, matching her rhythm. Her muscles clenched around his cock as she came in a slow, satisfying orgasm, prolonged by her own fingers, continuing to rub her clitoris in just the right spot. Christian groaned and she could feel the movement of his come, moving from his balls and along the length of his cock. He gripped her hips and pulled her hard onto him, filling her completely.

As they relaxed in each other's arms in the aftermath of their lovemaking, Josie felt unexpectedly content. Their time together had flown by, and she felt very relaxed and comfortable with him. As much as she didn't want to spoil the moment, she started to become conscious of the time as she needed to get to work. Sensing her change in mood, Christian jumped out of bed and set off to make coffee and croissants. Josie showered and dressed.

They were running late, so Christian insisted she took her breakfast in the car. He dropped her off directly outside the offices, reached over and gently kissed her on the mouth.

"I meant what I said last night, Josie," he told her, stroking the side of her face with his finger.

"Which bit," she replied, trying to make light of the situation, frightened by what he might say.

"You know exactly which bit. Now off you go like a good little PR girl. I've all that mess you left to clear up at home."

She swatted him gently with her hand and blew him a kiss as he drove away, watching her from the side mirror. As she turned into the office courtyard, she was embarrassed to see Thomas. He had arrived at the same time and had been watching her intently. Thomas held open the door for her and gave her a knowing wink, as if to say, "I know what you've been doing, young lady." Feeling herself blushing from head to foot, she made her way as quickly as possible to her office, feeling like a teenager caught kissing for the first time!

CHAPTER 6

Once she switched on her PC and checked her voicemail, Josie carried on with the work Thomas had left for her. Later she broke for lunch and joined the other secretaries in the usual local bistro. She felt that at last they had begun to accept her, with the exception of Sally, of course.

"What's Mervyn Bradley like?" she asked, during lunch.

Odette, as usual, was the first to offer an opinion. "Well he's American, in his fifties and looks a bit like one of the Marx brothers. He rents office space from us and his rent includes secretarial support. Most of his clients are American companies, but with offices in Europe, so he needs an English speaker really. Sally was supposed to help him with the admin tasks, but it was beneath her. He seems OK, he's nothing special."

"I've helped him out a bit," added Charlotte, "and he's always very kind and supportive. Most of his clients are from High Tech industries, so I didn't really understand their business, but the secretarial work was pretty straightforward."

Still on a bit of buzz from her involvement with the Four Seasons account, Josie thought the work for Melvyn sounded boring, by comparison. But she was astute enough to realise that she needed to keep her feet firmly on the ground, to avoid making mistakes or upsetting anyone. After all, she was still very new to the job.

That afternoon Véronique came to see her, and informed Josie that they would be presenting the proposals to Hélène, Jean-

François and the rest of the team on Tuesday afternoon, at their offices on the Boulevard Haussman.

"Who's on our team?" Josie asked Véronique.

"Me, you, and of course Bernard, he is a very experienced senior account manager. Jacques will also support us, but more as a figurehead. But we will need someone else to help with the admin, etc…"

"Won't I be doing that?" asked Josie

"No you won't. You'll be part of the account team, and you'll be working your butt off making this happen. Who do you think we can ask to help with the admin? I know most of the girls are pretty busy most of the time. You work with them, what do you think?"

"Well you could ask Marguerite. I've got to know her quite well and she's wasted in the accounts department. I'm sure she'd jump at the chance, provided Madame Raymonde was in agreement.

"Good idea, Josie. She seems a sweetie, though I don't really know her that well."

Josie nodded.

"Hmm, leave Raymonde to me. I'm sure I can persuade her to free up some of Marguerite's time. Don't say anything to her yet though, let me sort it out first."

As Josie was packing up to leave that evening, Véronique asked her to come up to her office.

"I've spoken to Raymonde and she's fine. She was very complimentary about Marguerite actually. But, before I spoke to Raymonde, I very casually asked if any of the other secretaries wanted to help out on one of my accounts. They didn't even ask which one, they just all claimed to be extremely busy. So if you like, you can ask Marguerite yourself."

"That's great news," Josie said smiling at the older woman, "and thanks, Véronique, for all your support. I really do appreciate it."

"You won't be thanking me when I'm bombarding you with work and keeping you here all the hours God sends. Now go and have a good weekend and we'll all meet on Monday and run through the final proposal."

Josie just managed to catch Marguerite as she was leaving the office.

"Hi Marguerite," she said, "let's walk to the Métro and you can tell me all about your date with Yves."

"Yves couldn't make last night, he had to cover Claude's shift. We plan on going out tonight instead. I'm really looking forward to it. How was your evening with Christian?"

"Lovely thanks," Josie replied, not going into any detail; she didn't want Marguerite to think she was too forward. "You know Véronique is putting together a special team, to handle the launch of the new Four Seasons hotels? Well they, we rather … need some dedicated admin support. I suggested you. Véronique has cleared it with Raymonde and if you want you can be part of the team."

Marguerite seemed taken aback at first, but then gave Josie a big smile. "That sounds fantastic. I must admit I do get a bit bored, working in the accounts department, even though everyone is lovely to me. I was actually thinking of looking for something else, as I really don't want to admit defeat and go back into the family business just yet. But if I can work on a real account, with you, that would be great."

"I'm so glad," replied Josie, giving her friend a hug. "We'll have such fun. And don't worry about the other secretaries. Véronique asked them first and no-one volunteered."

"I wouldn't want to upset them, especially Odette."

The girls both laughed. As they reached the Métro, Josie told Marguerite to call her over the weekend and tell her all about her date.

"Thanks again, Josie," said Marguerite, kissing her friend three times on the cheek.

"You've brought a breath of fresh air into my life. Even Luc, who isn't the most sensitive soul, says so."

Josie could feel herself blushing at the mention of Luc's name and didn't dare say anything in case Marguerite picked up on just how attractive she found her brother.

"It's nothing to do with me, just fate!"

As Josie travelled the few stops home, her thoughts turned to what she was going to say to Chrissie about Claude. Initially, she had planned on not saying anything, but her friend had called her during the day, and asked what Christian had said. Josie felt so sad for her that she thought she should at least say something.

As she emerged from the train and headed up the stairs to the exit, she had the odd feeling that someone was watching her. She turned to look but couldn't see anyone she recognised or anything untoward. Still, she felt a chill run through her. As she emerged onto the street, the sun was just setting behind the towering apartment blocks. Shielding her eyes, Josie looked around her and was completely startled to see Sally Marsden-Lloyd, at the entrance to the Métro, across the main boulevard, talking animatedly on her mobile phone.

Her first instinct was to cross the road and confront Sally. But as she attempted to cross the road, busy with commuter traffic, Sally disappeared down the stairs and into the Métro station. Josie decided not to follow her but to continue on home. She didn't like it one little bit. She made a mental note to find out why the Canadian girl was in the vicinity of the apartment and seemed to be following her. It could have been entirely innocent, but Josie didn't quite think so.

At home, Chrissie wasn't back from work, so Josie took the opportunity of having a long soak in the bath with a cold glass of wine, music blaring. When she eventually emerged, her flatmate was in the sitting room, with a glass of wine.

"Hi Josie, how was your evening with Christian?" asked Chrissie.

"Really lovely thanks," she replied, bracing herself to answer any questions about Claude.

"Did you manage to ask him about what's up with Claude?"

Josie had prepared her story.

"Apparently, there's some issue with an old friend of the family and he has had to spend his spare time with his parents, sorting something out. Christian seems to think it will all be sorted out by the weekend and told me that Claude was planning to see you over the next couple of days."

"He's asked to meet me Sunday lunchtime, though why not tonight or tomorrow night, I don't know."

"I think he's covering the night shift tomorrow and Saturday with Christian," Josie replied, hoping her friend wouldn't question her any further.

"I still don't understand, why couldn't he tell me what was going on? I mean, I would have understood if he needed to help his family out. I'm not a tyrant and I don't have a possessive bone in my body. I just don't get why he doesn't trust me enough to tell me."

"Men are strange creatures, Chrissie," Josie added, hoping Claude had really sorted himself out. "Who knows what's going on in their heads half the time?"

"Maybe, but I just don't get how cold he suddenly went. I guess I'll find out on Sunday, but it's killing me, not knowing!"

"I bet," replied Josie, turning away to pour another glass of wine, so her friend couldn't see the look of concern in her eyes.

"Well I guess it's you, me, a bottle of wine and some pizza," Chrissie said, trying to put on a brave face.

"How do you fancy going to the Kickmeon tomorrow evening? We haven't been there in ages and it's always such a good laugh," suggested Josie, trying to think of a way to distract her friend from thoughts of Claude.

"Great," she replied, "sounds wonderful."

The Kickmeon was a nightclub which the girls visited often. Entry was free before 10 pm and afterwards it was only a few euros to get in, which included a free drink at the bar. Drinks after that were expensive, but the music was very good and the club had a large dance floor, which was unusual for most Parisian night spots. Usually, by the time the girls made it to the Kickmeon, they had had a load to drink anyway and just tended to dance the night away.

They phoned the local Pizzeria, just a few metres down the street, and Chrissie popped out to pick up the order. Whilst she was out Josie called Christian, before he started his night shift, and told him what she had told Chrissie about Claude.

"That sounds fine," he replied. "I haven't seen Claude yet, but I'll let you know tomorrow if he tells me anything. Do you want to meet for lunch tomorrow? I should have recovered from the night shift by lunchtime!"

"I'd love to! Where shall we meet?"

"Top of the Métro, at the Champs Elyées," said Christian.

"Look forward to it - and don't crash any planes!" Josie said, "See you tomorrow."

After pizza and another bottle of wine, the girls began watching TV, but as usual, the phone didn't stop ringing. First it was Daniel, asking what they were up to on Saturday evening. Chrissie managed to fob him off, saying they already had plans. They didn't want him cramping their style. But she did invite him over for supper on Sunday evening.

"What if you're still out with Claude?" Josie asked her.

"Well you'll have to carry on without me."

"Great!" Josie replied, "That's all I need. An evening with Daniel quizzing me about you and what you're up to!"

The next day, Josie went to meet Christian. He was already waiting at the exit to the Métro when she arrived. His face lit up when he saw her approaching, and Josie was also really glad to see him.

"Where are we going?" she asked as they set off down the avenue, arm in arm.

"Wait and see."

He led her a bit further along the Champs Elysées, and down one of the many side streets. After a couple of turns, Josie was completely lost. He then stopped in front of the entrance to a small bistro, simply called 'Chez', and opened the door for her to go in first. The place was tiny, just like someone's front room, with only a handful of tables and chairs.

Christian was greeted warmly by a large lady wearing a white apron and they were given the only free table. The atmosphere was very intimate.

"How did you find this place?" Josie asked him once they were seated and a small blackboard with the day's specials was balanced on a chair in front of them.

"A friend of the family owns it. That's his wife, Jacqueline, who greeted us. Jean-Claude used to live near us in Provence but met a Parisian woman and moved to the big city. He cooks and she waits on the tables. It's virtually impossible to get a table here but I was lucky that there was a last minute cancellation. The food is exquisite, as are the wines. Unfortunately I can't drink today, because of work, but you certainly can."

The choices on the specials board were extremely appetising. Josie chose a goat's cheese salad as a starter followed by rack of lamb and a small carafe of the house red. The food was excellent and, at the end of the meal, Jean Claude came out of the kitchen to talk with them. Christian introduced him to Josie and he was charming, with a twinkle in his eye.

"I hope you're keeping this young pup on his toes," he said to her. "I remember him as a little boy, playing with his aeroplanes in his parents' garden. He always loved planes, so there was no surprise about his chosen career. He's a good chef too but then he did learn at the hands of the master."

"Don't let my grandmother hear you say that, Jean-Claude. You know she likes to take all the credit for my exceptional culinary skills," Christian replied.

"Have you met Christian's family yet?" Jean-Claude asked, turning to Josie.

"No, not yet."

"I want to keep her to myself for a while," Christian said to the older man, "otherwise my family will have us married off with at least ten children planned."

"True, knowing your family, that's probably the best move. Well Josie, it was lovely to meet you, and Christian, please give my best regards to your family. Let me know if they come to visit and I'll make sure I can fit you all in."

"Thanks Jean Claude."

As the couple left the restaurant, Josie asked Christian to tell her more about his family. She had picked up a few snippets over the past few weeks but the details were fragmented and she was intrigued by Jean-Claude's comments.

"My family is a bit larger than life, I guess," he told her, as they strolled, hand-in-hand, towards the Métro. "My father's family owns a number of olive groves in Vence, not far from Nice, that's how I know Claude because his family owns land next to ours. My father is an only child and his parents were really proud of him, especially when he chose to become an architect. He was one of the most highly respected architects in France at one time, but a very quiet, private man too. He met my mother when he was working on a local project. They had a whirlwind romance and were married within a few months of meeting each other. Maman basically runs the estate's business and accounts. Father has no time to oversee the day to day things, so my second cousin handles the estate management. My grandfather died a few years ago but my grandmother is still alive and basically rules the roost. Fortunately, my mother and grandmother get on like a house on fire. Otherwise I don't know how we'd all manage."

They both stopped to kiss, a long lingering passionate kiss, Josie felt a warm satisfying glow and they held hands as they continued walking.

"My mother's family all live close by and own a number of confectionary factories. Family get-togethers can be quite overwhelming. Even I find them exhausting and I'm used to them."

Once again, Josie felt that her simple, middle class British family seemed very tame by comparison.

"They sound lovely," she told him.

"What about you? I know you have a sister, what about your parents?"

"Not nearly as exciting as yours," she replied. "My Dad is an accountant and my mother is a housewife. We've always lived in Bristol. I was glad to move away when I went to University. My sister Ella is nearly twenty-one and still at University, she's studying psychology. My grandparents have all died and I only really knew my father's parents as my mum's family died quite young. And that's it really."

"Didn't you say your sister was coming to visit?"

"Yes, she's supposed to come over at Easter but it depends on funds and whether my father will contribute to the trip. Ella's a typical student, she naturally spent all of her grant during her first term," Josie rolled her eyes, "so she's dependent on my father, a student loan and what she can earn behind the Student Union bar to survive. She seems to manage well enough. I guess we all do when we have to."

By this time they had reached the Métro and needed to take different train lines to reach their respective homes. Christian pulled Josie into his arms and gave her a lingering kiss on the mouth.

"I really enjoyed your company today, Josie, as I always do. I'll call you tomorrow afternoon when I wake up. I hope all goes well with Chrissie and Claude. He was very quiet at work last night and I didn't like to ask him what was happening."

"I enjoyed today too. I'll let you know what Chrissie says as soon as I know myself. Either way, it's best for both of them that this is resolved. I just hope they'll both be happy."

As they were getting ready later that evening, Chrissie started to knock back the wine faster than usual.

"Steady on Chrissie," Josie said to her. "You don't want to get slaughtered before we go out."

"Well I'm going to enjoy myself tonight, as a single girl, because that's what I feel like, and I'm just having a few drinks to get me in the mood."

"OK, I just don't want to have to bring you home early because you can't stand up!"

The girls had a few more drinks in a bar on the boulevard St Michel before heading for the Kickmeon. Chrissie had slowed down her drinking, but was quite merry when they arrived at the nightclub. The place was really quiet and so the girls ordered drinks and sat at the bar, singing along to the music. Within half an hour the nightclub began to fill up and a group of four guys came in, positioning themselves at the far end of the bar. One of them was Luc, Marguerite's brother. He spotted Josie before she saw him and came over to speak to her. Despite the amount of alcohol she had consumed, she still felt shy and self-conscious when he spoke to her. Practically stammering, she introduced him to Chrissie and he invited the girls to join him and his friends.

They managed to secure one of the alcoves in the nightclub and this time it was Luc who made the introductions. His friends were old school mates and they had met up for a reunion; one of them, Pierre, worked in the US, but was home for a visit. The men were pretty drunk themselves and so the group was lively and talkative. As the place filled up, they danced together for over an hour, fooling about on the dance floor. When they returned to their seats, Josie realised that Luc had disappeared and asked one of his friends where he had gone. He just shrugged his shoulders but had a cautious look in his eye. A few minutes later, Josie spotted him coming back and he nodded at his friend. The young man joined him and they headed for the men's loo. Josie found the whole thing quite strange.

After a little while, Luc and his friend re-joined them. Josie knew instantly, from the sparkle in their eyes, that they had taken something. She was very anti-drugs. The brother of her oldest school friend was a heroin addict and his habit had put the family through hell. She caught Chrissie's eye and nodded towards the ladies' loo.

"Excuse us," she said to the young men.

In the loo, Josie told Chrissie what she suspected. Her friend just shrugged.

"As long as they don't try and get us to take anything, then it's up to them what they do."

"I know," Josie replied, "it just makes me feel uncomfortable, that's all. To be honest, I can't see what I saw in Luc any more. I mean he's quite good looking but he's very arrogant and really loves himself. The others seem okay though. Come on, let's go back. I hope whatever Luc and his friend have taken doesn't turn them into idiots."

As they returned to the table, two very attractive French girls joined Luc and the group. Luc put his arms around both girls. Josie thought he looked completely stoned.

"Come and meet my latest admirers," he said to Josie and Chrissie. "This is Francine and Odile. Say hello girls, to my English admirers."

Josie and Chrissie introduced themselves to the French girls and turned together towards the bar.

"He really rates himself, doesn't he," Chrissie said to her friend, ordering fresh drinks. "I don't know why you find him attractive."

"I don't anymore," Josie replied. "He was charming, in a flirty sort of way, when his family were around, but tonight I find him quite obnoxious. What shall we do? I don't fancy spending any more time with Luc and his mates. What do you think?"

"Nor me. Well, let's finish these drinks and have a dance, we don't have to stay with Luc and his crowd."

The two girls sat at the bar watching the crowd on the dance floor. Luc's friends came to ask them to dance again so they spent the next half hour bopping away with them. One of them tried half-heartedly to pull Josie to him and kiss her but she managed to avoid his advances and laughed at his over-exaggerated pretence of disappointment. The music switched to a slow number so the girls hastily made their way back to the bar, leaving the young men to their own devices.

They eventually decided to call it a night and ordered a taxi. It took only a few minutes to arrive. They said goodbye to Luc's friends who by this time were at the bar with another group of French girls but didn't bother Luc himself who was absorbed with his latest conquests.

On their way home in the taxi the girls discussed their evening. "Weird night," said Josie. "I've completely sobered up despite the number of drinks we had in the club. It must have been Luc and his absolute arrogance. He frightens me a bit. I don't know how I could have found him attractive."

"Oh he's very good looking and extremely assured and confident," replied Chrissie. "But I know what you mean. He's the sort of guy who seems used to getting his own way and would stop at nothing to get it."

"Maybe, the drugs thing really put me off, and the girls. I know we weren't strictly with them but I felt sort of discarded. Do you know what I mean?"

"A bit, yes, it's just how I feel about the Claude situation," said Chrissie, the sadness evident in her voice.

"Oh Chrissie," Josie took her friend's hand. "I'm sure it will all work out for you and Claude. Anyway, in only a few hours you'll find out what's been going on. Don't fret. He's a decent guy and must have had his reasons for not seeing you."

Chrissie just shrugged and for the rest of the journey gazed out of the window, lost in her own thoughts.

Josie sincerely hoped Claude had decided not to get back with his ex. Chrissie would be devastated and, based on what Christian said, she sounded like a grade one bitch.

They arrived at the apartment and Chrissie paid for the taxi, Josie rummaged in her handbag for her keys. She was distracted by a movement in the shadows from the building across the road. She looked intently but couldn't see anything. "Must be my imagination," she thought as she retrieved her keys and headed into the foyer of the flat. Nevertheless she still felt a bit uneasy. This wasn't the first time she'd felt uneasy. Most evenings, Josie opened the doors to her balcony for some fresh air during the night, especially in the summer. She liked to sit on the balcony and imagine what was going on behind the shuttered windows of the narrow boulevard. But over the past few weeks, every so often, she thought she'd seen or sensed a movement in the shadows, of the canopies overhanging the shop entrances across the road.

Josie had the same feeling at work. When she was on her own, in the Routage, or making her way to Thomas's or Isabelle's office, she sometimes had the distinct feeling that someone was watching her. She naturally thought of Sally, but surely there was no way the Canadian would bother to stalk her to the apartment, no matter what happened at work. Surely Sally had better things to occupy her time. Nevertheless, Josie felt uncomfortable and spent a good few minutes on the balcony scanning the street below her.

"Neurotic!" she scolded herself.

Chrissie headed straight for bed; she wanted to get up reasonably early to spend some time getting ready before she met Claude. Josie was pretty wide awake so she made coffee and took it into her bedroom. She stood for a while in the dark, looking out of the bedroom window again. The streets were quiet and there were very few lights on in any of the buildings. It was after two in the morning. Then she saw movement again and could just about discern the outline of someone lurking in the shadows across the road. It looked like a man and there was something familiar about him, even though Josie couldn't fully make out his face. The phone rang abruptly, startling her. Josie rushed to pick it up and Chrissie emerged from her bedroom, already dressed for bed.

"Who's calling us at this time of night?"

Josie held her finger up to her mouth, indicating for her flat mate to be silent. The caller had hung up as soon as Josie answered the phone. She immediately redialled to check on the last caller's details, but it came up with number withheld. She was now beginning to feel really uneasy.

"Chrissie, I think there's someone watching us from across the road. I thought I saw someone when you were paying for the taxi but I wasn't sure. Then from my bedroom I thought I saw someone again, and now this," she said pointing to the phone.

The phone immediately rang again. "Hello," she replied, picking it up after the first ring. Again the caller hung up.

"Who could it be?" Chrissie asked.

"I don't know," Josie replied.

"What shall we do?" asked Chrissie, who was now also alarmed.

"Is your bedroom light on?"

"Yes."

"OK, go into your bedroom and switch off the light. Then wait there. I'll make a big show of stretching in front of my window, I'll partially pull the blinds and make it look like I'm getting into bed and switch off the light. Then we'll crawl along the floor and see if we can see someone opposite. If we do, we'll call the police from my mobile."

"OK," said Chrissie, "but I'm scared, Josie."

"Look, it could just be a coincidence, and my over-active imagination, but just in case follow my plan. It's not like we're in the building all on our own. The Beaudoin's are just next door and

116

there will be people in the other apartments. Don't worry Chrissie. I'm sure it's probably nothing."

Chrissie switched off her bedroom light and crept back into the hall. Josie made a big show of shutting her blinds, leaving enough of a gap for the girls to peer through and then switched her own bedroom light off. She beckoned silently to Chrissie and the girls crawled along the floor and peered out onto the street.

"Can you see anyone?" Chrissie whispered.

"No, can you? And why are you whispering?"

Chrissie started to giggle. "I don't know. This is very Famous Five isn't it, Josie?"

Josie also started to giggle. The girls did their best to hold back their laughter but ended up, practically hysterical, on the floor. Their laughter was again interrupted by the sound of the phone ringing. This time Chrissie answered.

"Hello, madhouse incorporated here. Who's speaking?"

Again the caller hung up. Josie rushed back to her bedroom and flung open the blinds. She was convinced she saw a man's shadow move in the darkness across the road.

"Right, we have a couple of options," she said to Chrissie. "If whoever is calling is the same person who is standing across the road, then hopefully they know we are on to them. We could go down together and confront them."

Chrissie shook her head.

"Yes, probably not the brightest suggestion. We could call the police," said Josie, "but we don't have anything specific to go on, except for the phone calls. Why don't we wake the Beaudoins?"

"None of those are particularly great ideas," replied Chrissie.

The girls decided to watch the street, discretely, from behind the safety of the blinds in Josie's bedroom. Suddenly the silence was broken by a police siren in the distance. Josie and Chrissie looked at each other in surprise. Suddenly, a figure emerged from the shadow of the building opposite and began running down the street toward the Gare St Lazare.

"Could you see him? Do you know who it was?" said Chrissie. Josie hesitated. Though she couldn't be a hundred percent certain, she was pretty sure she knew who it was, but she didn't want to panic her flatmate.

"No, I didn't get a good look at him. How about you?"

"Me neither, but it was definitely a male."

Josie nodded.

"So what are we going to do now?" Chrissie asked. "I mean he might come back. What if there's only one of us here? That would be really scary."

"I think we should tell the police," said Josie. "We'll explain what happened. They may not do much about it, but at least we will have registered our concerns. Let's do it in the morning when our heads are a little clearer."

Chrissie agreed, but looked anxious. Josie yawned and started getting into bed. "Come on," she said, "Hop in. I think we'd both sleep better if we stay together."

Chrissie slipped off her dressing gown and climbed into bed. It took a while for them both to get to sleep, each preoccupied with their own thoughts.

CHAPTER 7

When, eventually, Josie drifted off to sleep, her dreams focused on dark figures and shadows. She awoke with a start and checked the alarm clock. It was only 7 am but she felt wide awake. Chrissie was still fast asleep so Josie slipped out of bed, trying not to disturb her friend.

She made herself a cup of tea and sat alone in the sitting room, reviewing the events of the past evening. She decided to call the police straight away. Josie was very disappointed with the lack of importance the policeman, at the other end of the line, seemed to place on the incident. In retrospect, she realised, they should have called last night. The policeman informed her that they couldn't be one hundred percent sure there was anyone meaning to cause them distress or harm. He did however make a note of her call for the record.

Josie thanked him for his time, and realised that the phone call she intended to make the next day was more important than ever.

It was a lovely March day; she went into Chrissie's bedroom and sat on the balcony, watching as Paris sprang to life. A text message, arriving on her mobile, interrupted her thoughts. It was Christian. He was on his way home, to sleep, but would call her later and hopefully they could meet up. She sent a text back, 'great x', and headed for the shower.

When she emerged from the shower, Chrissie was up, drinking tea at the dining room table and anxious to discuss last night's drama.

"I called the police first thing," Josie told her, "but there's very little we can do, we have no proof that the person was actually watching us, or trying to frighten us, or even if they made the phone calls. We should have called the police last night really."

"Never mind," said Chrissie, "hopefully it's nothing to worry about."

Josie guessed her friend had other things on her mind, like meeting Claude at lunchtime.

"I'm going to chill, catch up on some phone calls and do some reading," said Josie, stretching out on the sofa, yawning. She hadn't slept much and was tempted to go back to bed.

"I'm probably seeing Christian later, after he's caught up on his sleep. Didn't we invite Daniel around for supper this evening?" Chrissie yawned and nodded. "Well we better cancel or he'll turn up and we could all be out."

"Worse still we could all be in!" said Chrissie laughing.

"You call him Chrissie, he won't whinge at you and give you a hard time."

Chrissie brought the phone into the sitting room and dialled Daniel's number. He answered almost immediately. After the usual greetings, Chrissie explained that they had both made other plans without consulting each other and asked if they could postpone. Josie could only hear one side of the conversation but it sounded like Daniel was giving Chrissie a hard time of it after all. When she eventually hung up she was not best pleased.

"He asked if we had a good time last night and said that it must have been late when we arrived home because he called several times but there was no answer. Perhaps it was him calling after all. I didn't like to press it in case he asked too many questions, and you know Daniel," Chrissie rolled her eyes, "he'd be around in a flash, trying to protect us, and probably insist on staying over a few days." Josie nodded.

"He was definitely angling to find out where we went last night," said Chrissie, "he even wanted to know where we're going today. I couldn't bear to tell him. Anyway I've rescheduled for Tuesday evening, is that OK for you?"

"I'll have to play it by ear," replied Josie. "We have the big pitch to Four Seasons on Tuesday afternoon and I don't know what time that will wind up or if we'll go out afterwards. So it could be just you and him."

"Great," said Chrissie, pulling a face. "Now I'm off for a shower. I'm so nervous and I really want to look my best today – even if I am going to get dumped."

"Why do you say that?" Josie asked.

"Gut instinct I guess. I just feel as though something really 'big' has been going on in Claude's life. I don't appreciate him blanking me these past few weeks. I'm not sure I want to be with a guy who can do that at the drop of a hat."

"Well, wait to see what he has to say first, before you go jumping to conclusions and giving him the famous Chrissie cold shoulder. At least give him a chance to explain."

"What do you mean, the Chrissie cold shoulder?"

"You know full well what I mean, going all cold on him just because you're miffed."

"Well I am miffed, mega miffed actually, and I hate the fact that a mere male mortal has made me feel like this."

Josie burst out laughing at Chrissie's haughty look.

"Oh Chrissie," Josie said. "You really are a cool one. I'd be desperate to find out what's been going on and I'd do my best to be warm and understanding. Obviously Claude really likes you and you really like him, you've been fretting about it all week. So don't let your pride get the better of you. Give the man a chance."

Chrissie managed a smile. "I know you're right. And even though I've only known Claude for a short time, he seems a really genuine guy. I'm so messed up. I've never felt like this before. I'm not handling it very well."

"Well go and make yourself beautiful, you're meeting him in a couple of hours."

While Chrissie prepared herself for her date with Claude, Josie pondered what she would do. She decided to call Marguerite and see if she was free to go for walk, but there was no answer from her friend's land line or mobile.

It was at times like these that she missed Libby, so she made herself a coffee and settled down to call Libby in England. She was delighted to hear from Josie and once they had caught up with the major office gossip, including how stressful setting up the London office had been, Libby told Josie she would be coming back to Paris at the end of the month. JC had organised a job interview for her with Crédit Suisse bank. She had already had a phone discussion and was due to meet the Director for a formal interview.

JC had indicated that the job was virtually hers but Libby was being very careful not to be too confident.

She also told Josie that she had ended the affair with Matt as Lia was pregnant again and she finally realised that he would never leave his wife. He was basically frightened of her and had admitted as much.

"I don't want to waste any more time on him," Libby said. "Quite frankly, I find him quite pathetic now. So it's a new start when I come back to Paris. Even if the Crédit Suisse job doesn't come off, I can always temp for a while until I find a permanent job. I've saved quite a bit of money and so I'm not panicking, at least not yet anyway."

"Good for you. I can't wait to have you back. Hey, you haven't told me how things are working out with the JC, Muriel and wife triangle?"

"Well JC is living with Muriel in a flat in Regent's Park. His wife and kids are living in a house in Richmond. Muriel has been helping a bit with the office set up but has really been more of a nuisance than a help. However, she does have a flair for interior design and the offices look fabulous," Libby said sounding a little surprised. "So she's thinking of setting up as a sort of interior design advisor. I'm not sure how she'll do as essentially she's pretty lazy but you never know, if she's doing something she enjoys then she may make it work. She certainly looks the part and I think the British people may think it's pretty cool to have a stunning Parisian model designing their offices or homes. So watch this space."

As the girls ended their conversation, Libby promised to call Josie the following weekend for another update. Josie picked up a magazine and glanced distractedly through it. She was really bored and found it difficult to just chill and enjoy her free time. Josie decided to try calling Marguerite again. This time Luc answered the phone.

"Hi Luc, its Josie here. Is Marguerite in?"

"Hi Josie, how are you? Did you enjoy last night? Sorry I was so distracted, but, you know, these women just seem to find me irresistible!" he said laughing.

"Really," she replied, "well there's no accounting for taste, is there?"

The words were out before she realised what she'd said.

Fortunately, Luc was so laid back that he saw the funny side.

"OK, I guess I deserved that. Did you have a good time though? I know my friends thought you girls were great fun."

"We had a good evening thanks, and your friends were really good company."

If Luc noticed the dig, he chose to ignore it.

"Marguerite's out for the day with my parents. They're visiting my grandparents in Fontainbleau. But if you're at a loose end, I'm free this afternoon."

"I'd rather spend the afternoon suspended upside down over a pool of sharks," she thought to herself. "I'm fine thanks Luc, just wanted a quick word with Marguerite. I'll catch up with her tomorrow at work."

"I could leave a message asking her to call you this evening."

"It's OK. I'll be out with my boyfriend this evening."

Josie purposely stressed 'boyfriend'. She wanted Luc to know that she wasn't single or available.

"Lucky man," he replied. "I hope he deserves you, Josie."

Luc's comment confused her momentarily. Why should it matter to her what Luc thought. She decided to ignore his words and ended the conversation quickly. Chrissie came into the sitting room to say goodbye.

"You look fabulous, Chrissie," said Josie. "Now remember my advice, don't get all hoity-toity. Give him a chance to explain himself first. It's probably something and nothing anyway."

"It must be something significant, Josie. It was strange of him to go off like that. Anyway I'll find out soon enough."

"Call me or text me as soon as you can."

"OK, see you later."

It was such a lovely day, Josie decided to go for a walk on her own. She headed towards the Parc Monceau. There was an open air café there where she could sit and read her book. She was halfway through Prophecy of Ravens by Ken Blakemore and was hooked. Josie particularly liked the central character, Lara Johnson, she was strong and feisty and ran rings around all the men in the book. The walk was pleasant and Josie was enjoying her own company. She reached the park after about twenty minutes and was glad to sit down and watch the people go by. She ordered a coffee and started reading her book but found it difficult to concentrate. A family sat next to her and the children were noisy and boisterous.

The mother kept trying to calm them down, but with no luck. Josie smiled at the mother who smiled back with a look of exasperation on her face. She was nursing a baby who looked really sweet. Josie felt quite broody. "One day," she thought to herself, but the thought triggered an alarming suspicion. "When did I last have my period?"

Things had been so hectic of late with work and such a busy social life; she couldn't remember when she was due. Josie looked at her pill packet which she always kept in her handbag. She had finished taking the last one four days ago and her period should have started by now, she was never late. "Shit," she whispered under her breath. Josie checked her watch; it was only 1.30 pm so the supermarket should still be open. She paid for her coffee and headed for the Monoprix on rue de Villiers which was the closest supermarket. It stocked most things and she hoped it stocked pregnancy tests.

Josie found the test kits on the health and beauty shelves. There were about ten different kinds, all guaranteeing, 99% accuracy. She opted for a middle priced one and dashed home to do the test. She read the instructions carefully twice through to make sure she understood what she needed to do. Whilst she was nervously waiting for the test results to show, Christian called her mobile.

"Hi Josie, what are you up to?"

Josie was tempted to tell him, but thought better of it. It would sound flippant and if she was pregnant she would need time to think about what she was going to do.

"Hi Christian, I'm just on the other line at the moment. I'll call you back in a few minutes?"

"Sure, hurry up though. I really want to see you."

"I won't be long, promise."

Josie really needed to know the test results before she could speak to him sensibly. She headed back to the bathroom and looked at the tube which she had left on the side of the bath. The test showed 'not pregnant'. Josie didn't know whether to laugh or cry. She was relieved, naturally, but for a split second she was disappointed. She couldn't understand why. An unplanned pregnancy was not on her agenda, particularly with such an exciting new job. Also, she and Christian were only in the early stages of their relationship and this would probably have frightened him off.

That thought made her feel quite miserable. She quickly called him back.

"Hi, sorry about that. How are you feeling? Have you had enough sleep? Have you eaten?"

Christian was taken aback. Josie wasn't usually quite so gushing. He sounded pleased though.

"I'm fine Josie. What are you up to?"

"Nothing really, I've been waiting to hear from you. I went for a walk earlier but I'm home now. Chrissie is out meeting Claude."

"Have you eaten?" he asked, ignoring mention of Chrissie and Claude's rendezvous. Josie realised that in all the excitement of her false alarm, she had forgotten to have lunch,

"Actually, no I haven't."

"OK. I'll pick you up in half an hour and we'll grab a pizza somewhere."

"Great, see you shortly."

Josie popped into her bedroom to check her appearance and freshen up. She sat on the balcony to wait for Christian and passed the time watching commuters enjoying the mid-afternoon sun. True to his word, Christian arrived within thirty minutes, and as he got out of his car Josie shouted to him from the balcony. He looked up at her and waved. She felt inordinately pleased to see him and shouted that she'd come down straightaway. He shook his head and pointed to a couple of carrier bags he was holding. Josie pressed the intercom button to let him in and opened the apartment door. Having run up the stairs he burst into the hallway and handed her the carrier bags. He had brought cheese, bread, tomatoes, wine and a huge crème caramel.

"Lovely. Come on I'm starving."

"Hang on, where's my kiss?"

Christian took her in his arms and kissed her gently on the mouth. She put her arms around his neck and kissed him back. He pushed his body in close to hers and she could immediately feel his erection against her leg. Josie pulled back from him a little and tilted her head questioningly to one side. He needed no further encouragement and lifted her quickly into his arms and carried her to the bedroom. He dropped her unceremoniously on the bed and was on top of her in an instant, pinning her down with his hands and legs and kissing her deeply. She pretended to struggle beneath him but then gave herself up to his kisses and caresses. He undressed her quickly and then flung off his own clothes. It was as if he was desperate for her and Josie felt a deep ache inside. She needed him and quickly. She manoeuvred herself underneath him so his penis brushed her vagina lips. Lifting her hips she pushed herself onto him and they both let out a groan of pleasure. She entwined her legs with his and he moved slowly, getting deeper and deeper with every thrust. He cupped her buttocks in his hands, pulling her further onto his shaft. Josie could feel herself coming and gripped his shoulders hard as the tremors of her orgasm ran the length of her body. Christian thrust deeply inside her, one more time, and she gripped him tightly with her muscles as he came inside her. He collapsed on top of her, breathless, unable to speak. Josie caressed his shoulders and upper body, gently, with the tips of her fingers. He took her hand and kissed the palm.

They didn't speak. They just lay in each other's arms, lost in their own thoughts. After a few minutes Josie shivered. "Are you cold?" he asked her, cuddling her tight to his body. "A little, yes." The French doors that opened from her bedroom onto the balcony were still open. The curtains had started to billow as the wind picked up outside. Christian covered them both with the quilt and asked her how the evening had gone the night before. Josie told him everything, including the incident with the 'lurker' and her suspicions about who it could be.

"Well you've done the right thing, informing the police. And you must make that phone call tomorrow. I wished you'd called me."

"You couldn't have done anything and I didn't want to panic Chrissie unnecessarily. It's her I was most worried about. Speaking of whom, I still haven't heard from her. I hope things are going OK with Claude. Has he said any more to you?"

"Not really. He looks pretty awful. I know that he's spoken with Dominique. It didn't go very well. That's all he's said. He'd kill me if he knew I'd told you."

"Don't worry. I won't let on when Chrissie tells me. She was ready to give him the elbow this morning, but hopefully, when she hears what he has to say, she'll be more understanding."

"I feel sorry for Claude," said Christian. "He's one of those guys who have everything going for them. Good looking, wealthy background, intelligent, but rotten luck in his personal life. And I don't just mean the situation with Dominique. Claude had a twin brother, who was quite ill from birth, and died when they were nine years old. Claude always felt that his mother blamed him for his brother's death. Sort of took all the good health. So Claude has tried to overcompensate over the years. He wouldn't compromise on his job though. I think eventually he realised that whatever he did, he could never make up for the loss of his brother. So he's just got on with his own life."

Josie didn't say anything, but she hoped that Chrissie would be supportive of Claude too. She thought he was a really nice guy and a good partner for her friend. Christian, spooning Josie, pulled her tight against him. After a few moments, Josie could feel his erection growing hard against her buttocks. She reached back and caressed his cock, slowly and gently, feeling him getting harder and harder between her cheeks. Christian gently moved his hand over her belly and towards her mound, quickly finding the hard knob of her clitoris. She was still wet from their earlier love making, his finger slipped effortlessly inside. Christian rubbed her from her arsehole to clitoris in purposeful movements. Josie moved in rhythm with his strokes. Christian rolled onto his back, pulling her on top, her buttocks resting against his thighs. Christian held her hips and slipped his penis inside her, at the same time manipulating her clitoris. He teased her continuously by pulling out of her until the tip of his glistening cock caressed her swollen lips, tantalisingly, barely touching her, despite her urgent thrusting, then pushing deeply back inside.

Pushing his hand away, Josie licked her fingers and began to caress her clitoris, rubbing harder and harder, caressing the base of Christian's penis at the same time. She pushed and pressed harder and harder until she felt the tell-tale pounding in her ears. The exquisite release of her juices exploded deep inside her. Josie's lips contracted around his shaft. Christian thrust deeper and harder into her, crying out with the release of his own orgasm. Their heavy breathing finally subsided. Josie made a move to the side of the bed but Christian held her firmly, nuzzling her neck and caressing her breasts.

"Please, no more," she said, removing his hands gently from her body and rolling away,

"I'm not going to be able to walk tomorrow at this rate... and you are insatiable!"

"Actually I'm starving," said Christian. "Come on lazy bones, let's eat."

"Don't you lazy bones me. You're the one who wanted to go to bed."

"Oh, and you didn't?"

Josie grinned at him. She put on her dressing gown while Christian dressed. She was starving too. Christian headed for the bathroom while Josie began preparing the bread, cheese and tomatoes.

"Josie, what's this?"

He was standing in front of her with the pregnancy test in his hands. She thought about lying and saying it was Chrissie's but she guessed he wouldn't believe her.

"Josie?"

"Ah, well I'm a few days late and I'm never late. So I panicked and did a pregnancy test but it came out negative. Look."

"Were you going to tell me?"

"Christian, there's nothing to tell. I literally did the test just before you arrived and it's negative. So there's no problem, nothing to worry about. "

"And if it hadn't been negative?"

"I don't know. Panic, despair, happiness, I really don't know."

"Josie, you know how I feel about you. I can't force you to feel the same way. But I hope eventually, one day you will. So please, if you're concerned or worried about anything, especially something like this, you must tell me. I'm here for you, whatever the circumstances."

Josie's eyes welled up. Christian took her in his arms and held her close.

"Sweetheart, don't cry. Sorry, I didn't mean to sound so harsh. I just care about you so much and seeing that test thing was a bit of a shock."

"Actually Christian, when it showed negative I was quite disappointed, in a way. I know we've only been together a short time but I do care about you too, you know."

Josie meant what she said. She had genuinely been disappointed when the test showed negative. On her way back from the park earlier she had pictured herself, Christian and their perfect little baby, a happy family, living in big house in a Parisian suburb. It was this thought that made her realise that she did see a future with him. He kissed her gently on the top of her head and held her even tighter. They stayed like that for a few minutes, neither wanting to break the closeness they were enjoying. It was the rumble of Christian's stomach that rudely interrupted the tender moment.

"I'm sorry, but I haven't eaten, not since yesterday evening and it's nearly 5 o'clock now."

"Come on then, tuck in. Do you want some wine or are you going to drive home tonight?"

"It's up to you. I'm not in work until noon tomorrow so it's not a problem for me."

"As long as you don't mind me getting up early and disturbing you then please do stay. I don't know what's going on with Chrissie and Claude. I thought she would have rung by now."

"I guess they have a lot to talk about," he replied.

Josie nodded, but couldn't help but feel concerned. She was tempted to text Chrissie but decided to wait a bit longer, in case she interrupted a delicate moment. After they had eaten and cleared away, they snuggled up on the sofa and dozed in front of the TV. Christian suggested going to the cinema or out for a drink, but Josie preferred to stay in. The evening had turned chilly and besides she was getting more and more anxious about Chrissie. Josie decided to take a bath. Then after that, if Chrissie hadn't called, she would text her.

Whilst she was having a luxurious soak, the phone rang. Josie shouted to Christian to answer it. When she emerged a few minutes later he was still on the phone. "Here she is now," he said to the caller, handing Josie the phone.

"It's Chrissie," he whispered, smiling at her.

"Hi Chrissie, how'd it go?" she asked her friend.

"Very emotional but I understand now why Claude has been so distant. Listen, we're going to get something to eat and then come home, do you want to join us?"

"No it's OK. You spend some time with Claude."

"We're only going to the bistro around the corner so we won't be long. I think Claude will stay over so we'll have to have a proper catch up tomorrow evening."

"Well, looks like those two are OK," she said to Christian once she had hung up. "Are you sure you don't mind staying in?"

"What do you think?" he replied pulling her into his arms again and running his hands over her buttocks. Within seconds, he had slipped her dressing gown off and his hands were exploring her body, very softly and gently, touching every part of her. Josie had just pulled his t-shirt over his head and was undoing the zip on his jeans when they heard the key in the front door. Josie had just managed to get her dressing gown on when Chrissie walked in. She was all alone, no Claude anywhere to be seen. She looked awful.

"Chrissie, what's happened? Where's Claude?"

Chrissie just shook her head and burst into tears. Josie hugged her friend trying to soothe her but her body was so racked by sobs she couldn't speak. Christian left them and went into the kitchen, bringing back a glass of water. Josie made Chrissie sit down and drink the water. Eventually, she stopped crying and just looked at Josie and Christian in despair.

"Everything was great," she said. "Claude explained what had been going on with his ex-girlfriend and that he had told her there was no going back."

"He told me the full story," she added, turning to Christian, who nodded solemnly. "He told me he wanted to be with me and that not seeing me over the last two weeks had been awful. But he needed to sort out his ex and make sure she understood that it was definitely over. Anyway, she wouldn't accept it and has been giving him a really hard time, involving his family and everything. Finally, before he came back to Paris, he told her that she had to accept his decision and that he'd met someone else."

"How did Dominique take it?" asked Josie.

"She went ballistic apparently and threatened all sorts of things, ranging from trashing his apartment to suicide. But he stood his ground and, as you know, came back to Paris on Friday. Claude heard nothing, not a word, so assumed she had finally come to terms with the situation and would get on with her life."

"Well surely this is good news, why are you so upset?" asked Christian.

"Well today, after he told me, he asked me if I wanted to be with him. I told him that I did and the look on his face was so fantastic. It was like having the old Claude back, with a sparkle in his eyes and that gorgeous mouth smiling at me," Chrissie wiped the tears from her eyes. "We were heading for the restaurant when his mobile rang. It was his mother. He went completely ashen and was literally shaking. When he hung up, he just looked so desperate. I asked him what was wrong and he just shook his head. Then he told me that Dominique had carried out her threat."

"She killed herself?" asked a shocked Josie.

"She took an overdose. I don't know much more than that except that Claude said he had to go and sort it out. There was a note apparently, accusing him of all sorts of things. But she is still very much alive."

"Where is he now?" asked Christian.

"He headed straight for the airport and I came home. He barely even said goodbye to me. I just feel completely discarded and worthless. I know he's been through a hard time and he's a good man at heart, but I can't spend my time with someone who's at the beck and call of his ex-girlfriend."

Josie hugged her friend again. She just didn't know what to say. An awkward silence enveloped the three of them. Christian looked distraught and Josie knew he was torn between loyalty for his friend and concern for Chrissie's obvious distress. He gestured to Josie that he was going to make a phone call and, picking up his mobile, he headed for Josie's bedroom. She could hear the low rumblings of his voice but couldn't make out what he was saying. He came back a few minutes later.

"I've just spoken to Claude," he said. "He's in a right state. After he left Chrissie, he made it as far as the airport but turned around and is heading back here now. He's not going to Provence."

"I don't want to see him," Chrissie replied, standing up and confronting Christian. "He's hurt me enough already. I can't take any more." Christian looked shocked.

"Chrissie, I know you're upset," said Josie, "but think about how terrible you've been feeling over the past few weeks without Claude around. He obviously cares for you deeply and in a way his actions have been admirable. So he over-reacted initially to his mother's phone call, but again, given the history, that's not surprising either."

"What history?" asked Chrissie, rubbing her eyes and smearing mascara all over her face.

"The death of his twin," replied Christian. "He did tell you about that, didn't he?"

"Yes, but what's that got to do with this situation."

"It's his mother. She's always been hard on him for being the surviving twin and Claude has always bent over backwards to make it up to her," said Christian. "His mother loved Dominique and totally blamed Claude when the relationship went pear shaped. Even though it was evident to everyone that it was obviously not his fault. You need to cut him a bit more slack Chrissie, please. He's really been through it these past few weeks. I know he does care for you. He just wanted to make sure his past was sorted out before he took any further steps. You can't blame him for that."

"Oh I don't know what to think anymore. How can I be sure I'm the one he wants? It certainly didn't seem that way earlier."

"Just see him, Chrissie," said Josie, feeling very sorry for her friend. "You'll never forgive yourself if you don't. You'd always wonder what might have been."

"OK, I'll see him," she replied running her hands through her hair.

"Go and freshen up," Josie told her, standing up. "I'll make some sandwiches and open a bottle of wine. You must be starving."

"Not really, but thanks, Josie."

Once Chrissie had headed off to the bathroom, Josie asked Christian exactly what Claude had said. He told her that Claude had pulled into a lay-by on the approach to the airport and was just sitting there, mulling things over in his mind.

"I told him to get his arse over here quickly or he'd lose the one person he really cared about. I also told him that he needed to stand up to his mother and realise what an out and out bitch Dominique really was. Harsh I know but it seemed to do the trick."

"I don't know who I feel most sorry for. I know it's been awful for Claude but it's been hard for Chrissie too."

In no time at all, the buzzer sounded at the door. Josie checked who it was and pushed the button to let Claude in. He looked very upset and she told him Chrissie was in her bedroom. He knocked tentatively on the door, "Chrissie, it's me, Claude. Can I come in?"

Chrissie opened the bedroom door. He took her in his arms and buried his head in her shoulder. She couldn't help but stroke his head gently, like a parent comforting a child. Josie was riveted to the spot watching the tender scene unfold. Christian came into the hall, making her start when he touched her shoulder. He indicated for her to follow him back to the sitting room. After a few moments they heard Chrissie's bedroom door close and the muffled sound of conversation.

"Come on you, bed time. You've work in the morning and it's been quite an eventful evening."

Josie followed him into her room and as it had turned chilly she went to close the shutters. She thought she saw a movement in the shadows, but when she looked more closely there was nothing there. "Just my imagination," she told herself. They undressed quickly and hopped into bed. Christian held her gently in his arms and kissed the tip of her nose. "Good night Josie. Don't forget I like a cup of coffee in the morning." She swatted him gently and settled into his arms. She was grateful that he didn't try to make love to her. The events of the last few hours had unsettled her and she just needed to relax and sleep. During the night she half awoke to the sound of voices in the apartment but quickly drifted off to sleep again.

Josie awoke with a start when the alarm went off. She had been sleeping very deeply and dreaming of Christian and babies. She slowly edged out of the bed, not wanting to disturb him

"Oh no, you don't," he said, grabbing her around the waist and pulling her back down next to him, "Where's my good morning kiss?" She kissed him gently on the mouth and he pulled her closer.

"Christian, I have to get up. It's 7.30 already and I need to shower and wash my hair."

"OK," he said, reluctantly letting her go. "I don't know whether to drive you to work or stay here and wait for Claude to emerge and see if he needs anything. Assuming he is still here."

"Stay here, Chrissie will be up in a minute to go to work. Is Claude working today?"

"No, he's not in until Wednesday lunchtime. We're all out of synch because of the time he took off over the last few weeks. We'll be back covering the same shifts soon enough though. Maybe Chrissie will take a day off to be with him."

"Maybe. I'll stick the kettle on and have a quick shower."

When she returned to the bedroom, Christian had gone back to sleep but woke up when she put the coffee on the bedside table next to him.

"Claude is still here. His jacket's in the sitting room and there's still no sign of Chrissie so maybe she is taking a day off.

Stay and get some sleep, you can go straight to work from here if it's easier. There's plenty of food in the fridge, help yourself."

"I will, thanks. If I do see Chrissie and Claude, I'll let you know what they say."

"You better had," she said smiling, "call me in work as soon as you know whats what."

"Yes boss!" said Christian with a smart salute.

"And don't you forget it," giggled Josie, "I almost have you house trained."

Christian reached out and tried to pull her back onto the bed. She playfully slapped his had away.

"There will be plenty of time for that later," she said pouting and blowing him a kiss.

"Oh Josie, you drive me crazy," laughed Christian, burying his head in the pillow.

Josie quickly dried her hair, put on some make up and dressed in black trousers with a white shirt.

"Very smart," said Christian who had been studying her performing her morning rituals. "I'm impressed at how quickly you can get ready. Most women take ages."

"Years of practice, darling" she drawled smiling at him, "but I do like to take my time sometimes. Right I'm off. I'll speak to you later. Have a good day. And Christian.... thanks."

"Thanks for what?" said Christian clearly baffled.

She bent down and kissed him. "Just thanks."

CHAPTER 8

Despite the upset of the night before Josie felt good as she headed for the Métro. She had a great new job, a lovely, attractive, attentive boyfriend and hopefully a happy flat mate too. Then she remembered the 'lurker' and the need to make that all-important phone call. Josie also wanted to find out why Sally had been at Rue de Villiers the previous Friday, but didn't know how to address the issue. The girls were barely on speaking terms and she couldn't just ask her outright.

When she arrived at the office, she checked with Claire that the small meeting room was free and went to make her call. She didn't want to be disturbed. As she dialled the number, she started to feel a bit nervous. What if he wouldn't take her call? What if he didn't believe her? When the receptionist answered she gave her name and asked to be put through to the Managing Director, Monsieur Dupré. The receptionist asked what it was concerning and she told her it was a private matter concerning Monsieur Dupré's son, Thierry. She was put on hold for what seemed like ages but finally she heard him say, "Charles Dupré, can I help you?"

"Monsieur Dupré," she said hesitantly, "it's Josie James, Chrissie's flat-mate."

"Oh, hello Josie," he replied. She could hear the tenseness in his voice. "Is everything alright?"

"No, not really Monsieur, can I ask if Thierry is back in Paris?"

"Not to my knowledge. Why do you ask?"

"I think he's been lurking outside our apartment block in the early hours of the morning. And at the same time we've been getting strange phone calls. The caller just hangs up when we answer."

"Why do you think this is Thierry," he asked her, quite sharply.

"Because I saw him myself, Monsieur, he ran off when he realised we had called the police. I didn't inform the police who it was. But if this happens again, then I will have no choice but to tell them everything, including his attempted rape of Chrissie."

"Now, now, it wasn't as bad as all that, surely. Please Josie…If he is in Paris then I had no idea. I'll call him right now and tell him to stay away."

"You need to tell him more than that. Tell him I was that close to telling the police everything on Saturday night but I didn't want to frighten Chrissie. That's the only reason I didn't say anything. But it's not too late. I can still tell them."

"I'll tell him and I'll speak to his mother too. Thanks for not saying anything to the police, Josie. I really am very grateful."

Once again she felt sorry for the poor man. His son was obviously deranged and needed medical supervision.

"Well please call me back when you've spoken to Thierry and his mother. I want guarantees that this won't happen again."

"I promise I'll call you back as soon as possible."

She hung up and headed back to her desk, where she spent the next hour working on the proposal for the Four Seasons, ahead of the meeting. She kept looking at her watch and wondering why Charles Dupré hadn't called her back. She was about to call him when her mobile rang. It was him.

"Josie, Charles Dupré here. Look, I've tried to get hold of Thierry and his mother but neither is answering their mobiles or the house phone. Actually, I'm rather worried because my ex-wife doesn't go out much and it is very unusual for her not to answer the phone. So I'm heading to Rennes to see what's going on. I'll keep you posted."

"Thank you, I hope everything is alright," she replied.

When Josie hung up she felt even more worried than before. She didn't want to jump to the wrong conclusion but if Charles Dupré was concerned enough to drive to Rennes, then he must think something had happened. But she didn't have time to fret about the situation as she had the Four Seasons work to finish. She'd just have to let Charles Dupré sort it out. She carried on with her work and had it all finished and ready on time for Véronique. She emailed the document to her and made her way to the Routage for coffee. The room was empty so she called Christian. He was still at her flat having breakfast with Chrissie and Claude. She told him to call her when he was alone so she could tell him about the Thierry situation and asked if everything was fine with Chrissie and Claude.

"Seems to be," he replied. "Chrissie's going into work this afternoon and Claude is going to speak to his mother and tell her not to get involved any more. Easier said than done I guess but he's determined not to give in and go home. His main concern is that Dominique will turn up in Paris and cause a scene here, but he'll cross that bridge if it comes to it."

"Right, good, I'll speak to you later then. Have a good day," she replied.

As she hung up, she realised that Sally had come into the room. "Morning Sally," she said politely, but Sally ignored her. Josie just shrugged her shoulders and continued drinking her coffee. She was determined to not let Sally get to her. Then Véronique burst into the room.

"There you are Josie, great work on the Four Seasons pitch. I've sent an email back to you. If you can just make a couple of changes, then you can print copies off ready for the meeting."

"Sure," she replied, "I'll go and do it now."

Véronique waved triumphantly, obviously pleased with Josie and headed back to her office.

Josie caught a glimpse of Sally's face, and if looks could kill... Josie was beginning to feel out of her depth. The Thierry situation had unnerved her and she was still intrigued as to why Sally was at her Métro stop the evening before. She decided to broach the subject.

"Sally, I was just wondering, was it you I saw at Métro Villiers last Friday night, around six-ish?"

Sally looked cross.

"What are you talking about Josie? What on earth would I be doing in an arondissement like that? I live in the 16th as you well know. You certainly won't find me in that sort of area. It's full of prostitutes and transvestites."

Josie couldn't disagree with her, it certainly wasn't the best of neighbourhoods. But she loved the fact that the area was so interesting and colourful. Even late at night she felt safe walking home.

"Sally, I saw you with my own eyes, so don't give me that bullshit. What were you doing there?"

Sally smirked unpleasantly. "So what if it was me? Do you have something to hide, Josie? I've made it my business to find out all about you. Affairs right, left and centre and now you're messing about with some air traffic controllers. I wonder what Monsieur Fredet would say about all of that?"

Josie couldn't believe her ears. Perhaps she was wrong. Maybe it was Sally who was stalking her and not Thierry. But she wasn't going to let this psycho bitch get to her.

"Honestly Sally, you must lead a pretty sad and shallow life if you've nothing better to do than to check up on me. Jealous, are you?"

Quick as a flash, Sally threw herself at Josie, grabbing her hair and pulling her face close to hers.

"How dare you?" she snarled, her face too close for comfort. "I was the top dog here until you came along, you English slut. Don't think you can just flutter your eyelashes and push out your boobs and all the men will come running. I know your sort. I know what they're like here. You better watch your back. I'm going to make it my mission to get you fired."

Sally released her grip on Josie's hair and sauntered from the room. It took Josie a good few minutes to compose herself. She couldn't believe how much Sally hated her and how bitter she felt about Josie's appointment at Renseignements. As she made her way back to her desk, Josie passed Claire in reception who was talking to a tall, dark haired man with a substantial moustache, wearing a crumpled but expensive suit.

"Josie," said Claire. "This is Mervyn Bradley. Mervyn, this is Josie."

"Delighted to meet you, young lady," he said shaking her hand firmly. He had a strong American accent and a humorous glint in his eye.

"Pleased to meet you too, Mervyn. I've heard a lot about you." Although Josie still felt a bit shaky, she was determined to maintain a professional demeanour.

"Excellent. I gather Jacques has agreed that you can give me a bit of admin support when I'm in town. It's not too strenuous, just organising me a bit really. So come on up to my office when you're ready and we'll have a chat."

"I'd be delighted," she replied. "Give me half an hour to finish something for Véronique and then I'll be up."

Back at her desk, she told the other girls that she'd met Mervyn and that he seemed very sweet. Josie omitted to tell them about her confrontation with Sally. The girls agreed that Mervyn was a sweetheart, but he was also incredibly disorganised. Josie finished the work for Véronique, printed off copies for the meeting and then headed for Mervyn's office.

Josie knocked at the door and walked in. Mervyn was on the phone, legs up on the desk, coffee cup in hand, and chaos reigned. There were piles of papers wherever you looked, all over the desk, on the chairs, on the floor and then piles of files on top of filing cabinets and book shelves. He gestured for her to sit down and she had to lift a pile of papers off the chair before she could sit. He was ages on the phone and Josie was getting quite irritable, not just with him, but with the state of his office. She hoped it wasn't her job to sort this mess out, but suspected that it probably was. He eventually hung up and apologised to her profusely. He then started to tell her about his clients and what his job entailed. It sounded rather boring to Josie as most of his clients were either in the high tech industrial sector or telecommunications. It certainly wasn't as glamorous as the Four Seasons account. When he had finished his spiel she asked him what he expected of her.

"Well, I travel a lot, I need someone to check my post, when it comes in, and sometimes there are some important contracts and documents that will need fedexing. I'll need you to check my voicemail messages too. Most get directed to my mobile but sometimes one or two slip through the net. I really need to get this office sorted. I know it's a mess and I can't even claim to find things myself. So I really do need a good clear-out."

"OK," said Josie. "The post and voicemail are easy. I'll open your mail and then email you with the details, you can let me know where to send stuff, or whether it can wait until you get back. Ditto the phone calls. But it's going to take hours to sort this office out. I'll need some guidance as to what is essential and what isn't, and a full client list too."

"That's fine, Josie, I'll let you have the list later today. As far as what's essential and what isn't, anything dated this year or last year should be filed. Anything before that can be archived, just by client name, no more than that. And I will pay you over-time, cash in hand, if that helps."

It certainly did. She had bought some new clothes before she started at Renseignements and her credit card bill had become scary, so some extra cash would definitely help.

"Well I'll probably come in one day next weekend and make a start at least."

As she headed back to her desk she saw that Marguerite was on her way out to lunch.

"Hey, Marguerite, wait for me. I'll come with you if that's OK?"

"Great, I called in earlier but the girls said you were with Mervyn."

"I was, but now I'm free. Come on, let's go. I'm dying to hear how you and Yves got on."

As they settled at the table Marguerite told Josie that she and Yves had got on really well and she was seeing him again on Thursday evening. "My brother's not too keen though. I don't know why. He was quite rude to Yves when he came to pick me up, being overprotective I guess."

"We met Luc and his old school friends out on Saturday night," said Josie.

"Did you? He didn't say."

"Well, he was with some other people, but we enjoyed his friends' company."

"How are things with Christian?" asked Marguerite.

"Fabulous, he's a lovely guy and we're getting on really well."

"Yves told me that Christian was head over heels about you. Apparently he confided that he'd never met anyone like you before. I agree with him. I've never met anyone like you before, either."

"Don't be silly," replied Josie, secretly quite pleased to hear that Christian thought so much about her. "I just enjoy life and want everyone around me to enjoy it too."

"I heard about Claude. How's Chrissie taking it?"

"Chrissie's fine. They met yesterday but Claude had a call from his mother to say his ex-girlfriend had tried to commit suicide. He started to head for the airport but changed his mind and came to our place to see Chrissie. So I think they're fine. Sad story though."

"Yes tragic," Marguerite nodded, "Josie, who were the other people Luc was with on Saturday night?"

Her question held a hint of concern.

"I'm not sure, just some old friends and some girls. I don't know if he knew them before or if he met them that night. He's very popular with the girls, your brother."

"I know, he always has been, he's never really settled with one though. I only ask as Luc has some friends whom my parents don't approve of. He's been a bit of a tearaway in the past, you know, drinking, partying and taking drugs sometimes. Since he had the drink driving ban he's calmed down a bit. I know my parents worry about him though. Still, he has a mind of his own and they can't protect him all the time."

Josie suspected that Marguerite was not telling her everything about her rebel of a brother. But she didn't want to push for more information, it was none of her business.

"I did call you yesterday to see if you wanted to go for a walk, but Luc told me you were out."

"Well he didn't tell me that either," replied Marguerite, clearly exasperated. "I'll have words with him when I get home."

Josie laughed. "Don't worry about it. Not passing on phone messages is definitely a trait of the male species. I know my mother and father have huge rows about it."

The girls chatted idly over their lunch and then they returned to the office. Josie headed for the meeting room with all of the print-outs ready for the Four Seasons rehearsal. The meeting went well and Véronique thanked Josie for her hard work in getting everything ready.

When she returned to her desk, there were a number of missed calls on her mobile plus a voicemail message from Charles Dupré. She listened to the message. He sounded very distraught and asked her to call him back right away, which she did. He answered after just one ring.

"Josie, thank goodness. Listen. I'm in Rennes. When I got to the house it was empty. One of the neighbours informed me that my ex-wife was in hospital. So I went along and indeed she is in hospital having her appendix out. Thierry was supposed to tell me about it as she was rushed in over the weekend but needless to say he didn't. But we don't know where he is. He was meant to contact me to arrange to come and stay while his mother is in hospital as she doesn't trust him to stay in the house on his own. But he didn't. I guess he was in Paris if you saw him but he hasn't been in touch with me. So I don't know whether to wait here to see if he turns up, or come back to Paris. What do you think?"

"Well I don't know," Josie replied, deeply concerned, "He's your son, you know him better than me. I just don't want him hanging around our apartment."

"I've tried to call his mobile but it's switched off. I've left several messages telling him to get in touch with me but he hasn't. I've even said I'll call the police if he doesn't get in touch soon which I really don't want to do."

While he had been talking, Josie had been thinking.

"Monsieur Dupré, I don't want to involve the police either, but we can't have Thierry behaving like this and frightening us. I'll go home this evening as usual and hopefully the others will be home too, and if anything suspicious happens I'll call you first. So perhaps you'd better get back to Paris, unless of course you hear from Thierry first. If you do, please let me know."

"OK Josie, and thanks," he replied. The concern in his voice was tangible even over the phone. Josie felt the whole thing was like something out of some badly written police novel but she couldn't help but worry. Thierry was a loose cannon and she didn't want him firing in their direction.

Josie decided to call home. "Hi Chrissie it's me, everything OK now?"

"Fine thanks, Josie. Yesterday was very traumatic, and thanks for your support and understanding. Christian was fantastic too. Claude's still in a bit of a state but he's adamant that he's not going to let Dominique control his life, nor his mother. I'm waiting to hear from him actually as he was due to call this afternoon. He's picking me up from work tonight and I'm staying at his place. I don't think he should be alone at the moment."

"That's good of you Chrissie, please send Claude my best regards," Josie didn't want Chrissie to know about Thierry, she felt her friend had been through enough over the last few weeks. But neither did she want to spend a night on her own at home. Christian was working until 10 pm. Josie sent him a text, asking him if he would stay over. He replied, almost instantly, that he would and that he'd get there around 10.30pm. She still felt a bit uncomfortable and asked Marguerite to come home with her for supper, straight from work, but unfortunately she had other commitments. So Josie resigned herself to an evening in on her own until Christian came over after work.

At home, she was starting to prepare supper when the phone rang. It was Daniel confirming the arrangements for the following evening. In all the excitement, the girls had forgotten about him.

"Sorry Daniel, it's been a bit hectic over the weekend. I'm not sure if Chrissie is going to be here tomorrow, you'll have to check with her. Look, I'm making supper for myself, why don't you come and join me tonight instead?"

Daniel pointedly asked if Chrissie would be there later. Josie told him firmly that she wouldn't as she was staying with Claude. So he declined her invitation.

"Charming," she thought. Although Josie realised that Daniel had not felt entirely comfortable with her, ever since the Angie episode. The previous New Year's celebrations had all got a little out of hand and Josie had ended up in bed with both Angie and Daniel. Nothing had happened, though not for lack of persistence on Daniel's part. She was tempted to tell him about Thierry. Daniel had been the one to rescue Chrissie, the last time, but he'd start to get overprotective and would be around all the time. She promised to get back to him when she'd spoken to Chrissie and arrange to meet up. Josie often felt that dealing with Daniel was like dealing with a spoilt child.

After supper she had a long, hot shower, put on some comfortable clothes and settled in front of the TV. The girls didn't subscribe to a cable or Sky channel. They didn't watch much television and felt it wasn't worth the expense. But that particular evening Josie wished they did as there was nothing on the terrestrial channels. She picked up her book and began reading but soon dozed off on the sofa.

She was woken by the sound of someone ringing the doorbell. In her half sleepy state she automatically answered the door, assuming it was one of the neighbours, as the downstairs intercom hadn't rung. Josie opened the door wide and was abruptly pushed back into the hallway by two strong arms. It was Thierry. She was dumbstruck. How could she have been so stupid? He closed the door quickly and stared at her with absolute hatred in his eyes. She tentatively touched the pocket of her tracksuit bottoms to check she had her mobile phone. He noticed the movement which brought a sneer to his face.

"Alone tonight?" he said, his voice was strained and croaky and he looked like he'd been sleeping rough. His hair was plastered to his head and his face bore several days of dark stubble.

Josie didn't dare speak, so she just nodded. This seemed to egg him on further and he launched into a furious and fast tirade about her and her 'prostitute' flatmate. Spittle sprayed out of his livid mouth as he cursed Chrissie, who didn't appreciate a real gentleman, but who would open her legs for any man who showed her the time of day. His language was foul and Josie didn't understand everything he said though she picked up the gist of it. Spittle hung from the sides of his mouth as he continued to deride her and her friend. He seemed to know a lot about their comings and goings and she guessed that he had been watching them for some days. While he was ranting and raving, he walked disjointedly around the hallway, sometimes putting his face up very close to hers. He smelled awful but she didn't turn her head away. She continued to look him directly in the eye, challenging him.

Eventually he stopped shouting at her but she didn't dare move. Josie had no idea how long she had been asleep and didn't know what time it was. Perhaps Christian was already on his way over? She had contemplated making a run for the bedroom just behind her but didn't want to anger him any further. The last thing she wanted was to be trapped in there with him. Thierry seemed to be contemplating what to do. He approached her again and ran a finger down the length of her neck and very close to her breasts. She continued to stare at him but it took all of her strength not to flinch and push his hand away.

"I'd fuck you here and now," he said to her, "but I'm not interested in sloppy seconds. You English girls are all sluts. French girls are far less eager to get a man's cock inside them. They have morals. You don't even know what the word means."

"What do you want, Thierry?" asked Josie, speaking for the first time since he had pushed his way into the apartment.

"Don't speak to me, slut," he replied, slapping her hard across the face.

Josie reeled from the blow and was now really frightened.

Seeing the fear in her eyes, he began laughing at her.

"Not so cocky now, are we. Not faced with a real man."

He approached her again and stretched his hand out towards her breasts. With strength brought on by sheer and utter fear, she grabbed his hand and bit into it deeply. He yelped with pain and pulled his hand back. Josie saw an opportunity and kicked him as hard as she could in the groin. Even though she had no shoes on, he doubled over with pain and she quickly headed for the apartment door. She managed to get it open before he recovered and tried to pull her back. She wedged her foot in the door as Thierry tried to wrestle it shut, and began shouting for help. Her voice sounded small and pathetic, like in a bad dream when you call for help but no sounds emerge. Josie tried to shout louder, holding onto the door for dear life and struggling with Thierry.

Thierry grabbed her hair and tried again to pull her back into the hall but she continued to resist, all the time shouting. Josie hoped the Beaudoins were in and that someone would hear. She sincerely hoped they didn't think it was those mad English girls partying again. She could feel her hands losing their grip of the door frame. Thierry dug his hands into her hair, pulling her head right back and almost snapping her neck.

"Help, Police," she shouted one last time. Josie could hold on no longer and the pain in her head was excruciating. She let go of the door and, as Thierry kicked it shut, she thought she caught a glimpse of the Beaudoins' door opening.

"Help, Police," she shouted again as loud as she could. Josie didn't know if her neighbours had heard her or if they had seen anything. Thierry slapped her again and she could taste blood in her mouth. "You stupid bitch," he hissed, his face practically touching hers. "You'll pay for that."

Survival was all that Josie could think about. Even if the Beaudoins hadn't heard her, Christian was due anytime soon, surely. She just wished she knew what the time was. Josie didn't know if she was safer in the hall or if she should try to get into one of the other rooms. Maybe she could pick up a piece of furniture as a means of attack or even, god forbid, defence. Thierry was pacing around her again, muttering to himself. She managed to edge her way backwards so that her back was against the hall cupboard. Very slowly she moved her hand around to her back pocket to locate her mobile phone. She had just about managed to get it out of her pocket when he noticed the movement and struck her hard again. Her head reeled back against the hard wall and for a few moments she blacked out.

As she slowly regained her senses, she watched as Thierry put the bolts over the front door and disconnected the telephone cable from the wall. Josie was now convinced that the Beaudoins hadn't heard or seen her as surely they would have knocked on the door by now. She just hoped that when Christian arrived he would be concerned enough, when she didn't answer, to get into the apartment anyway.

"Just you and I now, Chrissie," he said, turning towards her.
"I'm not Chrissie," she replied.

"Of course you are. It doesn't matter what your name is, you English women are all the same, circuitée, gentil et tartes, slags. Well, this is what sluts get." He started to undo his belt. Josie was petrified but determined that this horrible maniac of a Frenchman was not going to rape her. He began to undo his trousers, moving closer, his groin in line with her face. Pinning her down with one arm, he undid his zip. Josie had never been so terrified in her whole life and was now bitterly regretting not informing the police about the previous incident with Chrissie. Thierry's penis was limp and flaccid but he started to masturbate as he held her down on the floor, his hand on her neck, making any movement painful and difficult. As he became hard, he moved his crotch towards her face, screeching at her to open her mouth or he'd kill her there and then. "No way," Josie thought to herself as she clamped her mouth together and struggled against the pressure of his hand on her throat. His erect penis brushed against her lips. The immense fear she felt seemed to give her an inner strength and she hurled herself at his legs, bringing him to the floor. Thierry hit his head against the door frame and was quite obviously badly winded. Within a split second Josie was at the front door, had it unbolted and was out in the corridor banging on the Beaudoins' door. Monsieur Beaudoin answered almost immediately.

"Help me, please," she screamed at him. He pulled her into the apartment and quickly shut the door. Josie collapsed against him.

"Don't worry Josie, you're safe now," he said. "The police are on their way. We heard you earlier and I saw that man pulling you into the apartment so we called them immediately."

All Josie could do was sob against the sturdy and reassuring shoulder of her neighbour. Madame Beaudoin, who had been in the sitting room looking out for the police, joined them and told them that they had arrived. Within a few moments there was a knock on the door. Monsieur Beaudoin opened it and explained quickly that there was an intruder in the next apartment but that Josie was safe with them. Two policemen headed for Josie's apartment whilst another asked if she could tell him what happened.

"His name's Thierry Dupré," she told him, her voice still heaving, from intense sobbing. "He pushed his way into the apartment, hit me and I think he was going to rape me."

"You know him, then?" the policeman asked.

She nodded and began to tell him about the night out with Chrissie and the ensuing incident when she saw him spying on them.

"I have his father's telephone number," she said. "He's been really worried about him. I told him I'd let him know if I saw him outside our apartment. I just didn't expect him to do this."

The policeman and the Beaudoins made reassuring noises. Madame Beaudoin handed her a glass of brandy. The policeman then left her in the care of the Beaudoins to go and check what was happening next door. He returned within a few minutes and asked Josie for Charles Dupré's phone number.

"Have you got him?" Josie asked as she checked her mobile for the number.

"Not exactly," he replied. "The man in your apartment is threatening to throw himself off the balcony if we go near him. He's clearly unstable so we've sent for back up. Are you OK here?"

Josie nodded, "I really should let my flatmate know what's going on, and my boyfriend is due at any moment."

"What's his name?"

"Christian, Christian Lecourt. What time is it?"

"It's nearly 10.30," replied Madame Beaudoin.

"We'll send him up when he gets here," said the policeman.

Josie nodded and dialled Chrissie's mobile, but it went straight to answer machine. Josie hung up. This wasn't the time to leave a message. Just as she hung up, Christian came bursting into the room.

"Josie, are you OK? What the hell's been going on? The

police told me there'd been an incident!"

"Christian," she cried out, bursting into tears again, as he put his arms around her and held her tightly. They stayed locked together for ages, until Josie's sobs subsided enough for her to tell him what had happened. The Beaudoins left the room so they could be alone.

"The bastard, wait until I get my hands on him. Oh God, Josie, you poor thing. I wish you'd gone to my place instead. If I'd only realised what he was capable of."

"It's not your fault Christian. I should have been more careful. I shouldn't have opened the door."

"Come here," he replied, pulling her close.

They were interrupted by her mobile ringing. It was Chrissie.

"Josie, are you OK?" her friend asked. Christian gently took the phone from her and quickly explained what had happened. Josie gestured for him to give her the phone so that she could speak with Chrissie herself.

"I can't believe it," her friend said. "Look, Claude and I are on our way over now. Stay there at the Beaudoins until we get there."

"It's OK, Chrissie, I'm fine. Christian is with me. There's no need to come over. I guess the police will want to interview you at some stage."

"We're coming over, Josie. I don't care what you say. It's my fault you're in this situation. See you soon."

"Chrissie and Claude are on their way over," she told Christian, still feeling very shaky.

"Look, I'm going to find out what's happening next door," he replied.

"No, don't leave me, please."

He took her in his arms again to reassure her and stayed with her until one of the policemen returned.

"What's happening?" they both said in unison.

"No change so far. We've contacted the young man's father and he's on his way. We have special people to deal with this sort of situation and they've just arrived. Will you be OK to wait here a while longer? We are going to need to take a statement from you and your neighbours."

"I'll be fine here," Josie replied. "And my friend who had the initial problem with him is on her way over. Will you want to interview her too?"

"Maybe, at a later date, but that's really a different issue and wasn't reported at the time, so we can't take that into account at the moment. If she does want to report the incident she still can, but it would have been better to have done so then," he said sternly, "If she had, in all likelihood you wouldn't have had to go through what you went through tonight."

The policeman left, and soon after Chrissie and Claude arrived.

"Oh Josie, are you OK?" said her flatmate, rushing to Josie's side. "I'm so sorry. If only I'd done something before. I feel awful. But you should have told me about your suspicions. I wouldn't have left you at home alone if I'd known. I know you were trying to protect me but look at what could have happened!"

"I'm fine Chrissie. Just a bit shaken really but I'll be fine." No sooner had she spoken the words, she burst into tears again.

Chrissie hugged her close. The men left them alone but Christian returned a few moments later to tell them that Charles Dupré had arrived and wanted to see Josie.

"You don't have to see him if you don't want to," Christian told her protectively.

"No it's fine. It's not his fault what happened."

Christian went to fetch Charles Dupré and Chrissie also told her that she didn't have to see him.

"I'm surprised the police will let him see you as you haven't given a statement yet," Chrissie said.

Her thoughts were echoed a few minutes later when Christian returned alone.

"The police won't let him near you, Josie, and I'm glad. He's pretty upset and you've been through enough for one night. Anyway, Thierry is off the balcony and under arrest. They're taking him to the police station now. One of them will be in shortly to take your statement and then we can go home. They may want to see you at the station tomorrow as well."

Josie nodded. Then she remembered. "Shit, it's the Four Seasons pitch tomorrow afternoon. I can't miss that. I'll explain to them and go to the police station the next day instead."

"Josie, you're not going to work tomorrow," Christian said firmly, "after everything you've been through tonight? It's madness."

"Of course I am. Christian, all the ideas for this project are mine and I really want to be there. Also I don't want to let the team down."

"Well let's get your statement over with and then we can go to my place and discuss it."

"I'd rather stay here if you don't mind. It will be another hour before we get to your place and I'd need to pack a bag. Do you mind?"

"I don't mind Josie, but I'm staying with you. Are you going to be OK?"

"I'll be fine as long as you're with me. Are you and Claude staying too?" she asked, turning to her friend.

"Of course we will, silly. I'll go and let Claude know."

Alone again, Christian turned to Josie and said, "You are incredible, Josie. Anyone else would have just crumbled. Just don't take too much on. It's been a traumatic evening to say the least and it may affect you later. The shock of it all will catch up with you eventually. Just take care."

He cupped her chin in his hand and kissed her gently on the lips. Josie smiled at him, thinking, not for the first time, what a sweet, kind and understanding man he was. A vision of Max passed through her mind. She was sure he would not have reacted in the same way as Christian to everything that had gone on. Just this thought was enough to make her realise that she was completely over Max and was very lucky to have Christian in her life.

CHAPTER 9

As Josie gave her statement to the police officer, she felt quite numb. The events of the past few hours still hadn't really sunk in. Finally, after the officer was satisfied, he gave her permission to return to the apartment. Josie thanked the Beaudoins for their help and made a promise, to herself, to be a much more respectful neighbour in future.

Back in the apartment, Josie could tell the others were watching her warily for signs of distress, but in fact she felt quite light-hearted. Giving her statement to the police had been a catharsis of sorts. Josie was glad that the threat of Thierry lurking outside their flat was now gone. She had also received a text message from Charles Dupré, apologising for his son and saying that he hoped to speak to her, face-to-face, soon to apologise in person. Chrissie was going to the police station the next day to make a statement about the night Thierry attacked her.

It was 2 am by the time she was tucked up in bed, safe and secure in Christian's arms. Strangely she slept like a baby and awoke from a deep sleep when the alarm went off. For a moment, she just felt comforted by the closeness of Christian but then remembered what had happened the night before. For a split second she could feel her resolve wavering and just wanted to stay in the safety of her bed, but she knew she had to be strong and she desperately wanted to impress her new employers.

Josie forced herself to leap out of bed and into the shower. By the time she had emerged, Chrissie was also up and had made a cup of tea for her.

"Are you sure you're OK to go to work?" she asked.

Josie insisted that she was fine.

"What time will you be home?"

"I really don't know Chrissie. I think Véronique was talking about going on for a drink afterwards. I'll just have to see how it goes and let you know."

"Well I'll phone you and let you know how I get on with the police. I wonder if Charles Dupré will be in work."

"I wouldn't think so," Josie replied. "Poor man, he seems a genuine enough chap, shame about his son."

"Tell me about it. Anyway, he's under lock and key now and hopefully will be for a long time."

"We don't know that though, do we," said Josie, suddenly realising that Thierry would probably be released at some point, free to harass them again. As if reading her thoughts, Chrissie replied, "Even if he's given bail, I'm sure his father will take drastic action. Personally, I think he should be sectioned and I'll tell Charles Dupré that."

As she prepared herself for work, Josie couldn't help but worry about the situation with Thierry. She tried to focus on the day ahead and the Four Seasons pitch. Then she saw Christian, in the reflection of the mirror, watching her get dressed. She turned to him and smiled.

"Are you sure you're OK?" he asked her, the concern evident in his voice.

"I'm fine," she replied sitting on the edge of the bed. "I am, really Christian, and thanks for being so wonderful last night. I felt really safe and secure knowing you were here with me."

He pulled her into his arms and kissed the top of her head.

"Move in with me Josie," he said, "I could look after you all the time then."

Josie was shocked. She knew Christian liked her and she liked him, but it was still very early days to consider moving in together. He saw the look of surprise and then concern flit across her face.

"Sorry Josie. I don't know where that came from. It wasn't planned or anything. It's just that I was so frightened for you last night and I couldn't bear it if anything were to happen to you. I really do love you." Christian hesitated and Josie softly kissed him on the lips.

"The other day, when you said you didn't know how you felt," Christian looked deeply into her eyes, "about having our baby, well it made me realise how much I want you, not just now but to be part of my life in the future too. I don't want to rush you but it would give me so much pleasure to share my life with you on a more permanent basis. I guess my timing's all wrong. You don't want to make any life changing decisions after the night you've just had. God, I'm an idiot. Forgive me."

Josie didn't know what to say. Part of her was scared by the sort of commitment that Christian wanted. But she was also secretly pleased that he wanted to share his life with her. Josie realised that, over the past weeks, she had fallen deeply in love with him and that it was about time she told him so.

"Christian, I am really flattered. But as you say, it's very soon in our relationship, and the timing...to discuss this now, well it isn't the right time. But I do want to tell you, that I love you, very much."

She leaned over and kissed him on the mouth. He caught her face in his hands and kissed her back. When he eventually broke away, she could see a hint of tears in his eyes.

"I'll come and spend the weekend with you if you like and we can see how we get on 'domestically'," she told him, getting up from the bed and putting her shoes on.

"I'm working the early shift on Saturday, so I'll pick you up after work and we'll go to my place then."

"I'll probably go into work myself, on Saturday morning, and start sorting out Mervyn's office. You can pick me from there, if that's OK?"

"That's fine," he replied, "I can't wait for a weekend of domestic bliss!"

Josie arrived early at the office and was met by Thomas and Véronique.

"Josie, there you are," said the older woman. "Can you spare us a few minutes in Thomas's office?"

"Sure," she replied, wondering what was going on. Véronique looked a little worried, and she hoped it wasn't to do with her work on the Four Seasons pitch.

In Thomas's office, they sat on the sofas around the coffee table. Josie felt uncomfortable as they both seemed to be looking at her strangely. Then Véronique said to her, "Josie, your flatmate Chrissie phoned Thomas this morning. She told us what happened last night. She's very concerned about you and so are we. We don't think you should be here, you've had a very traumatic experience."

Josie didn't know whether to laugh or cry. She understood that Chrissie had phoned Thomas with her best interests at heart but she really didn't want to be molly coddled either, she just wanted to get on with her day as planned. The look of concern on her boss and colleague's faces was almost comical and it was all she could do to stop herself from laughing, but then they really would think she was traumatised.

"Thanks for your concern but I'm fine, really. I'd much rather be here and keep busy than be at home, on my own, jumping at every sound. Also, I really want to be part of the Four Seasons pitch, more than you can imagine, so please don't make me go home. Honestly, I really am better off here."

"Are you sure? You're not just putting on a brave face, because you're the new girl?" Véronique asked.

"Positive, I'm fine. Last night is over and done, I just want to get on with my work."

Thomas had been watching the exchange between Josie and Véronique intently.

"Josie," he said, "I accept what you say about being better off here but if at any time you change your mind or feel a bit overwhelmed, please don't suffer in silence. We'll do all we can to support and help you if you'll let us."

"Thanks Thomas, but honestly I'll be fine. Just one thing though, please don't tell anyone else. I don't feel up to being questioned. I just want to forget about it all and carry on as normal."

They agreed not to mention anything to anyone else and thanked Josie for her commitment to work. She found the whole thing quite surreal and overly formal. Josie had experienced this peculiar and particularly reserved French manner before. One minute they were great fun, but the second anything untoward occurred they took on a big 'doom and gloom', crisis approach.

As she headed back to her desk, she bumped into Mervyn in the corridor.

"I've just left the list of my key clients on your desk," he said. "Also, I have to go to the States tomorrow morning unexpectedly, can you spare me a few minutes this morning for a short briefing?"

"Of course," she replied, "let me just check my emails and make sure everything's ready for this afternoon and then I'll pop up. Oh and Mervyn, I'm coming in to make a start on your office, Saturday morning."

"Good girl," he replied, rather patronisingly. Josie wasn't sure about Mervyn Bradley. Her view was that he was an old charmer, used to getting people to do things for him. He played the part of a disorganised misfit, but she could tell he had a sharp brain.

Josie dealt with her work and then spent an hour with Mervyn going through his client list, what activities were currently on-going and getting all his contact details so she could pass on messages. It was soon lunchtime but Josie declined an invitation to join the other girls, she didn't feel like socialising. Instead she picked up a sandwich from the deli and returned to her desk to read through the Four Seasons information, one more time.

The afternoon dragged and she became more and more nervous as time went on. Chrissie phoned her just as she began to shut down her PC.

"The police interview was fine," she said. "I remembered more or less everything. They did have a bit of a pop at me, for not reporting the incident at the time. I do feel bad about that now."

"Don't worry, Chrissie, it's all done with now, thankfully. Look, I have to dash, the taxi will be here any minute."

"Good luck, and let us know how you get on."

The taxi was ordered to take them to Boulevard Haussman. Josie headed for the loos to check her hair and make-up. As Josie made her way to reception, to wait for the rest of the team, she was frustrated to see Sally chatting to Claire. Josie had decided to steer clear of the Canadian, as much as she could, and all she needed was another confrontation before the Four Seasons pitch. Sally gave her a patronising look and resumed her conversation with Claire. Josie decided to wait outside in the courtyard for the rest of the team, not wanting to be the subject of Sally's gossip or gaze. She could hear the two women chatting through the open window and was distraught to hear Sally mention her name, although she couldn't quite grasp what Sally was saying exactly.

Josie put it out of her mind as the rest of the team joined her. They hopped into the waiting taxi. "Everything OK?" Véronique asked Josie.

"Fine thanks," she replied unconvincingly.

"I know what's going on," Véronique said, "with Sally being a bitch, I mean. If you have any more problems come to me and I'll sort it."

"Thanks," replied Josie tentatively. She was used to fighting her own battles but wasn't sure this was one she could handle on her own.

"Don't stand for it, Josie. Sally's a pain in the butt. I mean it, if she gives you any more grief, come straight to me."

Josie just nodded. She really didn't want to involve anyone from the Renseignements management team in her petty squabbles.

The traffic was pretty light and they arrived at the Four Seasons offices with plenty of time to spare. The offices were very impressive and Hélène herself came to greet them in person. She made a big show of welcoming Josie, and the younger woman felt quite embarrassed by all the unsolicited attention.

They set up the presentation in the boardroom. Véronique took the floor and began outlining the agency's ideas. As she began her spiel, she took the time to say that, although the detailed plans had been worked up by the team, the initial concept was Josie's. Again Hélène gushingly thanked Josie for her efforts, making her feel even more uncomfortable than before. She did, however, catch the glimmer of a knowing smile on Véronique's face, which didn't help either.

Once Véronique had finished the formal presentation, she invited Josie to say a few words. Josie was well prepared and gave a brief summary of the overall presentation, highlighting in particular the publicity opportunities and endorsements. Especially the potential links between the hotel chefs and the celebrity chefs. Once she had finished, Véronique asked the Four Seasons representatives if they had any questions. The financial director asked about overall budget. Véronique indicated that details were in the dossiers, which she had handed out at the start of the presentation. So far Hélène had been very quiet so Véronique turned to ask her what she thought.

The older women looked thoughtful and didn't speak for a few moments, "As most of you know, I've always steered away from focusing on a 'seasonal' theme for our hotel launches, it has always seemed a bit too obvious. However, in this instance, I think the link to the seasons promotes the versatile image we are trying to portray. I especially like the emphasis on the haute cuisine. Getting our chefs to cook for celebrity chefs is a great idea. No doubt our people's noses would be totally out of joint, if it were the other way around. But, in particular, I love the idea of having the four openings consecutively on the same day, it will be very exciting to see it all happening by video link. I just can't decide which one I'll go to!"

The last comment was obviously said tongue in cheek but Josie couldn't resist chirping in. "Well you could make two of them, at least, if you used private air transport. Originally we'd thought of having one celebrity to cover all the openings but that would have delayed the events far too long."

"Yes I could, and I'd need a different outfit for each event. Thank you Josie, an excellent idea. Now let's take a look at how much this is all going to cost us."

Véronique ran through the budget figures and proposed timetable. "We need to make a start booking the celebrity chefs pretty quickly as time is not on our side." Josie noticed that Véronique didn't let on that they had already started making tentative approaches to a number of celebrity chefs. Jean-François hadn't said much during the presentation and ensuing discussions. While everyone else discussed the finances, Josie looked around the room and she caught his eye. He smiled shyly at her and she had the impression that he didn't really feel part of the Four Seasons team, more a relative tolerated only due to his parentage.

Hélène had obviously caught sight of the brief exchange between Josie and Jean-François and asked the young man what he thought of the presentation. He just shrugged his shoulders and looked down at the dossier which Véronique had given him earlier. Hélène looked exasperated and shook her head. Josie looked away. She was embarrassed for Jean-François but could also understand Hélène's frustration. The discussion eventually came to a close, and Hélène invited the Renseignements gang to stay for some champagne. Véronique gratefully accepted upon their behalf. The team stayed for a further thirty minutes, each enjoying a cold glass of Veuve Cliquot. Hélène cornered Josie and again complimented her on the presentation.

"As I said before, young lady, we could do with a bright spark like you in our organisation. Unfortunately, we can't always choose who we employ and so have to balance on-going nepotism against genuine talent and ability."

As she was speaking, Hélène was looking directly at Jean-François, who was standing on his own, looking out of the window over the boulevard below. Again, Josie felt sorry for him. Hélène turned her attention back to Josie. "Would you like a tour of the offices?" she asked.

Josie was taken aback. She didn't want to offend Hélène, but neither did she feel entirely comfortable going off with her, especially on her own. Before she could answer, Véronique joined them and she quickly told her about Hélène's invitation. Véronique raised her eyebrows and gave Hélène a steely look.

"Another time, Hélène. Josie and I have to get back to the office, for a meeting with Thomas. I'm sure you understand. Thanks for the champagne. I'll call you tomorrow with details of the chefs who are available and willing to participate?"

Hélène didn't seem at all put out. "Excellent. We'll have to leave the office tour for another time then," she said, running her index finger briefly up and down Josie's arm. It was all the younger girl could do to stop herself from flinching. As they emerged outside the building, Véronique asked Josie how she was bearing up.

"I'm fine thanks but I'm really tired now. I think I'll head home if that's alright with you?"

"Sure, you take it easy Josie. And thanks again for your contribution today. It was very well received."

Josie smiled her thanks. Then she remembered that she had to go the police station first thing in the morning and asked Véronique if she would remind Thomas.

Back at home, Chrissie was in the sitting room waiting for her. She gave her friend a big hug, no words were needed. Josie was so tired she could barely speak. Chrissie made them a quick supper and then both girls went to bed. Christian was working late again and she sent him a text, informing him that she was going to bed and would call in the morning. He replied, saying that he missed her, with lots of kisses. As her head hit the pillow, she fell asleep straight away.

Josie's sleep was disturbed, fraught with bad dreams, particularly linking Thierry and Hélène so that they almost merged into one person. At one point she awoke with a start, having dreamed that she was locked in a room with Thierry and Hélène and they were fighting over her. She looked at her alarm clock. It was almost 1am and the apartment was deadly silent. She needed to use the bathroom, but didn't put on the light, as she didn't want to wake Chrissie up. Josie passed through the sitting room towards the bathroom and found herself face to face with a semi-naked man. Josie screamed. In the darkness, she hadn't realised it was Claude. Chrissie came running out of her bedroom stark naked and put the light on. By this time, Josie was practically hyper-ventilating with fear.

"What's happening?" Chrissie asked.

"I think I scared her," he said, obviously embarrassed by the whole scenario and the fact that he was standing there in only his boxers.

Chrissie made Josie sit down and gave her a glass of water. Eventually her breathing subsided and she apologised to Claude.

"I'm so sorry, I just didn't realise you were here. I thought it was…. well, you know."

"I'm sorry too," he replied. "I thought you were asleep."

Chrissie began to reprimand Claude which made Josie smile as she was stark naked.

"Oh please," Josie said, "I'm fine now. I just didn't realise he was here, and it was dark."

Then she started laughing. Both of them looked at her as if she was demented, and that made her laugh even more.

"Josie, I think you need to see a doctor," Chrissie said. "I think this whole episode has upset you more than you realise."

"Oh Chrissie, honestly, I'm fine. I can just see the funny side now." Chrissie sat down next to Josie. "And don't you think you ought to put some clothes on?"

Chrissie ordered Claude to go and find her something to wear and he gladly scurried off back to the bedroom.

"Jose, I know you can see the funny side of this but you did have a horrible experience last night and I don't think it's hit you yet. Just take it easy. And no arguments, I'm coming with you to the police station tomorrow morning … no, this morning. Charles Dupré has told me I can take as much time off as I like to support you."

"Oh, have you seen him?"

"No, but he phoned me at work. He was very concerned about you. He wouldn't put up the bail for Thierry, said he was better off locked up. He really wants to see you, to apologise personally, but when you're ready."

"So what happens now?"

"I'm not entirely sure. You'll have to review your statement tomorrow. I made mine today about the first incident. I guess he'll be charged with something and hopefully get put away. I don't know if it will be prison or some sort of institution. I didn't like to ask his father, he was dreadfully upset on the phone. He had to go and tell his ex-wife all about it and she was beside herself, apparently. Anyway, enough for tonight, come on back to bed. Would you like me to spend the night with you?"

"Don't be silly, go and snuggle up with Claude. I can tell by your lack of apparel you were obviously in the middle of things," Josie smiled.

"The moments passed and besides I'm knackered and we need to get to the police station as early as possible tomorrow otherwise we'll be waiting forever."

Josie found it hard to get back to sleep. She eventually drifted off, but when the alarm rang she felt like she hadn't slept at all.

They arrived at the police station and were seen immediately by one of the policemen who had been at the flat on the night of the incident. Josie ran through her statement, but found reliving the events of that evening quite distressing. She knew if this went to court it would be the same but hoped it wouldn't come to that. When she had finished checking the details and signing the paperwork, she asked the policeman what would happen next.

"Well, it depends. If Thierry pleads not guilty it could go to court, but I think his father is looking at putting him in some kind of psychiatric home. If he does, then we should be able to avoid a court case."

"I'll speak to Charles Dupré myself," said Chrissie. "Find out exactly what's going to happen to Thierry."

The policeman nodded.

As the girls emerged into the fresh air, Josie still felt inordinately tired.

"I think I'll go home for a lie down," she told her friend. "I'm exhausted and feel as though I could fall asleep right here on the pavement."

"I'll come with you. I don't want you to be on your own just yet."

"Chrissie, I'll be fine, honestly."

"No chance, come on. I've had the go-ahead from Dupré to take as much time off as I want and I am going to do just that."

Back at home the girls each called their respective workplaces and explained that they wouldn't be in. Josie spoke directly to Thomas, who was very concerned about her.

"You take as much time as you need, Josie. We only want you back here when you feel fit and well enough to come back."

"I'm just really tired, Thomas. A good sleep will sort me out and I'll be in tomorrow."

After a quick bite and a cup of tea, Josie undressed and slid under her duvet. No sooner had her head hit the pillow she was fast asleep. She slept for more than eight hours and was only woken up by Chrissie shaking her gently.

"I've been checking up on you," she said. "You didn't even murmur. I thought I'd better wake you up now though as you haven't eaten much today and may not sleep through the night otherwise."

It took Josie a good few minutes to come around and sip the tea Chrissie had brought her. When she finished she got out of bed but felt very dizzy and light headed, so she sat back down again.

"See what I mean!" said Chrissie sternly, "Do you want me to bring you supper in here?"

"No, I'll be fine. Anyway I need the loo. I just need to get my second wind."

This time when she stood up she felt much better, although still a little wobbly.

As she made her way into the sitting room, she was surprised to see Daniel there.

"Hello Josie." He stood up and gave her a shy, tentative hug. "How are you doing?"

He looked a bit sheepish but Josie didn't understand why.

"I'm fine Daniel, thanks for asking."

"Look Josie, I'm really sorry I didn't take you up on your invitation to supper the other night. I feel so bad now. I wish you had said that you were concerned about being on your own."

"Daniel, please don't worry about it. If I had been concerned

I would have said something to you and I know you would have come over. I just didn't realise what state Thierry was in. Trust me, it wasn't your fault."

Despite her words, Daniel still bore a hang-dog expression and she couldn't help but feel a bit sorry for him. All through supper the phone didn't stop ringing. Josie felt she had to tell her family what had happened and had called her mother earlier that morning. The news had spread quickly back home in Bristol and her father, her sister and one or two of her old school friends called to check if she was alright. After supper, she phoned Christian who had just arrived home from work.

"Hi babe, how are you doing?" he asked her, the concern evident in his voice. "Chrissie told me you were asleep when I called earlier."

She told him she was fine but that she was still really tired and going straight back to bed. He advised her to stay off work for a few days but Josie told him she preferred to go in and keep busy, and anyway she wanted to be involved in the Four Seasons project.

"Workaholic," he said teasingly.

They agreed that he would come over the following evening as he was on an early shift.

Again Josie fell straight asleep and slept right through until her alarm woke her. She felt really refreshed and ready to get on with life.

Josie was in work by 8am and popped straight upstairs to see Véronique. She wanted to check if she had missed anything on the Four Seasons account. Véronique wasn't in her office so she went to see Thomas to tell him she was in. He seemed very surprised, yet pleased to see her. He invited her to sit down on one of the sofas and he sat next to her. Josie felt a bit uncomfortable as he was sitting very close. He asked her how she was feeling and again told her she could take as much time off as she needed.

"Honestly Thomas, I am fine, really. I just needed to catch up on some sleep – I'm right as rain today."

Josie tried not to look at him directly as his gaze was very intense, his eyes probing her own. She shuffled a bit on the sofa, edging as far away from him as possible. She didn't feel threatened, just very hot and bothered by his close proximity.

"You are a remarkable young lady," he said patting her knee. His touch burned red hot through the thin material of her trousers.

"You have certainly made a mark here at Renseignements, Josie. Even Mervyn Bradley is singing your praises and he's not usually very forthcoming in that respect.

"Well, that's very nice of him."

"The only thing is, and I am telling you this as both a friend and your boss, Sally has made a complaint about you to Jacques Fredet. Now Jacques isn't a stupid man and he can see Sally for what she is, but he and her father go back a long way and he doesn't want to upset him. I gather he's been pretty ill lately."

Josie was horrified. "What has she been saying," Josie asked, remembering the accusations that Sally had hurled at her the evening before.

Thomas looked uncomfortable, Josie realised that her gut instinct was correct and that Sally had obviously been making accusations about her character, in particular her sexual exploits.

"I don't care what she's been saying, Thomas, she barely knows me and is just causing trouble because Véronique invited me onto the Four Seasons team and not her. To be honest, I think she's been following me."

Although it sounded bizarre, Josie told Thomas about seeing Sally at her Métro Station and the Canadian denying being there. She hoped her boss didn't think she was being paranoid, particularly in the wake of what had happened with Thierry. But Thomas seemed to take what she said seriously.

"What I suggest is that you avoid Sally as much as possible. She's only here for a short time anyway. Jacques and I are going to come up with a project which she can work on and that will keep her busy."

"But she has nothing to complain about. I've worked hard and done my job. This is so grossly unfair. I could make a complaint about her, after some of the things she's done, but I wouldn't dream of it."

"What sort of things."

"Well nothing that much really, just snide comments. But I'm sure she deleted my Chemfast presentation from the laptop the other day."

"She's told Jacques that you have been very rude to her in front of the other girls, and you purposely ousted her from the Four Seasons pitch by befriending Véronique. Now you and I both know that Véronique is her own person and no-one can influence her in that way. So nobody is really taken in by what she says. I just wanted to let you know, that's all."

"Thanks Thomas. I guess it's best to know your enemy. I don't know why but she seems to have taken an instant dislike to me."

"You just take it easy, Josie," he said standing up, "and any problems with Sally or anything else, you know you can talk to me."

Again, Josie felt uncomfortable under his intense stare. She was relieved to leave his office and head for the haven of her own desk.

"Véronique has been looking for you," Charlotte told her, "she's gone to Routage."

Josie turned around and headed back to Routage. Sally was in the reception area talking to Claire.

"Bonjour Sally, bonjour Claire," she said, hurrying past, not waiting for a reply.

She found Véronique in the Routage chatting to Daniel Bergerac.

"Hi Josie, how are you feeling?"

"Fine thanks Véronique. I gather you were looking for me?"

"Have you been ill?" asked Daniel, before Véronique could answer.

"Just a bit under the weather yesterday," she replied, "but I'm fine today."

"We need to sit down with Daniel and Thomas and look at your work load, Josie," Véronique told her. "Hélène Du Tilly is insisting that you are full time on the Four Seasons launch and would also like you to be involved in the day-to-day account too. This will definitely clash with the Chemfast conference in Brussels and I'm not sure what other clashes there may be with Thomas's work. Can you meet us after our management meeting this morning and we'll sort it all out then?"

Though her tone was professional, Véronique smiled at Josie.

"That's fine," Josie replied. "Just a thought, but it may be best if Sally takes over the Chemfast conference. She's involved anyway and knows the account."

"Not like you do though," Daniel butted in.

"I know, but sometimes a more objective overview can be better. Perhaps I'm a bit too close to it."

"Maybe," he replied, "we'll talk more, after the management meeting."

Back at her desk, Josie checked through her emails and her voicemail messages. She was shocked to receive a voicemail from Charles Dupré, asking her to call him back when it was convenient, and leaving his office and mobile numbers for her.

As neither Charlotte nor Odette were anywhere to be seen, she tentatively dialled his mobile number.

"Dupré," he answered abruptly.

"It's Josie, Monsieur Dupré. You left a message asking me to call you."

"Josie, thank you so much for ringing. Firstly, let me apologise to you for the ordeal my son has put you through. I know there is nothing I can do to change things and I really wish I had done more following the incident with Chrissie. Then this whole situation might have been prevented. But hindsight is a wonderful thing and I can't turn back the clocks. I would however like to tell you that Thierry has been released on bail and is now in a private clinic in Rennes."

"How long will he stay there?" she asked.

"As long as it takes to find out why he behaves as he does and hopefully to address this behaviour. Maybe he will never come out. I don't really know. I had no idea how unbalanced he was. It makes me sad. He really is a very intelligent boy and could have done so well for himself. Like all parents, I blame myself. I didn't spend as much time with him as perhaps I should have, particularly after his mother and I divorced. Whether that would have changed things, I don't know. I'll never know."

There was a long pause and Josie wondered whether she ought to say something, but thought better of it.

"I would very much like to meet you Josie, to apologise in person. And I need to talk to you about Thierry and the charges against him too."

"I'm not sure I want to meet you, Monsieur Dupré. It was a horrible experience and meeting you would bring it all back. What do you want to say about the charges?"

"Please meet me, Josie. Bring Chrissie too if you prefer. I do need to speak to you."

Josie suspected he wanted her and Chrissie to drop the charges against Thierry but felt she needed to discuss this with her friend first.

"I'll speak with Chrissie this evening and we'll get back to you."

"Thank you Josie, and once again, please understand how really sorry I am about what happened."

Josie didn't get a chance to call Chrissie straightaway. She had some urgent work to complete for Thomas and wanted to finish it before the meeting to prove that she was on top of everything. As soon as everything was in order she made her way to Thomas's office, for the second time that day. The other managers were leaving just as she arrived and all greeted her warmly.

"Come in Josie," Thomas said.

She sat down next to Véronique, facing Thomas and Daniel. "Us and them," she thought to herself, glad that she knew Véronique was on her side.

"Thanks for coming along Josie," said Thomas. "I know Daniel and Véronique have mentioned the reason already. They also told me your idea about Sally taking over the Chemfast Conference."

Josie could see that he was trying, but failing, to stop smiling.

"Daniel would rather you were involved due to your inside knowledge of the account. But also we can't afford to upset Hélène Du Tilly. Do you think JC would mind if you stepped down?"

"I'm sure he'd be fine about it. If I was still at Chemfast, you would have had to get someone else to organise the conference, so I don't really see that it makes much difference."

"Fair point," said Daniel.

"So that's the easy one, out of the way," continued Thomas. "Véronique reckons your involvement in the Four Seasons launch will take around three days a week of your time, up to the event itself. So we will advise Hélène that you won't be involved in the day-to-day account until the launch is over and we'll review the work load then."

Josie nodded, so far so good.

"Obviously, you will continue to provide day to day support for me and for Mervyn. That's not as easy to predict, in terms of work hours. I don't really want to tell Mervyn you are no longer available. It doesn't make us look very professional. I understand you have spent quite a bit of time with him, getting to know him and the accounts. Do you have any ideas or suggestions?"

An idea had been lurking at the back of Josie's mind since she had spoken to Daniel and Véronique earlier.

"I don't know how this would work exactly," she said, "but Marguerite who currently works in accounts is going to be providing secretarial support on the Four Seasons launch, perhaps she can help out on some other day to day work as well."

"So she would be working for you?" smiled Thomas

"Well when you put it like that...not for me exactly, more with me." Josie could feel herself blushing. She really hadn't meant it that way.

"Actually, I think it would be better if she worked for you," said Véronique. "That way you can plan and delegate as appropriate, with some guidance from us, of course."

Josie couldn't tell if Véronique was being entirely serious, or not. "What about her existing role though. How would we cover that?" Véronique asked Thomas.

"I know Marguerite doesn't feel stretched in the accounts department," said Josie, hoping that her friend didn't think she had spoken out of turn. "It's only really busy at certain times of the year and I know she was thinking of looking for another job as she felt she needed a new challenge. Perhaps she could manage most of her current job and support me... I mean us, as well."

"I'll need to speak to Paul Renard first but it does sound like a good solution," said Thomas. "I'll do that today. If they are OK with it, Josie, you can talk to Marguerite, as you two seem so close. Daniel, you can tell Sally that she's full time on the Chemfast conference, and don't forget to let her know that it was Josie's suggestion."

"I will," Daniel said with a knowing glance.

"Great, I'll let Hélène know what's happening," said Véronique. "You'd better come with me so we can look at what needs doing and when, Josie."

"Just a few other things," replied Josie. "I intend coming in on Saturday, to blitz Mervyn's office. If everything is agreed today, I'd like to ask Marguerite to come and help me. That way, she'll be able to familiarise herself with his accounts." Josie struggled a little to give voice to her feelings. "Also, I'm still very new here. I really appreciate the support you've shown me and the confidence you seem to have in me. However, it's taken a little while for me to be accepted by the other secretaries, so I would prefer it if we said that

Marguerite was working on the same accounts, for extra support, and not directly for me. Will that be okay?"

They all nodded in agreement.

"Fair point," said Véronique. "It's a shame those other girls haven't shown the same commitment and initiative as you, Josie."

The younger woman just smiled. Josie could hardly believe the way her career was progressing. The move to Renseignements was really starting to pay off and she was enjoying the work. Later that day Josie had the go-ahead to tell Marguerite of their plans. Once again her friend was extremely grateful for Josie's recommendation.

"My family think it's great," she told her. "They have visions of me becoming a real PR guru so I can promote the family business. But I must not get carried away, it's early days yet."

Josie asked Marguerite if she could come in on Saturday to help her sort out Mervyn's office. Marguerite looked mortified.

"I am really sorry Josie, but I can't this Saturday. Its Maman's birthday and we have a big family lunch planned. I can't get out of it really. I'd offer to come in first thing but it's a surprise for Maman and I have to be there to make sure everything goes smoothly."

"That's fine," replied Josie, secretly disappointed. "I'll make a start and then perhaps you can take over a bit next week."

Marguerite looked distressed.

"Honestly Marguerite, it's fine, really. I understand and I haven't got to grips with the filing myself yet, so it's probably better this way."

The rest of the day flew by but Josie left on time for once. She was still feeling really drained. Later, at home, Josie told Chrissie about the phone call with Charles Dupré.

"He hasn't been back at work since the incident," said Chrissie. "People are speculating as to why he's off but no-one knows the real reason, except for maybe his secretary, I guess. What do you want to do, Josie?"

"As much as I don't want to live through that again, I do think it may be a good idea to meet him, really for our peace of mind more than anything else. I'd like to find out what's really happening with Thierry. I think he wants us to drop the charges."

"Maybe, look I'll contact him, to arrange a meeting. What about tomorrow evening, after work? I'll pick somewhere neutral and not too far from home."

"Sure, just let me know where and I'll be there."

Later that evening, as she prepared for bed, she couldn't help but feel apprehensive about the meeting the next day. However, she realised that in some way it might help towards a closure of sorts. It might put some distance between them and the traumatic events of Monday night, hopefully the beginning of the end of the entire sad episode.

Ellis Rose

CHAPTER 10

Friday dragged by for Josie and she became more and more apprehensive about the meeting with Charles Dupré. Daniel Bergerac came to see her and voiced his concern, saying that she didn't seem to be her usual bubbly self. Daniel's concern brought tears to Josie's eyes, making her realise that, despite the bravado, the incident with Thierry was still playing on her mind and making her feel edgy. Once Daniel had left, after explaining that he had informed Sally that she would be running the Chemfast conference, the Canadian girl approached Josie's desk.

"I suppose you think suggesting that I take on the Chemfast conference would butter me up. Well, you're wrong. That was my account in the first place and you had no right trying to take over. If it wasn't for you making eyes at Thomas and Véronique I would also be working on the Four Seasons account. I've told my father all about you and how you've wormed your way in here. You have purposely gone out of your way to make me look foolish. How dare you."

Josie stood up, confronting her work colleague. "Look Sally, I've done nothing other than work hard and do everything that has been asked of me. I have had no intention of taking over anything and I'm really sorry if you think that. The last thing I want is to create bad feelings. Can't we put all of this behind us and work together rather than fight all the time?"

"Are you stupid?" Sally replied. "There's no place for both of us at this agency. And I'm going to see to it that it's me and not you that wins this battle."

Josie was incensed. "Really?" she replied. "Well Sally, let's take a look at the facts, shall we? I'm on the Four Seasons account and, as I feel so sorry for you, as you said earlier, I've passed the Chemfast contract back to you... so, my crumbs, wouldn't you say?"

Sally turned practically green. Josie began to turn away and didn't see the slap coming. Sally hit her really hard on the side of her head and, though reeling from the surprise of the blow, her instinct was to hit back. She raised her arm ready to retaliate but stopped when she realised that everyone was watching them. It was all just too much for Josie. The tension from the previous days, combined with the conflict with Sally, finally caught up with her. Pushing her aside, Josie ran from the office and into the ladies toilet. The other secretaries looked up from their work, bewildered. Claire caught a glimpse of Josie whizzing past and quickly followed her. Josie caught a glimpse of herself in the mirror, tears of mascara streaming down her face.

"Josie! Josie, what's wrong?" asked Claire.

Josie couldn't speak. Her body was wracked with sobs and she was shaking from head to toe.

"Josie, come on. It can't be all that bad. Please Josie, speak to me, I don't really want to have to call Thomas."

Josie didn't want Thomas or anyone else involved in this. They would just make her go home and she really didn't want to do that. She walked sheepishly out of the loo, wiping her eyes, and Claire gently took her arm and made her sit down. "What's up, Josie? It's not like you to be so upset!"

Josie still couldn't bring herself to speak, she just shook her head, the tears dripping onto her linen skirt and leaving dark stains. Claire continued to murmur soothing words of comfort and eventually Josie's tears subsided and she managed a weak smile.

"Sorry Claire. I've had an awful week and the fact that Sally totally has it in for me doesn't help. Everything is just getting on top of me."

At that point Thomas and Véronique arrived. They indicated for Claire to leave but Josie stopped her.

"No. Claire deserves an explanation and she saw what happened with Sally. She's been so kind. Please, Véronique, explain what's been going on."

The older woman briefly told Claire about the experience Josie had endured with Thierry, earlier in the week. Meanwhile, Thomas took over as comforter, asking Josie what happened with Sally. She explained as best she could, but it all sounded so lame and petty.

"I knew you shouldn't have come back to work so soon," he gently scolded. "You need time to get over this, Josie."

"Look," she said, "it's just that Chrissie and I are meeting Thierry's father this evening and I'm a bit apprehensive about that. That's all. I'll be fine, really."

"And Sally having a go at you didn't help, did it?"

They all turned to see Daniel Bergerac standing in the doorway. They hadn't heard him come in.

"I guess not," Josie replied quietly.

"What did she say exactly?" asked Thomas.

Josie told him what Sally had said, virtually verbatim. She knew it wouldn't be good for their future relations but then she had never intentionally tried to usurp Sally.

"Right," said Thomas. "I'll deal with Sally. Véronique, you stay with Josie until she's ready to go home."

"Actually, would you mind if I dealt with Sally, Thomas," said Daniel. "I was there after all, heard every word and saw her slap Josie."

"Okay, Daniel. But please make it clear that in this agency we don't tolerate bullying of any kind and that all decisions about Josie's involvement in all accounts have been made by management. I'll have a word with Jacques too as he really does need to know about this."

"Can I just go back to work now?" Josie asked.

"I really think you need to go home," said Thomas. "Also, all the other girls will be wondering what's going on and you don't want them to be probing you all afternoon."

"I'll tell you what," said Véronique, "I have a meeting this afternoon with an agent who represents a number of celebrity chefs. Why don't you come with me? Claire, could you tell the girls about what's happened. I know you didn't want everyone to know, Josie, but really they are a good bunch and will be very understanding."

Josie just nodded her head. She was more than happy for Véronique to take over and a meeting at the agent's office sounded quite exciting. Véronique left Josie to freshen up and returned a few minutes later with her coat and bag.

"Charlotte is switching off your computer, so come on, let's go. The meeting isn't until this afternoon, so we have plenty of time for some lunch first."

The rest of the day was great fun. Josie really enjoyed Véronique's company. The meeting with the agent was a real eye opener with Véronique trying to negotiate rates to which the agent was never going to agree. But her principle was to start low, allowing more room to compromise. After the agent negotiations were complete, Josie still had the rest of the day before the meeting with Chrissie and Charles Dupré.

"Come on, it's Friday afternoon. Let's bunk off and do some retail therapy," said Véronique. "Nobody is expecting us back at the office."

The women spent the rest of the afternoon trying on clothes in the big department stores on the Boulevard Haussman. Véronique had a very individual style and made Josie try on things she would normally never have dreamed of putting together. One outfit in particular looked stunning, black leggings, a short burnt orange dress with a buttoned up black crop top over the top of the dress.

"Wow, that looks fabulous on you," said Véronique, when Josie came out of the changing room. The older woman also looked great in a severely cut, black trouser suit with nothing underneath the jacket. "You must buy it."

Josie looked at the price tag and winced. The outfit did look great and it was very different from the more traditional styles she usually wore.

"I guess that's what my credit card is for," she said to herself, grateful that she was working overtime that weekend for Mervyn Bradley.

Once they had completed their purchases, the two women stopped in the store café for a coffee. Josie's mobile bleeped and as soon as they sat down she checked her text messages. It was from Marguerite, saying that she had heard about what happened and wished Josie had told her. She ended the message by saying that she was thinking of her. Josie replied saying she would call later to explain.

After a delightful afternoon they parted company, with Josie thanking Véronique again for her support and for a great time. The older woman gave Josie a hug and told her that anyone else would have gone to pieces after what had happened, and that she was very brave. Josie hugged her back, thanking her again. As Véronique leaned in towards Josie, to give the ritual three farewell kisses, Josie unintentionally moved her face towards the other woman. The movement caused their lips to brush accidentally. Josie quickly stepped back, blushing from head to toe. Véronique too seemed taken aback but then started laughing. Seeing the funny side of it, Josie also laughed.

"Don't worry Josie, I know you prefer men. I can tell a mile off what a woman is into and you are definitely a man's woman. Shame though, you would definitely have potential as a lover. I can tell you would be very passionate."

"Well, Véronique," replied Josie, still smiling, "if it doesn't work out with Christian, you never know, I may come knocking on your door."

As she headed for the Métro, Josie called Marguerite and explained that she simply hadn't had the chance to tell her before but also that she just wanted to put it out of her mind.

"Sally's had a right telling off," said Marguerite. "She came out of Daniel's office in floods of tears. I get the feeling that she may not be staying at the agency right through the summer now."

"Well I hope it isn't just because of me," Josie replied. "I can't stand the woman but I don't want to be responsible for her leaving."

"I'm sure what happened with you was just the icing on the cake, Josie. Nobody is going to miss her, that's for sure."

Despite Marguerite's words, Josie couldn't help but feel bad about Sally and decided that on Monday she would speak to Daniel and to Sally herself if necessary.

She arrived at the café promptly and both Chrissie and Charles Dupré were already there. The events of the past week had really taken their toll and he looked older and greyer in Josie's eyes. He stood up and shook her hand very formally.

"Thank you for agreeing to meet me, Josie, and once again, may I apologise for my son's unacceptable behaviour."

Josie just nodded. She felt very sad for the poor man. He had done nothing wrong, himself, except perhaps over indulge his son. They ordered drinks and Charles Dupré told the girls that Thierry was in a private psychiatric hospital in Rennes.

"He's undergoing an assessment at present, so it's early days, but the doctors believe he is suffering from severe depression leading to emotional dysregulation. The prognosis is not good and even after treatment starts Thierry will be in hospital for a very long time."

His voice cracked as he spoke these last words and it seemed as if he was about to break down, but he pulled himself together and carried on.

"I am here today to ask both of you if you would consider dropping the charges against Thierry. I can provide you with evidence from the doctors that he will be under treatment for years to come, if you want me to. And I give you my personal assurance that my son will never come near either of you ever again."

"That's all very well Mr Dupré, but you told us that once before," said Chrissie harshly.

"I know, but I had no idea of the extent of my son's mental illness. To be honest with you, after that episode Chrissie, my ex-wife, and I did everything in our power to get him back on track. He went twice a week to a psychiatrist and he was never left on his own for long periods of time. However, when she was rushed into hospital Thierry, in his confused state, obviously headed straight back to Paris."

Josie had listened carefully to Charles Dupré.

"Monsieuer Dupré," she said calmly, "I, we, really do sympathise with you and understand that you naturally want to protect your family, as much as you can. But, in all truth, we have no guarantees that once Thierry is out of hospital, whenever that may be, that he won't do the same again. I don't mean necessarily to Chrissie and me but what if he does the same to other women in the future?"

"Please believe me, every measure will be taken to ensure this doesn't happen again," he replied. "I won't be around forever and normally one would want one's children to outlive them. So I have set up a guardianship through my lawyers to ensure that, if Thierry ever does leave the psychiatric hospital, he will never be in a position to behave in the same way."

As they had agreed the night before, Josie and Chrissie told Charles Dupré that they would consider dropping the charges. But both felt that they were too inexperienced to make that decision on their own and informed him they would be consulting a lawyer before reaching a final decision.

"Of course, that's very sensible," he replied, the relief evident in his voice. "I can provide you and your solicitor with all the medical records and reports from the hospital. Just let me know where I should send them."

"We will, and Monsieur Dupré, believe me, the last thing in the world either of us wants is to relive those horrible moments in court. But as I said, we couldn't live with ourselves if, through lack of action on our part, Thierry was free to act in the same way again."

He just nodded, the sadness evidently weighing him down.

"I'll be back in work on Monday, Chrissie, so as soon as you've found a solicitor, let me know and I'll arrange for all the paperwork to be sent straightaway."

There was an odd urgency to his tone which both girls noticed. Once he had left, Chrissie said to Josie, "I guess he wants this sorted out as quickly as possible. I can't blame him but we mustn't feel forced into doing something we don't think is right."

"I'm conscious that it's going to be a harder decision for you though, Chrissie. I mean, you work for the man."

"I know," she replied, "and with the best will in the world, if we do decide to press charges then it will make it very difficult. But that's jumping the gun a bit. We need to find ourselves a solicitor and see what he or she has to say first."

"I think we should ask Dan if he can recommend a firm," said Josie.

"Good idea, we'll give him a ring when we get home."

Later that evening, the girls called Daniel and he recommended the firm where Max's former girlfriend, Anna, worked.

"They are up there among the best," he said, "and there are a number of Brits working there and you may find it easier to deal with an English speaking person."

Chrissie agreed with him and told Josie that she would call the firm on Monday.

The next day, Josie made it into the office a little later than usual. There was no-one else in and she was glad that Claire had shown her how to de-activate the burglar arm. She made herself a coffee and then began to sort through the paperwork in Melvyn's office. At first sight it looked a complete mess, but there was some logic to the way the files and papers were stacked and so sorting through the current and old stuff wasn't as bad as it at first seemed. Josie was concentrating so hard on the task in hand that she didn't hear the door to Melvyn's office open and was startled when Thomas spoke her name. She dropped the bundle of papers which she had just sorted onto the floor.

"Oh my God, Thomas, you gave me a fright," she said, feeling a bit silly as she bent down to scoop up the papers.

He stooped down next to her to give her a hand.

"Sorry Josie," he said. "I didn't realise you were in today. The front door was locked but the burglar alarm wasn't on; I thought we had intruders."

"No problem. I thought it best to lock the door as I knew I'd be up here on my own all morning."

"Are you sure you're up to this?" he asked her. "I mean, you've had a terrible week."

Although she recognised that Thomas's concern was genuine, Josie was getting a bit fed up of being molly coddled, despite her tears the day before.

"Honestly Thomas, I am fine. I guess everything just came to a head yesterday but the meeting with Charles Dupré went well so that's out of the way now. So please, stop worrying about me."

He was standing very close to her and she could almost feel the warmth emanating from his skin. He reached over and pulled her close, gently tucked her under his chin, and stroked her back.

"You're very courageous, Josie," he said.

Josie thought for a split second he was going to kiss her. But if that was his intention he quickly had second thoughts and backed away from her towards the door. A flash of movement caught Josie's eye. There was someone outside the office, she was sure. Catching her glance, Thomas asked what was wrong.

"I swear someone was eavesdropping on us," she replied, edging her way toward the office door. She guessed Thomas thought she was being paranoid again but he nevertheless gave her the benefit of the doubt. They both approached the half open door but there was nobody to be seen. "I must be far more jittery than I thought," said Josie.

"Maybe," said Thomas, a sceptical look on his face.

"I could have sworn I saw someone. Not someone, a female

definitely, but I might have been mistaken, sorry."

"No worries. Well, when you're ready for a break and fancy a coffee give me a shout, I'll be in my office."

She nodded and smiled at him. As he left, she couldn't help but feel relieved. Thomas Frolin was a very attractive man and there was definitely a spark between them. But Josie had no intention of getting involved with a married man, who was her boss to boot. Also, she really did love Christian and would do nothing intentionally to hurt him. Although it still bothered her that Thomas could have such an effect on her. As she carried on sorting through the papers, Josie remembered that she wanted to speak to Thomas about Sally. So after another hour of work she made two cups of coffee and took them up to his office.

Thomas was on the phone but indicated for her to come in and sit down. He ended the call and joined her on the sofa.

"Thanks Josie. Sorry I became distracted. I should have brought you the coffee."

"That's fine Thomas. Listen, I wanted to talk to you about Sally. I gather she's going to be leaving earlier than planned and I just wanted to say that, if that's the case, I sincerely hope it's got nothing to do with me. I know we don't get on but I really would hate to think she was leaving just because of that."

"I'd be lying if I said her behaviour yesterday wasn't part of it. But to be honest it hasn't really worked out from day one. She's upset all the secretaries, including Claire, who never gets in a flap. She doesn't really pull her weight, but is ready and willing to take praise for the work of others and basically her French isn't really up to standard. Yesterday, after Daniel spoke to her, she went crying to Jacques but I'd already spoken to him and so he backed us up. Jacques has also spoken to her father, who didn't really seem that bothered whether she stayed or came home. So it looks like she will be going earlier than planned. She will still help with the Chemfast conference, before leaving."

"That doesn't make me feel any better. I mean, really my outburst yesterday was the catalyst in a way. Is there anything I can do to make her stay longer?"

"Josie, we don't want her to stay longer. As I've just explained, she's a bit of liability and so once the Chemfast thing is over, she'll be going pretty soon. I just hope she pulls her weight for Daniel on that. She'll have to if she wants a reference from us."

As Josie left Thomas's office, she was still feeling bad about the Sally situation. No matter what Thomas said, she still felt partly to blame for the decision. As much as she knew it was the right thing to do, she knew she wouldn't be able to bring herself to speak to Sally about the situation. It just wasn't worth the hassle. Josie carried on working until lunch time when Thomas popped back up to tell her he was leaving.

"See you Monday Josie, and don't stay too late, you need to relax and chill a bit."

"Don't worry, Thomas. My boyfriend Christian is picking me up this afternoon and, like you say, I'm really looking forward to spending the rest of the weekend relaxing."

"It sounds serious, this relationship of yours."

"I guess so, yes, it is."

"Lucky man," he replied, winking at her. "Are you going to be OK here on your own?" he asked, genuinely concerned.

"That's the second time he's said that to me," thought Josie to herself.

"Of course," Josie beamed, feeling more confident than she really felt. She wasn't going to let the likes of Thierry or Sally get to her. "I'll wrap up shortly and head off."

She settled down at Mervyn's desk to eat her lunch, which she had bought on the way in, then sent a text to Christian, telling him how much she was looking forward to seeing him later. He replied immediately, saying 'ditto'.

By late afternoon she had had enough. She felt distinctly uncomfortable being in the offices on her own, so decided to pack up. She made sure all the lights were turned off and the alarm set, and closed the main office door behind her. It felt like a gesture, but as she headed across the courtyard she looked up towards the office windows and could have sworn that she saw a shadow moving quickly back from one of the top floor windows.

A few stops later, Josie arrived at Villiers and popped to the supermarket, around the corner, to pick up some treats to take to Christian's place. Whilst she waited for him outside the Metro, she called Chrissie to check what plans she had for the next day. Her flatmate was seeing Claude and Josie suggested that perhaps all four of them could meet up the following evening. Chrissie agreed to call her the next day to confirm.

Christian was uncharacteristically a few minutes late and

apologised profusely.

"Don't worry," she said, "you're here now."

The couple spent a relaxing evening at Christian's flat, cooking, watching TV and eventually making love. As Josie drifted off to sleep that night she felt very contented and settled. The evening had passed quickly and she had enjoyed Christian's company tremendously. He had been caring and attentive but funny and teasing too. He really made her laugh and feel very special and she hoped she was able to make him feel the same way in return. His family were due to come and visit the following weekend and he asked if she would join them for dinner at his friend's restaurant the following Saturday evening.

"I'd love to." Although she knew nearer the time she would be nervous meeting his family.

The next day was spent in similar fashion. Between heavy rain showers they managed a romantic walk through the park. They met the others for a drink on Sunday evening and, although it was more convenient to go back to her flat, she went home with Christian as she was enjoying the time with him so much. Later in bed, Christian asked her if she had enjoyed the weekend.

"Absolutely wonderful," she replied kissing him gently. "I really needed just to rest and be taken care of and you have done just that. So thank you, Christian. It's been lovely."

"The offer still stands, Josie. I would love you to move in with me."

"Don't you think it's a bit soon? I mean we've only known each other a couple of months and only really been together for a few weeks. Don't you think we should spend a bit more time together first and be absolutely sure about this?"

"I've never been more certain about anything in my life. I love you, Josie, and I want to spend the rest of my life with you."

"I love you too Christian, and this weekend together has made me realise that more than anything. But I am not going to rush into this in my usual style. I want to spend as much time as possible with you so we can really get to know each other and be sure that any decisions we make in the future are the right ones."

"I know you're right Josie, but I want you now….."

"And you've got me now," she replied putting her arms around his neck and moving her naked body closer to his. His response was immediate and within seconds he was making love to her for the second time that night. Josie responded to his caresses with passion and eagerness. She wrapped her legs around his waist, pulling him deeply inside her and held him there as she writhed against him. He held her buttocks in his hand, pulling her deeper onto him until it felt like they were fused as one. He leaned forward to kiss her and at that moment Josie had never felt so close to anyone in her life. Tears welled up in her eyes.

"Are you okay Josie?" he asked, relaxing his grip on her slightly.

"I love you, Christian," she said, and smiled at him through her tears.

He smiled and continued to hold her, moving more gently in and out of her. She could feel her orgasm building and gripped his arms to control her herself. As her breath subsided and her limbs stopped trembling, Christian slipped out of her, resting his hardness against her stomach. He kissed her deeply, his tongue as tantalising in her mouth as his cock had been moving inside her. Josie reached to touch him, but he gently took hold of her wrists and held her hands above her head, as he kept kissing her. Christian's mouth moved down her neck to her collar bone, covering her skin with butterfly kisses. Josie instinctively pushed her breasts forward, his mouth lapped, nipped and sucked each of her nipples, sending hot vibrations to the core of her womanhood. After several minutes of excruciating pleasure, he released the hard, swollen buds and his tongue trailed gently down her belly, darting into her belly button. Christian grabbed her buttocks and literally pulled her mound towards his mouth, his tongue gently caressing the tip of her nub.

Josie could feel herself coming again, but he stopped licking, sitting back on his haunches, taking in the view of her body. As their eyes locked, he moved his fingers deep inside her and slipped his thumb into her anus. Josie rocked against his hands. She was so wet and so turned on. Josie felt as if she was undergoing an out of body experience. Christian's eyes bored into her as he continued to manipulate her. He was in total control and she loved it. She came hard and fast against his hand, wetting the sheets with the intensity of her orgasm. Christian gently slipped his fingers from inside her and licked them, like a child with a lollypop, then offered up her love juices for her to taste. Josie gently sucked his fingers, he took hold of his cock and rubbed the head against her swollen lips.

Josie could barely stand the sensation. With a quick movement, he grasped the root of his cock and thrust it deeply into her, hard and fast. She cried out with the sensation. He filled all of her and, as erotic as it felt, Josie also felt closer to Christian than she had ever felt with anyone else in her young life.

He began to thrust harder and harder. Josie could feel herself coming again. Sensing her orgasm, he kept on pumping into her until he reached the point of no return. As he released with a strangled sigh, he laid the full length of her, resting his head on her breasts. Josie stroked his head gently. She really did love this man who made her feel so special in so many ways. But she also knew she was being sensible by holding back on his offer to move in together. It was very early days and though her heart was telling her to go for it, her head remained the stabilising influence. Christian moved off her and pulled her against him, back into the spoon position again, as they drifted off to sleep without further words.

They both had work the next morning, and while finishing breakfast Josie told Christian all about Sally and asked what he thought she should do.

"I'd leave well alone, the mad bitch" he said. "There's obviously more to her leaving the agency early than the issue with you."

"But I feel so guilty."

"Don't. What have you done?" he said with a Gallic shrug.

"Well, nothing really, except take great pleasure in her being put in an awkward position and laughing about her with Véronique."

"Well then, she's a grown woman, Josie, and responsible for her own actions. It's not your fault at all. Anyway she sounds a complete mad bitch and deserves everything she gets."

Josie still couldn't help but feel a bit guilty but decided to take Christian's advice and not say anything to Sally. She would just avoid her as much as possible.

Later that day they had a review meeting with Four Seasons on the opening and so Josie spent a busy morning preparing for it. Instinctively she did most of the preparation herself as she found it easier and quicker. But she did pass on some work to Marguerite, who was delighted to be involved. Marguerite had gone out with Yves again on the weekend and they were getting on really well, although apparently Luc was still not happy about his sister seeing Yves.

"What's he got against him?" Josie asked.

"I don't think he has anything against Yves. Luc just hates any man I get involved with. He's overly protective, I guess."

"Control freak more like," Josie thought. The more she heard about Luc de la Fontaine, the more she disliked him. Yes, he was very attractive but he was also arrogant and, she suspected, rather domineering.

Josie told Marguerite about the Sally situation and her friend agreed with Christian's view, that she was not to blame. Josie had managed to avoid Sally all day and had purposely stayed close to her desk to ensure she didn't bump into her. As she was finalising the details of the Four Seasons report, Thomas phoned her and asked her to come up to his office. When she arrived, he told her that at the Directors' meeting it had been agreed to give her a small pay increase, due to the additional role she had taken on. But that it might be a good idea to keep it to herself, for the time being at least. Josie beamed back at him. "Thank you Thomas, and please thank the others for me too. I won't say a word but I really do appreciate it. Thanks again. Thank you!"

"Calm down, it's only a small increase, but you definitely deserve it. It was Véronique's idea actually, but everyone agreed."

Thomas then talked about some work he needed her to complete for him. By the time she arrived back at her desk she had just about managed to stop grinning inanely. Véronique stopped by and asked her to come into the Routage, with the report, for a quick run through over a coffee. The two women were engrossed in the report and didn't notice Sally come into the room until she spoke to Josie.

"Daniel has asked me to have a word with you about the Chemfast conference and to ask if you can give us some background on the members who will be presenting at the conference. Here's the list."

Sally's tone was very curt and Josie could practically feel the hatred emanating from the Canadian woman. She felt bad enough about Sally as it was, and she didn't want to alienate her even further.

"Give me two minutes, Sally. Véronique and I have nearly finished here and then I'll go through the list with you."

Sally nodded and proceeded to make herself a coffee whilst waiting for Josie to finish. Véronique raised her eyebrows questioningly at Josie, but the younger woman ignored the query and continued with the report. When Véronique left, Josie felt very uncomfortable alone with Sally.

"Let's have a look at who's on your list, then." She managed a weak smile. Sally handed her the list and Josie spent a few moments reading through it.

"Well, Giovanni Spontini is a really nice guy, but he's getting on a bit and needs to be told very clearly how long he has to speak for. He does have a tendency to go on a bit and overrun. Carlos Santos is great, he won't need much guidance and he's an excellent speaker. Is he presenting in English?"

"They're all presenting in English, remember. The Americans insisted."

"Oh, I wasn't aware of that. Sorry."

"So you're not always little Miss Perfect then!"

Josie chose to ignore the remark.

"Well, in that case you better make sure Giovanni is up to speed. He presents far more slowly in English, and is not terribly confident with the language. The others are all fine. I don't really know the German guy very well. He only joined the sales team a few weeks before I left. I could ask my friend Libby though, she'd knows him better."

"Don't bother, I'll ask JC myself," Sally replied, taking the list from Josie's hand and leaving the room without a hint of a thank you.

"I guess Christian and Marguerite are right," she thought. "Sally is not worth fretting over."

Véronique collected her and the rest of the account team, and together they took a taxi to the Boulevard Haussman where they were again greeted personally by Hélène du Tilly. This meeting was different from the previous, they were now getting down to the nitty-gritty and there was a lot more to get organised than Josie first realised. She also recognised that Hélène was no pushover and queried every decision, every cost and every argument Véronique put before her. Josie was exhausted by the time the meeting was over and was tempted to go straight home. But she had promised Thomas that she would finish the work he gave her earlier and was determined to do so. It was early evening by the time she finally wrapped up. A couple of the account managers were still chatting in the Routage and she said goodnight and left. She was grateful to arrive home but surprised that Chrissie wasn't there. She checked her mobile which had been switched off since the Four Seasons meeting and there was a message from Chrissie, asking her to call on her mobile. Josie tried Chrissie's mobile, but it was switched off. Josie also tried Christian's phone but reached his voicemail.

"What's going on?" she said to herself, bewildered.

Josie sat on the sofa, half watching the TV and half listening out for her friend. After a few minutes her mobile rang. It was Chrissie.

"Hi there, where are you?" she said to her friend. "I was starting to get worried."

"Josie, there's been a terrible accident," she said gravely, not knowing how to lessen the blow of what she needed to tell her friend. "It's Christian and Claude. They've both been involved in a car accident. Claude is okay, but Christian… he's been badly injured. He's been taken to the University Hospital. They're going to operate as soon as possible," she sobbed.

The room spun and Josie found it difficult to catch her breath. Finally she managed to blurt out, "I'm on my way," and, grabbing her coat and bag, headed straight out of the flat in a blind panic. Josie ran at full tilt for the taxi rank near the Gâre St Lazare.

"Please let him be OK, please let him be OK," she repeated like a mantra, willing the taxi to go faster through the late evening traffic. She shoved a handful of Euros, without bothering to count them, at the taxi driver and leapt out of the cab. Chrissie, ashen faced, was waiting for her at the entrance to the hospital.

"Chrissie, what's happened? How is he?"

Her friend led her into a quiet waiting room and sat her down.

"It's pretty bad Josie, but he's in the best hands now. They've just taken him into the operating theatre. The doctors have told us that it will be a good few hours. Let's go and find the canteen and I'll explain what happened."

Josie felt completely numb. She followed Chrissie along the corridors of the hospital, in a trance. The thought of losing Christian made her feel physically sick. Once they sat down, Chrissie explained that the men had been heading home from work, and as they were joining the Périphèrique a motor cyclist lost control of his bike and skidded right in front of them. Claude was driving and swerved to avoid him, but lost control of the car, which hit the central reservation. Claude wasn't too badly injured as his air bag opened. But for some reason Christian's didn't work. The impact of the car hitting the barrier caused his seat to dislodge and his head hit the windscreen.

"What have the doctors said?" Josie asked, a rising panic starting to overwhelm her.

"They said he was lucky he didn't go right through the windscreen. But he's had a severe blow to his head and the x-rays show that a blood clot has formed between the brain and the skull. They are operating on that now. They did say that they had got to him quickly so the chances of a successful operation are pretty good."

"Oh my God," a sob caught in her throat, "Christian. I can't believe it, Chrissie. Did the doctors say anything else?"

"Not really, they were obviously anxious to get him into theatre."

Josie could tell that Chrissie was struggling to stay calm.

"What about Claude?"

"He's badly shaken up, naturally. He's phoning Christian's family to let them know."

Josie could feel the tears running freely down her face.

"I just can't bear the thought of him lying there on the operating table. Did you see him?"

"No I didn't, but Claude did. Look, here he comes now."

Josie looked up. Claude looked terrible his clothes were stained with blood. He had a cut over his eye, his arm was in a sling and he was limping badly.

"Josie," he said simply.

Josie stood up and put her arms around him. She knew he wasn't to blame and at that moment in time he was the closest person to Christian. He looked on the verge of tears himself.

"I've spoken with Christian's father and he and his mother are flying out first thing in the morning. There are no flights tonight, unfortunately. They were all for getting in the car and driving but they will get here just as quickly by flying in the morning. I've promised to keep them posted on developments. They are completely devastated. It's very difficult when you live so far away…." Claude's voice faltered.

"Claude, you saw him. How was he?"

"Unconscious, Josie. He didn't regain consciousness before going into theatre. But the doctors said that was expected. They seem to think it will all be OK. But they did tell me that until they operate they won't know the extent of the damage."

Claude wiped his eyes and sighed.

"What do you mean damage?"

"They can't rule out the possibility of brain damage at this stage. Also, there could be other side effects like epilepsy or amnesia. These are classic symptoms, although Christian may not have any," he sobbed, "they just don't know yet."

Chrissie sat down, stunned.

"And the operation, will he survive the operation?"

Claude just shook his head, indicating that he didn't know. Josie felt a great blackness descend and was convulsed with sobbing.

Until a few moments ago she had a good life, great friends and a new job she was excelling at. Josie had finally found someone, in Christian, that she truly loved. This was the man she thought she would marry and have children with. This was the man she wanted to share the rest of her life with. Now her dreams lay in ruins and she felt her life was over before it had even begun.

Chrissie took her hand, "You have to be strong Josie. You have to be strong for Christian."

"What now, what if...?" sobbed Josie and gripped her friend for comfort.

ELLIS ROSE
ONE NIGHT IN PARIS

Josie James lives in Paris with her British Flat mate, Chrissie and works with another Brit, Libby. They live the high life going out to bars, restaurants and clubs, usually at the expense of their friend Daniel, a filthy rich banker who is besotted by Chrissie. Daniel treats them to a champagne-fuelled day out at the glitzy Tour de L'Arc de Triomphe at Longchamps racecourse. Josie meets Max there, whose addiction to women is constant and insatiable. With a body built for sin, and more charm than should be legal for one man to have, they begin a steamy but secret relationship as Max already has a girlfriend whom it quickly becomes evident he has no intention of dumping.

One night in Paris, they meet a group of French air traffic controllers and for two of the girls, this meeting is set to change the paths of their lives forever. Chrissie begins dating Claude, but the relationship is put in turmoil by a rape attempt on Chrissie by Thierry Dupree, the disturbed son of her boss who thinks English girls are easy.

Josie James, the luscious centrefold, with a little girl charm, a big girl body, and an appetite for all that Paris has to offer...Shameless raunchy sex, glitzy locations and a sharp observation of social interactions will have you focused until the final paragraph...

ELLIS ROSE
LAST NIGHT IN PARIS

With Christian's slow recovery from a coma after the serious car accident, Josie finds herself torn between caring for her man and her career. The prestigious Four Seasons Pan-European launch is delicately poised and Josie is in the firing line if it all fails.

The pressures of juggling Christian with punishing hours and stress at work result in a major bust-up at Renseignements with Sally Marsden-Lloyd. This time Josie is not in a forgiving mood and the spoilt little rich girl may have bitten off more than she can swallow. The situation becomes impossible when a vile anonymous letter is circulated that accuses her of a sordid affair with her dishy boss Thomas, a serial womanizer. Valérie, his long suffering wife naturally goes ballistic and the agencies senior partner, Jacques Fredet is called upon to investigate the allegations.

Josie's wayward younger sister, Ella James proves an unwelcome distraction when she visits. Ella takes up with the intriguing but dangerous Luc de la Fontaine and goes missing on her final night in Paris. The glitzy Four Seasons event in Switzerland finally brings everything to a head and changes the path of Josie's life forever.

WHAT THEY SAY ABOUT ELLIS ROSE

"A sexy, funny, riotous bonkbuster…Switch off your phone, grab a glass of bubbly and escape into an outrageous world of sex, thrills, glamour and passion. You'll be addicted…" AMAZON

"Packed full of sauciness, sex and intrigue, this lively romp takes you on a colourful journey through the sparkling world of Paris, from the ultra-highs to the face-planting lows. If you're looking for a sexy, racy, riotous read, this is the perfect choice…" AMAZON

"The sex scenes will make even the most frigid and puritanical of us aware that we are alive, and I suggest that if you have a partner, make sure they are available…you will want to do IT while reading. It is a sexy, thrilling, glitzy bonkbuster and is the most fun you can have between two covers…" AMAZON

"Fast, shameless and mesmeric fiction…offers an intoxicating blend of swooning romance, raunchy sex and agonising love stories…" GOODREADS

"A 'no holds barred' exploration of tangled and graphic love lives, perhaps no one plays with the heart – and other body parts – as successfully as the scandalous Ellis Rose." AMAZON

"Another Night… adult contemporary romance that contains strong sexual content and sultry raunchy thrills…inject some heat into your reading…" AMAZON

♦ *ALSO FROM IPONYMOUS* ♦

THE FINDING
ALAN M KEEF

Jennifer Suffram is the daughter of an old established but slightly down at heel Cotswold farming family. She feels stifled by her fiancé, the patronising Richard, the hum drum plod of her life and decides on a once in lifetime trip to East Africa in an effort to 'find herself'. Rather than finding herself she finds David, a handsome young man with a mysterious past.

But finding him upon her return to England is another matter entirely, with no contact details she turns sleuth and the couple are reunited. Despite their brief acquaintance, when he suffers a serious injury he calls for her help and in a matter of days she finds herself acting not only as his chauffeur and personal assistant but almost as his wife. And before she can stop herself, she's swept up in an affair so sensual she ignores all the warnings...

To her surprise she finds she likes the atmosphere and the people engaged in the family engineering business in Carlisle with the exception of David's PA, Muriel, with whom she is instantly at loggerheads. Jennifer's confrontations with Muriel unearth dark undercurrents of deception, menace and sex that cast light on some shocking skeletons buried in David's past. Can their fledgling romance withstand the revelations...?

"Wonderful dialogue, colourful characters, breathtaking twists and a plot that allows no pause for breath...all is perfectly weaved together to create an irresistible story in which absolutely nothing is as it seems" AMAZON

"An addictive novel to be devoured in one sitting...the plot rattles along with gusto...a real page-turner" AMAZON

PROPHECY OF RAVENS
KEN BLAKEMORE

KILLER BUG ESCAPES LAB
Authorities in the US have confirmed that the deadly virus now sweeping through California escaped from a laboratory.
LOCKED IN WITH THE PLAGUE
Five brave doctors, sixteen courageous nurses, ten plucky health workers are sacrificing their lives at the Princess Diana Hospital, Leeds, for us. By the time you read this, they may already have been taken by the Superflu plague sweeping through our country.
TWO MILLENNIA – AND NOW IT'S THE END
We knew it would happen. Great Britain's population has dwindled to a few million, as has almost every other country's. We knew there was no health service there and that all telecommunications, food supplies, the currency and the transport system had broken down. But we clung to hopes – hopes that one day the Old Country would rise again. That prospect now looks very remote indeed.

This is Britain sixty years from now – a land slowly recovering, like the rest of the world, from three devastating epidemics. It's an island of only a few million people. It faces the prospect of a slide back into a new medieval age: a land of dense forests, superstition and darkness – a land of ravens.

Lara Johnson is the youngest-ever high court judge to be appointed in the city of New Warwick. In the company of a young woman reporter, Star Edkin, Lara decides to set off on a final quest to find her missing husband. They travel through a country on the brink of rebellion and fraught with the dangers of a nuclear disaster.

"A genuinely unsettling dystopian novel…prescient to the degree that today's newspaper headlines accurately mirror the plot…an ambitious and addictive novel" SUE SAVITT, Faber & Faber

Ellis Rose